KINDNESS
KILLS

KINDNESS
KILLS

DUNCAN OTHEN

Pleasant W rd
A Division of WINEPRESS PUBLISHING

Packaged by Pleasant Word, a division of WinePress Publishing, PO Box 428, Enumclaw, WA 98022. The views expressed or implied in this work do not necessarily reflect those of Pleasant Word, a division of WinePress Publishing. Ultimate design, content, and editorial accuracy of this work are the responsibilities of the author.

ISBN 1-4141-0306-9
Library of Congress Catalog Card Number: 2004097736

Acknowledgments

I want to thank two knowledgeable people who helped me with my research: James Brosius, Chief of Police in Chagrin Falls, Ohio, and Dr. Elizabeth Belraj, Cuyahoga County Coroner.

I also want to thank four other special individuals for their valuable advice about certain sections of this novel: Greg Dorner, Al Wilson, Ann D'Agostino, and Jeanne Othen.

This book is dedicated to Jeanne, Sean, and Shana.

BOOK ONE: THE TORMENTED

Chapter One

When Sally Malloy noticed the clock in the store window she realized she only had twenty minutes left to live. She knew they would kill her at one o'clock if she failed at her assignment. She had been ordered to find the secret location by then or die, and with the deadline rapidly approaching she knew it was hopeless. They had deliberately given her vague directions, and she had no idea where to go.

She noticed her shadowy form on the window and shivered involuntarily, knowing it was probably the last time she would see her own reflection. She moved closer and squinted at the glass, seeing the lined, tired face of a woman in her fifties who had a look of helpless terror in her eyes. In a way, she was glad to be so frightened. Maybe her fear could somehow inspire a sudden idea that would save her life.

Sally finally turned away from the window and hurried along the sidewalk on Western Avenue, breathing heavily from increasing anxiety. A damp wind from Lake Michigan swirled around the tall buildings of Chicago and pushed from behind as if urging her to hurry. The cold temperature didn't bother her; she had on a heavy coat that was torn in a few places but quite warm, and a gray woolen hat she had selected from a shelter's clothing bin because it complemented her long gray hair.

Not many people walked the streets in this part of Chicago after midnight and she was oblivious to the few she passed. She kept glancing back at the towering buildings in the Loop which loomed above her in the distance, their lights gleaming through the darkness like thousands of evil yellow eyes silently watching her.

She had been told that a dramatic event would occur at one o'clock in the morning in an alley somewhere in this section of town; something she alone must witness; a tragedy the entire nation would hear about from the news media. That was all they said, except of course, if she disobeyed they would torture her to death.

A few weeks ago she had shared a thermos of coffee with an elderly homeless man who had suddenly collapsed from a heart attack. She desperately tried to revive him, but he died anyway with an overwhelming fear shining in his eyes. She fervently wished she could have saved him and all the other homeless people who had died during the years she had spent living on the streets. And now, in the final moments of her life, she understood the lonely terror they must have felt at the end when they realized they had no chance of surviving.

Sally turned down a side street and walked one block, then headed north on Artesian Avenue. The street was flanked by crumbling brick buildings with broken windows, many of them abandoned. If this was a normal night she would go inside one and sleep till dawn, but she certainly didn't have that option now. It would be one o'clock in a few minutes.

She stopped and glanced up at two tall abandoned buildings that towered over her like enormous twin gravestones. Huge planks of wood covered the windows and obscenities were spray painted on the doors. The alley between the buildings was too dark for her to see beyond the entrance. Could it be the right one?

She looked up at the night sky, disappointed that the moon's soft glow was barely visible from above the black curtain of clouds. It would have been wonderful to have gazed on its inspiring ivory luster one more time. She stifled a sob as she walked into the alley, realizing this would be either the best decision she ever made or her last one. Her heart fluttered wildly as she stepped around the trash scattered along the ground and after walking a short distance, she saw someone. There was enough grayish light shining from the street at the other end of the alley to reveal a figure up ahead, searching through the contents of a garbage dumpster.

She approached as quietly as she could and finally stopped and took several deep breaths. "Hello," she said cautiously. The person didn't respond, still bent over the side of the rusty dumpster rifling through its overflowing contents. "Hello there," she said louder.

A man straightened up and stared at her blankly. She moved closer and even with the drab lighting she noticed how dirty his face and clothes were. He had a round face with a few wisps of blond hair on top, just like a baby. She remembered him from one of the shelters. His name was

Burt, a simple minded, heavyset middle-aged man with large, innocent blue eyes. She recalled that someone had once referred to him as "Street Claus" because he spent his days wandering the city streets giving away whatever food he had to strangers, especially other homeless people. One day last winter a street person had complained about the sub-zero temperature, and Burt quickly pulled off his own coat and shirt and handed the man the clothing, walking away down the sidewalk bare-chested and seemingly oblivious to the frigid wind and the raucous laughter of everyone he passed. He would have ended up with frostbite except a social worker saw him and took him to get another jacket. The last time Sally had seen Burt she noticed he was extremely disoriented, wandering around aimlessly and mumbling to himself.

He continued to stare at her in silence so she patted him reassuringly on the shoulder. "It's OK. I'm Sally, Sally Malloy. I was sent to find an alley." She paused, realizing that wouldn't make sense to anyone. "You're Burt, aren't you?"

Burt scratched at his chest which was covered with a torn and faded Chicago Bears sweatshirt. "I can't find it. Somebody told me it's in one of these alleys, but I look in all of them and it ain't anywhere."

"What are you looking for?"

"Shoes, boxes and boxes of new shoes. He say they in a big garbage can, but I can't find them no place."

"Shoes? Some shelters are giving them out for the winter. You want me to take you to one?" She paused, realizing with a jolt of fear that there wasn't enough time left to go anywhere.

He shook his head adamantly. "Shoes ain't for me. I wanna give 'em away. Gotta be here somewhere." He turned away and leaned over the edge of the dumpster. He began mumbling incoherently, and she listened carefully but couldn't understand anything he said. His words were jumbled up in a nonsensical order.

"Burt, is there anything you have to tell me? Anything to show me?" She waited in vain for an answer and resisted the urge to break down and cry. "Burt, if this isn't the right place they're going to kill me."

He ignored her, continuing to talk to himself in a low monotone while he pulled out garbage. She went over to a pile of crates and sat down beside them, well within their dark shadow, and leaned against the cold brick wall. She decided she would sit and wait. Watching someone sift through garbage could not be the important event they had wanted her to see, but it was past one o'clock now and too late to look anywhere else. They would be coming for her soon.

She wondered what would happen to her after she died. Would she simply cease to exist? Was there an afterlife like her Christian friends claimed? Was heaven a place too wonderful to describe, like a beautiful pasture for sheep with Jesus being the gate and the good shepherd? It was very confusing.

She closed her eyes and listened to the clattering sounds of bottles and cans being thrown on the ground and struggled to fend off the constricting sensation in her throat. She didn't hear anything different, it was a just feeling that made her open her eyes and peer over the crates. She saw a man standing behind Burt, glancing around the alley. He wore a long, shapeless beige raincoat and a hat that was pulled down over his forehead. She sensed a tremendous energy emanating from him, a raging inferno of adrenaline powered fury.

Burt continued pulling out trash, completely unaware that someone was behind him. She saw the man step towards Burt. A silver object gleamed in his hand as he grabbed Burt from behind and quickly pulled it across his throat. He slashed across several more times and Burt's arms flailed wildly until they suddenly dropped limply to his side. The man in the raincoat laid Burt down on the ground and crouched over him, whispering something she couldn't quite make out. She saw him pull out a piece of paper and put it in Burt's pocket. She put her hands over her mouth to stifle a scream.

A car horn blared in the distance and the man jumped up and looked behind him. He then turned around in her direction and took a few steps towards the crates, staring past them to the alley's other entrance. His face turned at an angle and the dim light shined on his profile for an instant, long enough for her to recognize him with a shiver of revulsion. It was him! He was the one!

She pulled her head down so he wouldn't see her and restrained herself from yelling with unbridled horror. She had found the right location after all. They had sent her to witness this murder.

She heard his footsteps crunch on garbage and she pressed against the wall, listening intently as her hands shook uncontrollably. She waited a long time without hearing anything else before she finally looked over the top of a crate and saw he was gone. Burt was lying on his back on the ground and she hurried over, groaning with sorrow as she knelt beside him. His throat was slashed wide open and blood was oozing out. His face was frozen in a terrified expression and his lifeless blue eyes stared up at her in silent accusation.

Tears welled up in her eyes. "I'm so sorry, Burt. I didn't know. I would have yelled for you to run."

She noticed the piece of paper the murderer had placed in his pocket; it stuck out enough that she could tell it was a page torn from a book, its edge smeared with blood. She turned and ran back out of the alley, stumbling over trash, too upset over Burt's brutal murder to feel any relief that her own life had been spared. It was incredible that now she knew something no one in the entire nation knew. She knew the identity of the Homeless Slasher; the serial killer whose murders were front page news; the one who had frustrated the police for two years now and brought fear and death to so many. If she hadn't seen his face so clearly in the light she wouldn't have believed it was him. It raised a multitude of confusing questions in her mind.

But it wasn't important that she understand everything, she would go to the police immediately and tell them his name so the murders could finally end. Suddenly, she felt as if someone punched her in the stomach, and she stopped running and knelt down on the pavement, moaning loudly. "So that's why," she said in a bitter whisper as she gasped for air.

She knew what their next order would be. They didn't even have to tell her. They would forbid her to reveal the murderer's identity to anyone. She would have to keep guiltily silent as other innocent people were slaughtered one-by-one. What better way could they devise to torment her? And if she disobeyed them, they would kill her in the most excruciatingly painful way ever devised.

Chapter Two

The voice droned on, confident and soothing. "You can make your dreams come true. You can accomplish anything. All you have to do is believe you can."

Ryan Dolan gripped the steering wheel tighter and swung his car over into the wrong lane. A huge truck rumbled straight towards him, its brakes squealing with an animal-like sound in a hopeless attempt to prevent the inevitable head-on collision. Ryan's lips curled back with contempt as he watched the approaching truck driver frantically gesture at him. The truck's horn blared in desperation and one second before impact, Ryan made a sharp left turn into a small parking lot, his tires screeching as the car spun out of control in a complete circle before finally coming to a stop.

The voice on the cassette tape continued on, streaming out of the speaker like an incessant breeze off Lake Michigan. "With the right attitude you can achieve anything. And how do you develop it? With our ten easy steps to a positive attitude. Please turn this tape over now."

Ryan drove his aging, rust-eaten car next to a large garbage dumpster and rolled down the window. He ejected the cassette, glaring at it as he held it up in front of him.

"How's this for being positive?" he said aloud. "I believe I can throw you in the garbage." He tossed the cassette out the window with one smooth motion where it bounced off the side of the dumpster with a faint clink and fell down on the cracked asphalt parking lot. "I missed!" He yelled out the window at the cassette. "I guess that proves you were wrong!"

He slumped down in his seat as another voice whispered to him in a sardonic tone. *You're smart to quit, it's too late for positive thinking to help you.* Ryan didn't respond because this ridiculing voice existed within his own mind, frequently interrupting his innermost thoughts with disparaging remarks that always ruined his rare happy moments. Worst of all, it was always right.

He turned off the ignition and glanced over at the small one-story brick building whose faded sign proclaimed it as, "The Brass Bell." It was just another nondescript neighborhood bar, one of hundreds in Chicago.

He glanced at his watch; it was fifteen minutes past noon, so he was a little late. He looked at the ten cars in the parking lot, all gleaming in the bright sunlight, and he immediately recognized the brown mid-size model that the Chicago Police Department used for unmarked cars. This meant the person he was meeting was already there, waiting inside the bar.

Ryan opened his glove compartment and pulled out a .38 caliber revolver and some bullets. He held the bullets for a moment and then tossed all but one onto the floor of his car. One was enough; it was all he would need. He slid the bullet into the chamber of the gun and was annoyed when he noticed his hands were shaking. The adrenaline pumping into his system made him feel dizzy and weak and that frustrated him. His rapid, throbbing heartbeats echoed throughout his body and he thought to himself with disgust that even though he had just turned thirty and was in excellent health, it would be just his luck to have his first heart attack now and ruin everything.

Of course it might end for him anyway in a few minutes. Lately he had been reading the Bible, desperately searching for understanding and peace to ease his tortured existence, but he doubted if he were worthy of the forgiveness and blessings it promised. He remembered reading that Jesus said that he who lived by the sword died by the sword. He wondered if the warning Jesus gave applied to guns as well.

He got out of his car, tucked the gun under his belt, and put on an oversized coat to conceal it. *Don't do it*, his voice jeered at him, *you're going to fail as always.*

His legs felt wobbly as he walked to the entrance of the bar and paused for a moment in front of the door. A hand suddenly clamped down on his shoulder, and he instinctively ducked and spun around to face a small man wearing tattered clothes with a cardboard sign hanging on his chest that said, "Need a job. I will work for food."

"Sorry friend, I didn't mean to startle you," the man said sincerely.

"Nothing startles me," Ryan said unconvincingly as he took a deep breath.

"Know any place that's hiring?"

"No. Sorry."

"Same story everywhere." The man shook his head with discouragement. "I moved up here for a job, but it fell through. Me and my wife and kids been living in our car for three weeks now. Well, sorry to bother you." The man turned away.

"Wait a second." Ryan reached into his pocket and pulled out his wallet, taking out all the bills that were inside. "Here's fifty bucks," he said, handing it all to him. "Wish it was more. I hope it helps a little."

The man's eyes brightened with gratitude. "Thank you. This is very generous of you."

"Not really," Ryan said, discreetly adjusting the gun under his coat so it wouldn't pinch his stomach. "After today I might not need it."

Ryan turned away and opened the door. He stepped into the dingy room and breathed in a familiar aroma of cigarette smoke and beer while he waited for his eyes to adjust to the dim interior. A dozen people were sitting along the bar drinking quietly or eating lunch while a mournful country song crackled from an unseen speaker.

After a moment he noticed the row of booths along the far wall and saw him sitting there, staring back at him with undisguised hostility. It was Detective Kevin Dolan, one of Chicago's finest, and also Ryan's uncle.

Ryan walked over slowly, hoping the gun's bulge wasn't noticeable under his coat, and that it wouldn't work its way out of his pants and fall to the floor with an embarrassing clatter. Kevin Dolan wore a dark suit and glared at him menacingly as he slid out of the booth. Ryan estimated his uncle weighed 280 now, still impressively proportioned on his six-four frame. As a kid he thought his uncle was the biggest man in the world and he expected to be the same size when he grew up but instead ended up 5'10". Not small, but not big either. He weighed 185 pounds, with an athletic physique but certainly not massive. In fact, in his opinion there was nothing special about him. Every time he looked in a mirror he saw ordinary brown hair and a pug nose that seemed much too short. Some women had told him he was cute, but he didn't believe it. A couple of times he had wondered half seriously if he should get his nose fixed, but figured they couldn't make a nose longer, just smaller.

"Did you make those calls?" Kevin Dolan asked with a skeptical frown.

"You haven't seen me in two years and I don't even get a hello?"

"I said hello on the phone. You didn't call them did you?"

Ryan resisted the urge to swallow, a blatant sign of intimidation that his uncle would surely notice. "I couldn't. It's my apartment's fault."

"Why?"

"Because it's such a mess I couldn't find my phone." He forced a smile. "If only I could afford a maid."

Kevin Dolan threw his hands up in the air in disgust. "I knew you wouldn't call them. You just want to be a lazy bum and roam around the country doing nothing."

"I'm not lazy, and I've been traveling, not roaming."

"You could make good money selling cars, you could meet some hot women working in a health club, or you could be a security guard. I had it all set up. You just had to pick up the phone and any one of those jobs was yours. What's the matter, aren't any of them good enough for you?"

"They're all good jobs."

"If you became a security guard you could even wear a uniform again."

Ryan winced as if he'd been slapped. "I appreciate what you're trying to do."

"Yeah, sure you do. I give you an opportunity to improve your miserable life and you spit on it. You're twenty-nine years old and you still haven't grown up."

"Actually, I turned thirty last month."

"Whatever. You'll never change."

"Yes I will," Ryan said, staring back with intensity. "Today is my turning point. One way or the other, things will never be the same for me."

Kevin laughed sarcastically. "Sure, kid."

"That's why I asked to meet with you." Ryan gestured to the booth. "Can we talk?"

"I'd rather take you outside and kick some sense into you."

"OK. When we're done talking you can beat me up."

"Don't get sarcastic with me."

"I'm sorry, I don't mean to be. I just want to ask you about something. You'll be real surprised, because it's very important."

Kevin paused and then shrugged at him with a skeptical expression. "OK then, let's talk. I can use a good laugh."

They sat down on opposite sides of the booth and Ryan leaned forward against the table, feeling the gun press against his abdomen. "You're still working on the Homeless Slasher investigation, right?"

Kevin nodded. "Along with fifty other detectives. What does that have to do with your messed up life?"

"The Slasher killed Burt Wojik three days ago."

"I see you read the papers, I'm real impressed. Yeah, a worthless moron named Burt. Victim number twenty-three."

"Did he leave any new evidence this time?"

"Nothing, just like all the others. He left another page from that book, but there were no fingerprints on it and no fibers."

"*Death Is a Blessing.*"

"Yeah, that stupid book about the homeless. He left page twenty-three this time. The next one will get page twenty-four of course."

"And he underlined the word, compassion."

"Yeah, just the one word that was in the middle of a sentence and as usual, with the same ink that's in a million pens sold in any drugstore."

"Do you have any good suspects?"

"We got nothing; no suspects, no leads, no evidence. We just get headaches and hemorrhoids."

"Then the news media is right."

Kevin snorted in disgust. "Don't talk to me about those parasites. It wasn't so bad last year when this wacko had only killed ten. But now that the story's national the heat is unbearable. Network crews are hanging around all the time, bugging us for interviews. The Mayor's screaming at the Chief, and the Chief's screaming at us."

"Have you learned anything from the victims?"

"Nothing you haven't seen on the news. He preys on the bottom of the barrel; the scummiest of the homeless, the mentally ill, the old, the sick. The only common denominator is they were all helpless street people."

"Nine were women, fourteen were men. A pretty even split."

"And this knife freak ain't a bigot, either; ten whites, nine blacks, three Hispanics, and one Asian."

Ryan nodded. "They're different ages, too."

"And they were killed in different locations; Uptown, the Loop, West Town, the South Side. He likes variety, that's for sure."

"He's lucky no one's seen him."

"Yeah, he's lucky and smart. He obviously picks his victims carefully then he kills them in out of the way places like alleys, abandoned buildings, and parks. We've talked to a bunch of street people and no one's seen anything."

"What kind of profile do you have on him?"

"Depends on what week it is. First the FBI said he was definitely white, then they changed him to black, now he's white again. First he was one of the homeless and now he's not. They say he's on a personal crusade and he's male like other serial killers, but that doesn't help any. I think they're just sitting around picking their ears like the rest of us."

Ryan stared at the beer on the table in front of his uncle. Amber bubbles were lazily drifting up to the foamy surface, it would be so easy to grab the glass and suck down huge swallows of salty carbonation.

"This is the first time I've seen you in a bar without a drink," Kevin said, reading his thoughts.

Ryan resisted an absurd urge to take his gun out and shoot the beer glass. "I'm trying to quit."

"That's very commendable; don't want a job, but trying to stay sober. At least that's half a start." He took a huge gulp of his beer and wiped his mouth with the back of his hand. "So, when are you going to tell me why we're here?"

Ryan looked up and felt an eyelid begin twitching in nervous betrayal. "I came back to Chicago for a reason. I want to help you find the Homeless Slasher."

Kevin stared at him in disbelief for a few seconds and then laughed loudly, his huge body shaking. Ryan felt anger rise within him so suddenly and forcefully that his vision blurred. "Don't laugh at me."

Something in his tone stopped Kevin's laughter and he looked at Ryan with disdain. "You're serious? Aren't you forgetting something? You're not a cop anymore."

"I don't mean officially." He struggled to speak in a controlled voice. "I'll work on my own; do your legwork, walk the streets, anything you want me to do."

"The only thing I want you to do is straighten out your life."

"I could help you find him."

"Finding the Easter Bunny would be easier than finding this guy."

"I'll work around the clock."

"Tell me kid, how did you come up with such a ridiculous idea?"

Ryan resisted the urge to look away from Kevin's contemptuous gaze. "Maybe I've got nothing better to do. Maybe I think saving the lives of future victims is a noble cause."

"That's about as noble as my armpit hair. Who cares about the homeless? I don't. They're all lazy, or lunatics, or both."

"How do you know some of them aren't just unlucky?"

"Cause I know." Kevin shook his head in amazement. "So, that's your motivation? You want to save worthless people?"

"I don't believe they're worthless," Ryan hesitated, "but that's not my only reason. I think I could have been a good cop and I want to prove it to the department, the city, and the whole country. But most of all I want to prove it to me."

"Forget it kid."

"Will you let me help you?"

"Be a security guard instead."

"If I start investigating on my own will you at least give me inside information so I'll have a better chance?"

"No way."

"I thought you'd say that." Ryan looked down at the table and rubbed the back of his head which was now giving him shooting pains in perfect unison with his pounding heart. He reached under his jacket, gripped the gun, and pulled it out.

He looked up and saw fear in Kevin's eyes, something he had never seen before. "Put that thing away."

"Don't worry I'm not going to use it on you. You're safe." He was impressed at how calm and controlled his voice sounded even while his hands were visibly shaking. "It's for me," he said as he put the gun under his chin, the cold barrel pressed hard against his skin.

"Put it down."

"Why? My life's a waste."

"You won't do it. You're bluffing." Kevin leaned forward slightly, his eyes narrowing with anger. "If you blow your head off you'll die a failure and you can't stand the thought of dying that way."

Ryan forced himself to grin. "Yeah, you're right. I'm bluffing so I can work on the case with you. I'm not going to kill myself." He pulled the gun away from his neck and pushed it against his left shoulder. "But I'm serious about this."

"What are you doing now?"

"If I shoot myself in the shoulder I'll bleed a lot, but I won't die."

Kevin banged his fist on the table. "All this for the idiotic homeless murders?"

"You'll have to write a report on the shooting. It'll be embarrassing for you when everyone realizes it's your long, lost nephew."

"Put it away!"

"Let me work on the case with you."

With surprising quickness Kevin suddenly reached out and grabbed the gun from his hand in one swift motion. He opened it up and took out the bullet and groaned. He lunged across the table and slapped Ryan across the face. "You make me sick!"

Ryan pushed himself out of the booth, his face stinging and his stomach churning with nausea. As he ran to the front door, he noticed the other people had turned around on the bar stools to watch, their faces seeming large and grotesquely twisted like distorted reflections in a carnival mirror. The blaring country music was now drowned out by the angry rushing sound in his ears, as deafening as a surging waterfall crashing down on jagged rocks below.

He pulled the door open, letting in a flood of blinding sunlight and through the thunderous noise within him he could still hear a familiar derisive voice. *Your uncle is right. You'll never find the Homeless Slasher because you're a failure; always have been, always will be. Nothing you do can ever change what you did that one unforgettable day. Nothing will ever change that.*

Chapter Three

Lydia Dupree resisted the urge to scream. Instead she leaned forward and drummed a finger on the battered table. "Tell me again what Burt said the night he was killed." She waited, struggling to keep frustration out of her voice. "Alvin, do you hear me?"

Alvin sat across from her, slumped protectively over a plate of scrambled eggs and hash browns. He was a tiny, wrinkled African-American man in his fifties wearing a sweater that was several sizes too big. He looked up at her with genuine weariness. "I already told you and the cops more times than I can count."

"Just one more time, Alvin, in case you forgot something."

Alvin looked around for some gesture of sympathy, but no one even noticed him. The other homeless men and women seated at nearby tables kept quietly eating their food. "My eggs will get cold."

"I'll get you more. Tell me again."

Alvin was about to say something but then paused and Lydia noticed his eyes brightened with relief.

"Ten more minutes, Lydia," a familiar voice said, and she clenched her fists in annoyance.

She turned to see Martin Sanders standing behind her, smiling with sadistic pleasure. He was a tall, thin man in his thirties with dark hair and a neatly trimmed beard that gave him an eerie resemblance to a young Abe Lincoln. "I know what time it is," she answered sharply, hoping her pessimism wouldn't be too obvious.

"Then you know it's hopeless. That's why you're wasting your last remaining minutes playing detective." He walked away with a smug expression on his face and Lydia turned back to Alvin, feeling her face redden with anger.

"You need to go somewhere?" Alvin asked hopefully. Lydia shook her head emphatically and he sighed with resignation and put down his fork, carefully wiping his mouth with a napkin. "I was sitting on a sidewalk down on Artesian Avenue. Burt comes up and says, 'Hey, gotta find those shoes. Where are they hiding?'"

"And you reminded him we have some shoes here at this shelter?"

"Yeah, right. I say that, but this Burt, he's a little gone you know. He says, 'Gotta give away shoes. Bunches of them waiting for me.' I don't bother asking why, I know that cat was crazy. Never hung around him but saw him at shelters sometimes, usually mumbling to himself and trying to give away candy bars and stuff. So I ask him where he's gonna find all these shoes and he points and says, 'That way. Somebody told me there's a bunch of boxes of them in a garbage can in an alley.'"

"You didn't ask who told him that?"

"No, I didn't care at the time. I just wished him good luck in finding them and he kind of rambled away down the street. I just rested there for another hour or so and then moved on."

"Did you notice anyone following him?"

"No."

"Do you remember anybody who walked past you after he left?"

"No. Plenty of people walked by but nobody I know or remember." Alvin shook his head. "I don't think old Burt knew where he was going. Poor harmless dude, I don't know why anybody would kill him or all those other street folks. I guess only God knows."

"Yes, and that won't help us at all. You can't count on God."

"You don't believe in God?"

Lydia frowned. "I've believed in Him since I was a little girl. I used to pray to Him all the time, but I'll never pray again. And it's His fault that I won't." She stood up. "I'll find this murderer without God's help."

Lydia looked around at the others seated at tables; all were dressed in worn or poorly fitting clothes. A few had contented expressions, but most looked tired and depressed with sagging faces and glazed eyes. They were an equal racial mix of white, African-American, and Hispanic, which was normal for their Logan Square location. Two-thirds of them were men and their ages ranged from 18 to 70. What disturbed her the most was seeing six women with small children; they represented the fastest growing category of Chicago's homeless population.

She noticed several new faces, but decided not to question any of them about Burt's murder. She was upset and would probably question them too aggressively and she didn't want to make them uncomfortable on their first visit to The Helping Hand. So instead, she walked towards the kitchen and took a deep breath before pushing the door open. The kitchen was large and cluttered with plates and cups stacked on the counters and Lydia inhaled the familiar aromas of scrambled eggs, coffee, and spaghetti sauce.

Martin was leaning over a boiling pot of spaghetti, but he immediately turned towards her and grinned sarcastically. "How did it go, Inspector Lydia?"

"The same as always. Nowhere."

"Don't worry, the Chicago Police will catch him eventually. Of course there might not be any homeless people left by then."

"I'm going to find him myself. I know I will."

Martin shook his head. "Such brazen confidence. Tell me are you equally confident you'll defeat me?"

"Yes," she said, moving to the counter and opening a box of doughnuts.

Martin laughed as he glanced at his watch. "Right. You have six minutes left; plenty of time." He walked over and gestured at the cupboard above her which had a piece of paper taped to it. "After all, maybe I miscounted." His lips moved silently as he scanned the list. "No, there's definitely seven on my list and only six on yours. That means I win, doesn't it?"

"Not yet." Lydia's stomach tightened as if she were suddenly plunging downhill on a roller coaster, but she forced herself to nonchalantly take the doughnuts out of the box and pile them on a plate.

Martin laughed again. "First of all, how about wearing something provocative? We'll have a quiet romantic dinner and then we'll go someplace where we can slow dance for a few hours. And finally, back to my place where you will finally confess you find me incredibly attractive and have fallen madly in love with me."

"Not a chance. You'll be lucky if I agree to the dancing and I'll wear five layers of clothes." She crushed a doughnut in frustration and hoped he wouldn't notice. Why had she so foolishly agreed to the bet? She should have known he'd compete so tenaciously that he might actually win. He had hooked her with a worthy cause though; a week long contest to see who could convince the most unsheltered people to stay in an overnight shelter. She had mistakenly assumed she'd win easily and get to help others at the same time.

She moved to a cupboard and pulled out a stack of napkins, conscious of Martin's eyes eagerly following her. She had often thought it would be an interesting experiment to shave her head and have her facial features altered into grotesque deformities. She could envision the stunned expression on the plastic surgeon's face when she told him she didn't want to be attractive, that she wanted him to change her perfectly straight nose into a crooked monstrosity, to put large hideous scars on her smooth complexion, and make her full, supposedly sensuous mouth twisted and deformed. She wondered if that type of surgery would make her life easier. If so, then it would be worth the pain and expense.

Many men had told her she should be an actress or model instead of a social worker, which always angered her because she knew her occupation was infinitely more meaningful than posing for cameras all day. Besides, she wasn't at all impressed with her own looks. In her opinion, her long, flowing red hair was so glaringly bright that it was positively garish and her snow white complexion made her look like a pale, sickly vampire. Her body was in decent shape, not too heavy or thin, but plenty of women had more voluptuous figures. Long ago she had decided men must have illogical standards of beauty to consider her so attractive. It frightened and disgusted her when a man looked at her with blatant interest, and it happened far too often. She wished instead that she could be totally ignored. It wasn't that she had no interest in men, sometimes she'd meet a man whose personality or looks were very appealing, but she'd stubbornly fight back any feelings of attraction. She didn't want a man in her life now and would not allow herself any relationship except platonic friendship. She hadn't explained this to anyone. No one would understand why someone twenty-five years old wasn't interested in romance. Her friends certainly wouldn't; it seemed like every time she accompanied one of them to dinner or the theater they told her about a good-looking guy their boyfriend or husband knew who would be a perfect match for her. They'd be happy to arrange a blind date; it wouldn't be any trouble at all. She would always force an appreciative smile and politely decline, saying she was just too particular when it came to men. It would be a waste of time to try and make them understand because they hadn't endured the horror, as she called it. Her life had once been dominated by that unspeakable horror. Even now it caused her to wake up sometimes in the middle of the night screaming incoherent words of terror.

"I promise we'll have a great time," Martin said, moving closer and putting his hand on her shoulder.

She recoiled and moved away. "I've warned you not to touch me!"

He blinked at her, stunned, his smile fading. The kitchen door swung open and a diminutive young Hispanic woman walked in with a small boy. She looked at Lydia with large, frightened eyes. "Are you Lydia Dupree?"

"Yes."

"I'm Maria Gonzales. I talked to you on the phone this morning. You said you could find a shelter for me and my son."

"Yes, Mrs. Gonzales. I'll be happy to help you." Lydia glanced at her watch and turned to Martin with a triumphant glare. "There's three minutes to go and this gives me eight. I win."

A few minutes later, Lydia stared at her in disbelief. "What do you mean you've changed your mind?"

Maria Gonzales sat on a folding chair on the other side of the desk staring at the neat stacks of paperwork. After a while she looked up with huge brown eyes but avoided Lydia's gaze, evasively glancing around the tiny office before feigning interest in a small bookcase against a wall and the poster above it showing children building an enormous sandcastle on a beach. A frail looking seven-year-old boy sat next to her with a worried expression. Lydia noticed the scab on his swollen lower lip and the ugly purple bruise under Maria's eye.

"My husband Carlos gets angry sometimes," Maria said softly, "but he still loves me. I'm going home now."

Lydia leaned across the desk. "Mrs. Gonzales, you told me on the phone your husband beats you frequently."

Maria nodded slowly, "Sometimes when he drinks or is in a bad mood. It's probably my fault. I must be a bad wife. If I was a good wife he'd be happy all the time."

"No, it's not your fault he beats you. Even if you were a bad wife, which I'm sure you're not, that still doesn't give him the right to assault you."

Maria shook her head. "Sometimes it's my fault he gets mad; I cook a lousy dinner or the house is messy or I don't look pretty enough."

"No," Lydia said, struggling to control her rising anger. "There is nothing you could do to deserve these beatings. It's common for an abused wife to blame herself, but believe me what he does to you is inexcusable."

Lydia shook her head, winning the wager against Martin was no longer important but helping this woman and her son certainly was. She got up and walked around the desk and put her arm around the boy. "Benito, how did you get that swollen lip?"

Benito looked startled and glanced at his mother who nodded at him in resignation. "I was playing too noisy," he said in a haltering voice. "My Dad hit me."

Lydia stared at Maria, her arm still protectively around Benito's shoulders. "If your husband ever hurts him again then it's your fault because you passed up this opportunity to protect him."

"Carlos will never forgive me if we leave him."

"I told you about the women's shelter this morning. It's a safe house for battered women and children. Your husband won't be able to find you or hurt you anymore. You can also press charges if you want."

Maria's eyes filled with tears. "I love my husband."

Lydia resisted the urge to make a disparaging remark. "And your son, do you love him?"

Maria nodded and wiped tears from her eyes. "Yes."

"Your husband will be notified that you've been removed to a safe place. If he agrees to counseling he'll eventually be allowed supervised visits. Maybe you can reconcile someday." Lydia hesitated. "My shift here is over. How about letting me drive you over to that shelter now?"

"All right," Maria said, nodding with dejection. "I'll do it, for my Benito."

Lydia hugged Benito and smiled with relief. "That's wonderful! Let's go."

But as she ushered them out of the office her euphoria quickly dissipated, crowded out by a familiar gnawing terror. After she dropped them off she would have to go home. Her hands shook whenever she remembered. Something she feared so much would be there again. It would be waiting for her.

Chapter Four

An unopened bottle of vodka was on the table, its clear liquid as innocent looking as pure water from a mineral spring. Ryan Dolan stared at it with a tormented expression. The early morning sunshine was filtering into his apartment and he picked up the bottle, tilting it at different angles so it would reflect the light.

He bought it last night to forget the traumatic encounter yesterday with his uncle, but by the time he got home he'd somehow regained enough willpower to resist opening it and went to bed early instead. His sleep had been filled with recurring dreams of children's eyes staring at him in silent condemnation until the blood flowed over them, covering them forever. More nightmares, he thought to himself, that's my reward for having self-control. He squeezed the bottle as hard as he could. Even though he was awake another gruesome vision could return at any moment to strangle him with anguish and remorse. "If you take one drink you'll take another;" That's what they say at Alcoholics Anonymous meetings. He knew if he poured just a few drops in his orange juice he'd end up draining the entire bottle and staggering around his apartment in frustration and rage until he passed out.

He had two other .38's besides the one his uncle had taken away from him. They were in a battered dresser drawer in his bedroom, loaded and ready. He doubted he could ever actually shoot himself, though. He didn't want to end his life, miserable as it was. *It would be for the best*; a harsh voice whispered within his mind, *you have nothing to live for, but you won't do it, you're a coward.*

He had pulled his suitcases out of the closet and put them on the bed. He could be all packed up in fifteen minutes. Take off for Vegas or New Orleans or anywhere else. Forget about trying to find the Homeless Slasher. Forget Chicago.

He glanced around his apartment as if it could offer him advice, but all he saw was a sparsely furnished room with a worn couch and a scarred coffee table that looked worse than usual with the bright sunlight streaming through his front window. The plain beige carpet on the floor was crushed down as if hundreds of steamrollers had thundered over it. The room was certainly too depressing to offer any advice about living or dying.

He noticed his Bible on the coffee table. He had grown up an agnostic and scoffed at Christians for believing in a book of fairy tales. But recently, he'd been reading it and was impressed with the personality of Jesus. His wisdom and charisma were far more appealing than he'd expected. He'd also read a couple of books on Christian apologetics and discovered there was much more historical and logical evidence that supported the Bible than he'd thought. He now believed that God and Jesus probably did exist. That was bad news for him because he also believed they would never forgive him. They really shouldn't, he thought, I'm not worthy of salvation. Not after what I've done.

If he decided to stay he would launch a one-man investigation of the homeless murders. He had read everything available on the twenty-three killings and filled up two notebooks with information. He was convinced the key to the case was what the Slasher left with the victims. Each one had a page from a book beginning with page one and continuing consecutively to page twenty-three. The book was a true story about the experiences of a writer who had disguised himself as a homeless person in New York City. Every page the killer left had a word or phrase underlined such as "more shelters" or "job training" or "government funds." The underlined words were either a statement about the plight of the homeless or a clever strategy to cover a hidden motive.

Ryan looked again at the bottle of vodka thinking how a few swallows might wash away his despair and loneliness. One drink couldn't hurt.

He forced himself to turn away and thought of how he would first visit all the murder sites which he had carefully marked on a map. He would also go to the newspapers and ask to see photos taken of the victims at those same locations, posing as a freelance writer and hoping no one recognized him. Then the time consuming part would begin, days and weeks of visiting shelters and soup kitchens, talking to anyone who knew the victims or had seen anything suspicious. The police were already doing that of course, but Chicago was a huge, sprawling city and they may have missed someone who knew something. Maybe he could discover something important and stop the senseless slaughter of innocent people. But he had also counted on his uncle supplying him with information the police withheld from the press. *That figures, nothing ever turns out right for you.*

He got up and walked over to the coffee table where he had left the large manila envelope, and his stomach tightened with foreboding as he approached.

The envelope had arrived in yesterday's mail and was badly crumpled. He knew it contained a manuscript of a play he had written, a drama about a man struggling to rebuild his shattered life. The envelope had the return address of a theater in Los Angeles, and he'd put off opening it because he knew it was just another rejection. He'd sent it out to thirty-six theaters so far and every one of them had turned it down. He had written two other plays in recent years which hadn't been produced either. The plays were a joy to write, but the continual rejections were devastating. It was unbearable to realize that the characters he had created would never come to life on any stage. That was always the best part, the characters. He understood how they thought and felt. He visualized them so clearly that he was always able to lose himself in their lives as he wrote; temporarily escaping from his own tortured existence.

He took a deep breath and opened the envelope telling himself there was always hope. *Yeah, right.* He pulled out the manuscript and quickly skimmed the attached note. It was just another standard rejection letter which meant the grand total of rejections was now at thirty-seven. At the bottom of the letter however, someone had scrawled a few words with a pen. "We can't use this, but keep trying! You have talent!"

Ryan stared at the words in disbelief. He'd been sending out his plays for years now, and no one had ever offered him any encouragement. He reread the words several times feeling as if he would explode with rapidly growing joy.

When he finally looked up, he watched in silent awe as the front wall of his apartment suddenly became hazy and seemed to melt away entirely, revealing the dark interior of a theater with seemingly endless rows of seats facing him. He squinted through the bright lights that now shined down on him and could see well-dressed men and women seated in the first few rows, the rest hidden in darkness while they watched, silently judging him. His apartment was now a stage for an imaginary audience, and that thought delighted him.

He grinned and saluted the audience. "Ladies and gentlemen," he said to them. "I promise to give you your money's worth!"

He hurried to his bedroom which was off-stage and returned carrying his two guns, walking quickly to the table where the bottle of vodka was. He put the guns down beside it and took the bottle to his kitchen sink where a week's dirty dishes were piled up. He twisted the cap off, tipped the bottle over the sink, and watched stoically as all the vodka poured down on the dishes.

"Probably the best way to clean them," he said to the audience with another grin. "Kills all the germs."

When the bottle was empty he tossed it into an overflowing garbage can next to the sink, knocking an empty cereal box to the floor in the process. Then he went over and picked up both guns and dropped them into the garbage can where they landed with a loud clink.

He pulled his car keys off a hook on the wall, grabbed a notebook, and headed toward the back door. He heard applause burst forth from his imaginary audience in a sudden cascade of sound, a fervent response from people who had just witnessed a magnificently performed scene. He paused and turned to see the faces in the first few rows smiling with unbridled expressions of admiration, rising as one as they continued to enthusiastically clap their hands.

You shouldn't have wasted that bottle, the voice shouted at him above the applause. *You failed as a cop. You're still a failure as a playwright, and you'll only waste your time tracking the Homeless Slasher.*

He opened the door and paused again, looking back at the audience exhorting him on. He bowed deeply and stepped out of his apartment into the cool, invigorating breeze.

Chapter Five

Lydia drove north on the Kennedy Expressway trying to dodge potholes so deep that her teeth seemed to rattle when her car ran over one. She had just left Maria and Benito Gonzales at the women's shelter downtown, and Maria had assured her with grateful tears that she would press charges against her husband and allow the social worker at the shelter to handle communication with him.

Normally she would feel elated at how well her day had gone. Although she hadn't made any progress on solving the murders, she had helped someone and won a wager against Martin at the same time. But instead, a painfully tight feeling in her stomach was slowly turning into nausea. She opened the window slightly to let in some cool air and slowed down a little. There was no reason to hurry home because she knew another one would be waiting for her.

The first one came four days ago, a plain white envelope, postmarked in Chicago, with her name and address typed on it. There was no return address. She had opened it and laughed when she saw there was only a piece of lined notebook paper on which a large letter "I" was written in ink. She assumed it was a strange joke and threw it away. The next day another one arrived in the mail, and she opened it to find another piece of notebook paper with the word "WILL" written on it with block letters. She decided then if it wasn't a joke it must be a bizarre marketing ploy by some business. So far the message was, "I WILL." "I WILL," what?

Two days ago another one came, and she opened it eagerly and saw that the word "GET" was written on the paper. The three consecutive messages now said "I WILL GET." She had a restless night, struggling to sleep while her mind pondered different explanations for the cryptic notes, some of them extremely frightening.

When she arrived home last night and found another envelope in her mailbox, her hands trembled slightly as she ripped it open. "YOU" was written on the paper. Four days of messages now spelled out, "I WILL GET YOU."

She only slept for a few hours, too frustrated to relax. As soon as she arrived at The Helping Hand in the morning she had confronted Martin, demanding to know if he was mailing her the mysterious notes but he looked at her with such genuine confusion when he denied it that she decided he was telling the truth. In working with him over the last six months she had noticed he was an unconvincing liar, unable to keep a straight face whenever he said something untrue. Judging by his reaction, he really didn't know what she was talking about. Besides, her instincts told her Martin wasn't sending the notes, it was someone from her past. Maybe even the man responsible for what she referred to as the "horror." What little sleep she had gotten the last two nights was filled with sickeningly graphic images of that time.

It was all God's fault. She had never expected so many horrible things to happen after she became a Christian. Ever since she was a small child her grandmother had taken her to church regularly and would often read to her from the Bible. She was only eight when she had prayed one night for Jesus to forgive her and come into her life. Her grandmother was delighted and began to have regular Bible studies with her, which were actually quite enjoyable.

Her mother never participated or said much about her beliefs. Her grandmother said she was a "backsliding" Christian who would return to her faith someday. Her father had deserted them when Lydia was a baby, and she had given up asking her mother about him. If she mentioned him around her grandmother she would just shake her head sadly and say she still prayed for him.

Lydia's mother had never finished high school and struggled to support them as they lived in a series of rundown apartments in Cleveland. Lydia was an only child, but her grandmother lived nearby and gave her enough attention that she didn't feel deprived.

Lydia was twelve when her grandmother died suddenly from a stroke. Her opinion of God did not change though; she knew her grandmother was in a paradise beyond imagination with all the loved ones who had gone before her. She missed her but she wasn't angry at God. She could accept the fact that He had allowed her grandmother to die. But she could never accept what followed.

Her mother remarried a few months later to Bobby Joe Miller. He was a tall man with a gold tooth and a penchant for drinking. Her mother drank with him frequently and

Bobby Joe would usually be in a bad mood and say cruel things, disparaging her mother's looks or anything she said. In time, he became more abusive and on a few occasions Lydia saw him shove or slap her. One night when she was in bed she heard her mother sobbing in the next room.

Lydia despised Bobby Joe for the way he treated her mother. She would sometimes imagine herself inflicting pain on him by various sadistic methods but she reluctantly stopped when she remembered Christians were not supposed to take revenge. They had to wait for God to do it. So she decided if she couldn't hurt Bobby Joe herself then at least she'd end the misery he was causing. It would be easy; all she had to do was pray. After all, Jesus said ask and you will receive, and the Bible was filled with examples of men and women turning to God for help. Surely God did not approve of Bobby Joe's behavior or want her mother to suffer. Every night at bedtime she prayed for God to intervene and change their situation for the better. She knew He would help.

One night Lydia was beading a macramé necklace to give to her mother on her upcoming birthday while she worked the night shift at a doughnut shop. She was sitting on the floor in their apartment living room; Bobby Joe was slumped in a nearby chair with a six-pack watching a baseball game. They had only lived there a few months but the walls were already marked up from the things that Bobby Joe had thrown.

He completely ignored her, which was a relief, only shouting occasionally at the TV when the Cleveland Indians would do something bad. When an Indian hit into a double play to lose the game he screamed and threw an empty beer can at the TV. He opened another beer and glared at her.

Lydia avoided looking at him and continued beading the necklace. She heard him walk over and could smell his beer breath as he stood over her.

"Hey, what is that ridiculous thing you're makin'?"

She looked up at him, feeling out of breath, as if she'd run up a flight of stairs. "It's for Mom's birthday."

He snorted and reached down and picked up the necklace, eyeing it with disgust. "You ain't got much respect for your mom."

"Of course I do."

"No you don't. If you did you wouldn't give her garbage like this." He flicked his wrist and the necklace went flying into a corner, some of the beads flew off and clattered against the wall.

"Why do you hit my mom?" She spoke the words before realizing what she'd said.

"What?" Bobby Joe stared in disbelief. "Are you mouthin' off at me?"

"No . . . I'm not."

Bobby Joe's upper lip curled. "Maybe you need a lesson in manners." He grabbed for her but she ducked under his arm and sprinted for her bedroom. A beer can sailed past her and splattered against the wall. She ran into her room, closing the door and locking it just as his body slammed into it. He yelled vile names at her and told her he was going to enjoy punishing her.

Lydia hurried over to her window, took out the screen, and climbed down the fire escape. She ran all the way to the doughnut shop, over a mile. When she got there she was so tired she couldn't speak for a few moments so her mom took her to a corner booth and gave her a glass of water and waited.

Lydia told her mother what had happened. Her mother listened in silence but her blue eyes clouded up with irrepressible anger. When she was finished her mother hugged her tightly.

"This isn't your fault, Lydia. He's gone too far this time." She took off her apron and walked determinedly out of the doughnut shop. "Stay here until I come back." It was the last time Lydia saw her alive.

Her mother had gone back and confronted Bobby Joe, and according to the neighbors, there was a lot of shouting followed by an ominous silence. Hours later when the doughnut shop closed a woman who worked there drove her home and walked her up to their apartment. They found the front door open and her mother lying on the floor with a broken neck.

Her anger at Bobby Joe was insignificant compared to the burning rage she felt towards God. She had prayed faithfully for Him to protect her mother, trusting Him completely. Bobby Joe was an animal and what he had done was consistent with his violent nature but God claimed to love everyone enough to send His Son to die for their sins. How much love did He show by letting her mother be murdered? She knew God could have stopped Bobby Joe, but instead He did nothing and for that she would never forgive Him.

The police never found Bobby Joe Miller. Lydia had no relatives so she lived in a series of foster homes, some better than others. It wasn't until three years later that she found a note that had been tucked away in the dress of one of her dolls. It was Bobby Joe's handwriting and it had probably been written the night of the murder. The note said, "I'll return for you someday! And you'll end up just like your mom!"

If only the police had found him, she thought to herself as she got off the Kennedy Expressway and headed north on California Avenue. And now the strange notes in the mail were bringing the memories back, but why? Was there a connection or was she being paranoid? Had her stepfather tracked her down after all these years to exact some twisted retribution?

Lydia clenched the steering wheel tighter and her breathing suddenly became labored, as if she were suffocating. Quit acting like a coward, she told herself. There may be another note waiting at home and it could be him who's been sending them. So what? I can deal with him or anyone else. I won't be a victim.

She deliberately inhaled and exhaled with slow deep breaths and chided herself for feeling so paralyzed with fear. She was reacting just like so many women did in old movies who always screamed helplessly or burst into tears whenever they were frightened, and that was something she had vowed never to emulate.

She continued driving and forced herself to think about the Homeless Slasher. It angered her that someone was murdering pathetic homeless people and getting away with it and after months of questioning hundreds of street people she still hadn't discovered anything useful. She'd never stop trying, though, because if she came up with just one good lead for the police all her efforts would be worthwhile.

Lydia turned into the driveway of a well-maintained two-story graystone building across from California Park. She had chosen it because it was only five minutes away from The Helping Hand and her apartment faced the park with its tall trees and spacious green fields.

She parked her car in the carport that she shared with three other tenants and walked around to the front of the building as her heart vibrated in her chest with annoying thuds. I'm not going to be intimidated, she told herself, no matter what this one says.

She climbed the front steps and paused by the door where a row of small mailboxes were mounted on the building. She took another deep breath, swallowed hard, twisted the knob, and removed a handful of mail. She quickly shuffled through the junk mail until she found another letter. It was the same as the others, a plain white envelope with her address neatly typed on it and a Chicago postmark.

She told herself she should go inside and calmly read it in the privacy of her apartment but instead her fingers involuntarily ripped it open and dropped the rest of the mail which scattered to the ground like wind blown leaves.

"I WILL GET YOU . . . what?" She pulled the piece of paper out of the envelope, unfolded it and saw what was written on it. Someone had written the word, "SOON!"

Chapter Six

"Where did you find the body?" Ryan asked.

"Right here in the doorway. There was a big puddle of blood on the ground, that's what got my attention." She spoke in a bored, flat monotone and Ryan wondered if discovering a dead body had affected her at all. She had told him she was twenty-three but she looked more like fifteen. Small and petite with pale, ghostlike skin that was so faded it seemed almost transparent. Her huge blue eyes stared at him with obvious distrust. Her jeans were worn and she wore an oversized black coat and a black derby. She had taken it off once to scratch her head and he was surprised to notice her light brown hair was cut in a buzz that was as short as a Marine's.

"She was on her stomach, right?" he asked.

"Yeah."

"Most of the other victims were found on their backs. Do you think she struggled?"

"How do I know? I was asleep, remember?"

"Yes." He leaned into the doorway and looked again at the graffiti scrawled on the walls and the broken crates scattered about on the dusty cement floor. He noticed a quick movement in a corner and saw a rat scurry through a pile of garbage. The room smelled like stale, decaying food. It was just another ordinary decrepit abandoned building on the South Side, no different than countless others throughout the city except for one important difference; a homeless woman had been murdered in this one.

"When do I get my twenty dollars?"

"In a few minutes," he said, trying to keep the impatience out of his voice. A real cooperative witness, he thought to himself sarcastically. Unfortunately, she was the only witness that had been found so far, and wasn't much of one at that. She had simply been sleeping nearby when the Homeless Slasher had murdered victim number twenty-two, Lucille Johnson, one month before Burt Wojik had been killed.

"Hey, man, I've already answered a million questions and I gotta go now," she said, glancing up and down the alley with a worried look. "I'm afraid. Somebody's been following me."

"Can you give me a description?"

"No, but I can feel them. I want to get out of here."

"You're safe with me here. And I'll pay you in a few minutes."

"I ain't gonna do anything else for that twenty dollars," she said, glaring at him with open hostility.

"Don't worry, Tina. You won't have to." He stepped down from the doorway onto the cracked pavement of the alley. "Show me again where you slept that night."

Wordlessly she led him down the alley that ran between two boarded-up brick buildings. Rain trickled down on them in a fine, misty spray and the dark gray clouds above blocked most of the late afternoon sunlight. She stopped next to some rusty garbage cans and gestured to a pile of wet, decaying cardboard leaning against the side of the building.

"This was my home for a week."

"Obviously, finding Lucille's body made you move."

She snorted and gave him a derisive glance. "I'd have moved anyway. It's not smart to stay too long in one place. Somebody can find you."

"Tell me again what you did that night."

"I already told you ten times. Man, what's your problem?"

"Just one more time. In case you remember something else."

"You're as bad as the police. They asked me the same stupid questions you have. Why didn't you just check with them? They could have told you everything I said."

"You shared a bottle with a friend."

"Yeah, right," she said shaking her head with disgust. "At her place in an alley a few blocks away. I staggered back here sometime in the middle of the night and went to sleep. I found the body in the morning and called the police." She held out her small, childlike hands expectantly. "Twenty dollars right now."

"In a minute. You didn't notice anybody when you walked back from seeing your friend?"

"No, I just wanted to crash."

"Are you sure you didn't hear anything that night? Nothing woke you up?"

"Nothin' man, I was out of it."

"And you never saw Lucille Johnson before?"

She shook her head. "No, there's a lot of people out on the streets."

"And you weren't even aware she was sleeping in this building?"

"I wasn't aware of nothin', man."

"Isn't it reasonable to assume the murderer might have seen you here and maybe even walked right past you?"

"Yeah, right, whatever you say. You finished yet?"

Ryan paused and looked down at the pile of wet cardboard. "Why don't you stay in a shelter, Tina?"

"You ever stayed in one?"

"No." He hesitated. "I have an apartment."

"Then you wouldn't know why."

Ryan leaned against the brick building and squinted up at the darkening sky as the cold rain tickled his face like soft needles. He had gone to all twenty-three murder sites since he poured the vodka down the drain one week ago. He had also been to the newspapers, posing as a freelance writer to see their pictures of the victims and the crime scenes. Every night he had stayed up late pouring over the countless facts he'd assembled while successfully fending off an increasingly powerful urge to have a drink. Now he had talked to the only person who had been nearby when one of the murders had taken place and it all added up to nothing. *Way to go. Ryan Dolan, the great investigator.*

He visualized narrow rows of theater seats stretching endlessly up the alley filled with men wearing tuxedos and women in formal gowns all holding umbrellas over their heads. He could sense their restlessness and boredom and saw a few of them rising to leave. Who could blame them? As a character on a stage he was obviously disappointing and depressing to watch.

He remembered the first play he wrote was about a man who deluded himself with hopeless, unrealistic dreams. Maybe he was like that. How could he have thought he had any chance of succeeding? He was a failed playwright and a disgraced ex-policeman who couldn't solve a crossword puzzle much less a series of mysterious murders. He only had foolish pipe dreams.

He looked at Tina with a sudden feeling of hope. "Did you have any dreams that night?"

Tina looked suspicious. "What kind of dreams? I won't talk about weird stuff for money."

"No, Tina, just a normal dream."

She shrugged. "That's one question the cops never asked."

"Do you remember having any?"

She paused thoughtfully for a moment. "Yeah, I did have one. So what?"

"What was it?"

"I dreamed I was sleeping here in my little house, which I really was, and I heard somebody say my name. So I opened my eyes and saw this strange dude called 'Bible Bob' crouching at the opening looking in at me. Then I dreamed he asked me if I was all right and it took me a few seconds to get my tongue working to say 'yes' and when I did he covered me up with my blanket and left. That was all."

"When you woke up in the morning were you covered up?"

"Yeah, but I must have done it myself. It was just a dream, man."

"Who is this 'Bible Bob'?"

"He's a street corner preacher, I see him around sometimes."

Ryan pulled his wallet out and smiled for the first time in a week. "Here, Tina. You've definitely earned your money."

Chapter Seven

The traffic light turned red at the intersection of California Avenue and Addison Street but Lydia accelerated her car right through, hoping none of Chicago's blue-and-whites were around to witness it. If they pursued her she would just have to keep going until she reached The Helping Hand because Stormin' Norman might be in danger again. Stormin' Norman was a diminutive elderly man with a scraggly red beard who claimed he'd been a cowboy in his youth and once single-handedly took a herd of Texas Longhorns all the way to Alaska just so the Eskimos could have a chance to taste fresh beef. A regular at breakfast, he was emotionally unstable, bordering on suicidal. One morning she had been late getting to the shelter and as she drove up she saw him lying spread-eagled on his back in the middle of California Avenue wearing only his underwear. She stopped her car and ran over to drag him to the sidewalk, where she demanded an explanation. He said he was depressed that breakfast was going to be late so he decided he might as well be run over. He had stripped down to his underwear so his other clothes wouldn't get ruined.

This morning she was late again. She had been too traumatized by yesterday's note to sleep so she studied the data she had collected on her laptop about the homeless murders, trying in vain to find a better strategy for her investigation. Her mind, however, kept returning to the threatening notes. If Martin wasn't sending them then her former stepfather was the only suspect she could think of.

Finally, she gave up analyzing the murders and decided to quilt instead. Quilting was one of her favorite ways to relax; her thoughts could freely wander on any subject while she created something beautiful and useful. Her latest quilt was a log cabin pattern she had always admired and it had to be finished for a Christmas charity auction next month. Sometimes friends kidded her about being so overzealously unselfish that even her hobbies had to be altruistic endeavors. But this particular night quilting failed to relax her, and instead she felt increasingly apprehensive as she wondered what the note writer's next move would be. So, after an hour she put her quilt down and sat on the couch, determined to think of something more important, like her shelters.

She was determined to open her own shelter soon. She would find a suitable building somewhere in the Loop and then solicit funds from religious organizations, corporations, and city, state, and federal agencies. If she had to crawl on her knees all the way up Michigan Avenue to obtain the necessary funds, she would do it gladly because more help was badly needed. She saw it every day in the demoralized faces of the men, women, and children who crowded into The Helping Hand. Her shelter wouldn't just offer meals and beds; it would provide job training, prompt medical treatment, and various types of counseling. The Helping Hand provided many of those things and she had applied for a job there to learn as much as possible.

A year after she started her first shelter she would open another one somewhere else in Chicago. Then she'd open one in another city and after many years of expansion would eventually have a nationwide chain to help countless poor people turn their lives around.

Whenever someone asked her why she was a social worker she told them it was her only justification for living. Seeing gratitude in someone else's eyes was an indescribable joy and after a long day of helping others she finally felt good about herself. It was the only time when she felt like her life had any value because she believed she must be a bad person for so many horrible things to have happened to her. Maybe someday when she had established her chain of shelters she could banish that negative feeling forever.

She finally fell asleep on the couch and since she had forgotten to set her alarm she woke up at six o'clock, an hour later than usual, and was disoriented from a disturbing nightmare in which Maria Gonzales was brutally murdered by her abusive husband.

She had hurriedly put on her clothes and ran out to her car in the early morning darkness wondering if Stormin' Norman was already lying on the street with a huge truck rumbling towards him. If she hadn't turned away from God when her mother had been murdered she'd probably be pleading with Him to help. There was no chance of that now. She would never pray again.

What a great way to start off the day, she said to herself, shaking her head. She drove through another red light at the Belmont intersection and was oblivious to the cheerful yellow and orange lights shining from the windows of the many houses and duplexes she passed, the darkness disguising the fact that some of them desperately needed a fresh coat of paint. As she crossed Diversey she saw that the street in front of The Helping Hand was empty and slowed up with a relieved sigh. Thankfully, Stormin' Norman was late this morning, too.

She turned her car into the narrow alley that ran along the side of the shelter and drove slowly to the tiny parking lot behind the building. The duplexes beyond the parking lot had their shades typically drawn as if the residents wanted to close their eyes to the shelter and the type of people it drew to their neighborhood.

She was relieved Martin's car wasn't there yet, if he knew she was late he would tease her unmercifully. She parked the car next to a garbage bin and wasn't surprised to see a man leaning against it; he was obviously the first of the homeless to arrive for breakfast.

She got out of her car and smiled at the man. "Good morning. If you want some breakfast follow me." She turned and took the keys out of her purse to open the back door of the building and heard him shuffle up behind her.

"You must be Lydia." It was a statement, not a question, and his voice was filled with contempt.

She turned towards him, her keys dangling limply from her hand. The man stood a few feet away glaring at her with intense anger. He towered over her at about 6'2" and weighing 220 pounds with a huge, muscular upper body that stretched the material of his tight sweater. He was Hispanic and around thirty years old with slicked back dark hair and black stubble on his face. His eyes were so dark they appeared to be black in color, like gigantic pupils dilated by hatred. She swallowed involuntarily and felt dizzy as an icy coldness twisted her stomach. The note writer, she told herself, this is him.

"Why are you sending me those stupid notes?" she asked in as defiant a tone as she could muster.

His expression changed from insolence to confusion. "What notes?"

"The little love notes you've sent me the last five days."

He shook his head at her. "Listen woman, I don't know nothing about no love notes or whatever you're talking about."

Lydia exhaled deeply, feeling relieved and embarrassed. Unless he was a trained actor, which was highly unlikely, his denial seemed sincere. "I'm very sorry. I had you mixed up with someone else. Can I help you with something?"

His dark eyes narrowed again with anger. "You are Lydia, aren't you?"

"Yes. What's your name?"

He curled his upper lip and moved closer, his huge neck bulging out of his collar. "I'm Carlos Gonzales. My wife Maria left me. Yesterday I found a note in our apartment with your name on it and this address."

"Oh, yes. Maria and Benito."

"That's right. I asked a few drunks up the street about you and they told me you park back here. I figured we could have a little talk. Just you and me."

Fear twisted her stomach again, but this time it was mixed with anger. "You don't have to worry," she said, struggling to keep her voice calm. "They're safe. They're staying at a shelter for women and children."

He pointed a finger at her. "I don't want them at no shelter. I want them home with me where they belong."

"Your wife told me you were having marital difficulties. She thought it was a good idea to move out."

"She's coming back. Benito, too."

She noticed a large blue vein popping out on his neck. "I'm sorry Mr. Gonzales but that's not your decision to make. Your wife decided . . ."

"My wife decides nothin'!" He interrupted, shouting. "She's coming home today and that's it!"

Lydia glared up at him. "Maybe if you treated her better she wouldn't have left."

He leaned his face closer to hers and she grimaced at his sour, alcohol-laden breath. "I didn't come here for a lecture. I came to get my family back!"

"If you give her some time and agree to counseling maybe . . ."

"Tell me where they are!"

Lydia shook her head emphatically. "No way, that's privileged information."

"Tell me where they are or you're gonna get hurt!"

Lydia clenched her fists in anger. "I'll tell you something else instead. I think you're a despicable animal who should be put in a cage."

His eyes widened. "Watch your mouth!"

"Get out of here now or I'm calling the police!"

"You ain't calling anybody!" He grabbed her coat and swung her around, slamming her into the back of her car. He instantly pushed up against her, pressing her against the car and grabbing a handful of her long hair. "Where are they?" he asked, tugging so violently that her head snapped back onto the car's roof.

Unbearable pain flared from her scalp as he pulled on her hair again. "Let me go!"

"No way! I'd rather pull out all your pretty red hair."

Lydia swung her fist at his face as hard as she could but he ducked slightly and her hand glanced off his forehead. She immediately reached out with her other hand, desperately slashing and poking at his eyes, but his other hand closed down on her throat and she struggled in vain to pull it away. She couldn't breathe and her hair felt like it was being pulled out by its roots when he suddenly eased his grip on her throat and allowed her to gasp for air for a few seconds.

"Where are they?" he asked confidently.

She glared at him determinedly. "I'll never tell you!"

He squeezed her throat tightly again and pulled harder on her hair as Lydia writhed in agony. He lowered his face to where it was almost touching hers. "You'll tell me! Or you're gonna be in the hospital for a long, long time."

Chapter Eight

Ryan believed he could take off and fly. It would be simple. All he had to do was visualize wings sprouting from the sides of his car and they would instantly appear, enabling his rusty vehicle to rise up off Belmont Avenue and float majestically above the early morning traffic like a gigantic bird of prey. But why show off, he said to himself and grinned with unbridled euphoria.

He had an old positive thinking tape on the passenger seat but he didn't need to listen to it. Tapes are for wimps, he told himself, not brilliant investigators. He paused, expecting to hear a caustic voice berate his new found confidence, but for once his mind was silent and he smiled as he turned off Belmont onto California Avenue.

Interviewing Tina yesterday was a major breakthrough and he considered it ironic that one of his plays had inspired him to ask about her dreams. All the hours of writing and the unending rejections seemed worth it now, even if he never got one of his plays produced. He had a lead, maybe even a suspect. If the person known as Bible Bob had been in the alley the night Lucille Johnson was murdered he might have seen something important. He might even be the Homeless Slasher.

After dozens of phone calls he found a social worker who had seen Bible Bob yesterday and said he had gone to a shelter near Logan Square. Ryan immediately called the shelter but unfortunately it was already closed for the night so he decided he'd go there early in the morning. With a little luck his suspect would be there eating breakfast.

He drove past a seemingly endless row of older homes with battered cars parked on the street in front of them and slowed down when he spotted a muffler shop next to a seedy looking travel agency, as he had been told. Directly across the street was a two-story brick building with a large sign in front proclaiming it "The Helping Hand," the shelter he was looking for.

There were no available parking spaces in the street but he noticed a gravel driveway on the side of the building and turned into it, driving slowly until he arrived at a small parking lot in back where he suddenly slammed his brakes.

A dark-haired man had a woman pressed up against a car with his hands on her throat and he turned and glared at Ryan. The woman quickly stomped on his foot and the man let go of her and bent over in pain but as she tried to run away the man dove at her and they crashed to the ground with her long red hair flowing beneath him.

Ryan shifted into park and scrambled out of his car. "Hey, what's going on?"

The man glared at him again as the woman trapped underneath him gasped for air with a dazed expression. Ryan hurried over to them. "Get off her."

The man pushed himself up slowly. "OK, amigo. Everything's cool," he said in a calm voice that contradicted the anger in his eyes. He stood up and Ryan noticed his thick neck and shoulders, obviously the product of years of body building.

Ryan leaned over the red-haired woman who was still lying on the ground. "Are you all right?" he asked. Suddenly the side of his face exploded with pain as a fist struck him with tremendous force and he fell down onto the gravel. He instinctively rolled over as a boot missed his eye by an inch as it kicked at him. As Ryan struggled to get up, powerful hands gripped his sweatshirt and shoved him so hard that he fell backwards against the building's brick wall, hitting the back of his head with a sickening crack.

He felt himself dragged up by his collar and then a forearm viciously slammed against his chest. Through blurry vision he saw the dark-haired man's face was inches away, his lips pulled back in a snarl. "Stay out of this," he hissed, his rancid breath warming Ryan's face. A fist crunched into Ryan's stomach with nauseating impact and he fell forward deliberately smashing his face onto the other man's chest and clinging to his sweater while he gasped for breath, knowing if he went down again the fight would be over.

When he knew he could maintain his balance Ryan quickly locked his hands together and exploded upward, striking his assailant under the chin. The man staggered backwards and Ryan lashed out with a hard kick to his stomach and he doubled over with a loud grunt. Ryan brought down his hand, aiming for the back of his attacker's neck but hitting his shoulder instead. The man charged forward like an enraged bull, butting his head into Ryan's chest and driving him back to the wall. Ryan winced with pain and regret that he had given up the martial arts a few years ago; all those deadly techniques were useless unless practiced regularly.

The man swung his fist in a sweeping right hook but Ryan ducked under it and hit him in the ribs with a solid blow and jumped away. As the man turned towards him Ryan delivered a perfectly executed kick to his kneecap and he fell into Ryan screaming with pain. They both landed on the ground and rolled over several times, punching and gouging each other. Ryan ended up on top and drew his fist back to deliver a debilitating blow when something hard crashed into the back of his head and he fell off his opponent into a swirling darkness.

Ryan heard a woman's voice speaking to him in a soft, soothing tone and he lifted his head up with a painful jerk. "It's OK, he's gone," she said with obvious relief. "He ran away. Limped away actually."

His vision suddenly cleared and he saw the woman was crouching over him with a concerned expression. Even though his head throbbed with thunderous pain he decided she was the most beautiful woman he had ever seen. Large sparkling royal blue eyes framed with naturally long eyelashes. She had a pale complexion that was a striking contrast to her bright red hair which was thoroughly disheveled but undoubtedly soft and luxurious to the touch. She had a fashion model's straight nose, high cheekbones and full, sensuous red lips. Her only flaw was a temporary welt on her forehead.

She gestured with embarrassment to a brick lying nearby. "I threw it at his head, but it hit yours instead. I was always lousy at softball." She smiled at him with gratitude. "My name's Lydia. Thanks for rescuing me."

"You're welcome," he said, his voice a hoarse whisper. "It was no trouble at all."

Chapter Nine

The policeman stared at Ryan with a puzzled frown. "We've met somewhere. I know we have." Ryan shook his head and hoped he didn't look as nervous as he felt. "I don't think so."

"I'm sure of it," the policeman said. "It'll come to me in a minute."

"I've just got an ordinary, familiar type of face," Ryan said, forcing a grin as a drop of sweat trickled down his spine. He had given the police a false last name and address but he was still worried they might recognize him. He never would have waited around and taken a chance if it wasn't for Lydia. He glanced over at her as she leaned against the doorway of her office looking back at him with a serious expression, seemingly oblivious to the way her stunning beauty both intimidated and thrilled him every time he looked at her. He decided it was worth the risk of the police discovering his identity just to be in her presence a little while longer.

Lydia thought Ryan was being modest in describing his own face as ordinary and familiar. She thought he was good looking with large, bright brown eyes that fascinated her. There was sadness in them that she could identify with and she wondered what personal tragedies or disappointments tormented him. She wished she could remove his inner pain, and not just out of gratitude for fighting off her attacker. He seemed to have qualities she valued highly; he was quiet, polite, and obviously cared about others. The only thing she didn't understand about him was why he had seemed so tense since the police arrived.

"Isn't that right, Lydia?" a familiar voice asked her.

Lydia blinked and looked away from Ryan. "I'm sorry, Augie. I wasn't listening."

Augie Rosen nodded at her sympathetically. "It's OK; you're probably still dazed from being attacked." He was a stocky white man of average height who was in his late thirties. He had dark, curly hair and coal black eyes that always gleamed with some type of emotion. She remembered with a smile that his emotional enthusiasm was one of the reasons she had applied at The Helping Hand, which he had founded four years ago.

"I was just explaining to the kind officer here," Augie said gesturing to the other policeman, a heavyset man sitting on her desk with a bored expression, "that he should be out combing the streets right now for this Carlos Gonzales instead of sitting here doing nothing."

The policeman glared at him. "There's another patrol car out there right now."

Augie leaned over and thrust his face into the policeman's. "But if two cars are out there you'll have twice as good a chance or are simple mathematical concepts beyond your grasp?"

"We have to finish interviewing the victim," the policeman said. "We'll catch this guy eventually."

"Sure you will," Augie said sarcastically, "after he's assaulted three hundred other people."

"Very funny," the policeman said, shaking his head with undisguised annoyance.

"You think that's funny?" Augie said with mock surprise. "Then I'll tell you something even funnier. There's a mass murderer who's been running around this city for two years now killing homeless people and you incompetent slobs can't catch him either!"

"We will," the policeman said.

"Right, after he's killed every homeless person in Chicago!" Augie said, throwing his hands up in frustration.

"Don't be subtle, Augie," a voice said with amused sarcasm, "tell them what you really think." The man walked into the room. He was a tall, African-American man in his thirties with a shaved head.

"Doesn't any of this aggravate you, Carl?" Augie asked.

Carl shrugged at him. "There's nothing I can do about it so why let it bother me?"

"Well, I could never have that type of attitude."

Carl shook his head. "I know, but it's the only way I can keep my sanity after ten years of working in shelters."

Ryan watched Augie turn back to the policeman and continue his harangue but he didn't listen, he was too conscious of the other policeman staring at him now with open suspicion, probably dangerously close to realizing with horrified disgust that he was Ryan Dolan.

Martin Sanders came into the office carrying some aspirin and a glass of water which he brought over to Ryan. "Here you go."

"Thanks, I've got a Hall of Fame headache," Ryan said, gratefully taking the aspirin and water from him.

"I hope the aspirin takes it away," Martin said. "Anybody who rescues my Lydia is a friend of mine."

Ryan noticed Lydia stiffen and move away as Martin tried to put his arm around her. "I'm not yours," she said emphatically.

Ryan swallowed the aspirin with a drink of water and turned to see the policeman watching him with a disapproving frown. He realized it would be foolish to stay any longer so he set his glass down on the desk, looking at Lydia with regret. "Well, I guess I'll be going now."

Augie Rosen clapped him on the shoulder enthusiastically. "Thanks for helping!"

Lydia smiled at him. "Let me walk you to your car."

Martin looked at him with obvious jealousy but Ryan chose to ignore it and shook his hand. "Thanks again for the aspirin."

He followed Lydia out of her office and glanced up the hallway at the eating area where homeless people sat at crowded tables quietly waiting for breakfast. Behind him he heard Augie's voice rise again in frustration. "I hope they don't arrest him for disturbing the peace," Ryan said, as they walked down the hallway towards the rear of the building.

Lydia laughed. "Quiet is not a word to describe Augie."

He tried to avert his eyes from her shapely form which even her loose fitting sweater and slacks couldn't disguise, and he wondered why her beauty made him feel so self-conscious and uncomfortable. *Because she'd never be interested in someone like you,* a familiar voice echoed in his mind.

Lydia opened the back door and they walked out into the parking lot where she had been attacked by Carlos Gonzales a short time ago. A frightening image of his angry face flickered before her until she willed it away.

Ryan paused by his car. "Are you sure you're OK?"

"Yes. Are you?"

"I'm fine." He paused and looked at her with concern. "You don't have to worry about that guy coming back here. I'm sure the police will catch him. If not today, it'll be soon. He'll mess up and get a speeding ticket or get in a fight in a bar and they'll have him."

Lydia realized she would probably never see Ryan again and was surprised at how much that disappointed her. She forced herself to smile at him. "I wish I could repay you for helping me."

"Well, there might be a way you could. Like I told the police, I came here looking for somebody. Maybe you know him, he's called Bible Bob."

"Yes, of course I do, he's become a living legend on the streets. He spends all his time helping the unsheltered homeless, bringing them food or medicine or encouragement."

"Is he here this morning?"

"No, but he was last night. He said he'd be working around Union Station today and we gave him some food to give away."

Ryan nodded with relief. "Thanks, you've just repaid me."

"Why are you looking for him?"

"Someone saw him near the murder location the night Lucille Johnson was killed. I want to talk to him about it."

Lydia stared at him with surprise. "I'm sure he has a logical explanation for being there. Why do you want to know?"

Ryan hesitated. "Well, I'll probably sound like Don Quixote and make you hysterical with laughter but the truth is . . . I'm trying to find the Homeless Slasher on my own."

"You are?" Lydia asked with genuine enthusiasm. "So am I! I haven't gotten anywhere yet but I talk to every street person I can about it. You ought to come over to my place tonight and I'll show you all the information I've compiled." Lydia paused, scarcely believing she had just invited a man over when she was determined not to have any close relationships with one.

"Do you really mean it?"

She saw the vulnerable look in his eyes and decided she couldn't disappoint him, not after what he had done for her. "Of course I mean it. I live at five sixty-eight California Avenue, apartment three. I'll expect you at eight."

"Then I'll be there. Thank you." He grinned and gestured to his car. "Well, I better go find this Bible Bob. Maybe I can have this case wrapped up by tonight."

Chapter Ten

The Great Hall of Union Station reminded Ryan of a huge church instead of a waiting room. It had dozens of long, dark brown benches which looked exactly like pews lined up in the middle of the immense cathedral-like room. The large skylight in the impressively high ceiling offered a glimpse of heaven above and its grayish light cast a seemingly benevolent glow on the clean white tiled floor below. The pay phones in the distant corners and a small newsstand near the entrance seemed out of place and a little irreverent.

But if it was a house of worship he decided it should be called the Church of the Bored. Hundreds of people were sitting in the pews or standing around and all seemed to have the same tired, passive expression. Those few who were hurrying off to catch their trains looked just as unhappy even though their tedious wait was finally over.

It was easy to spot the homeless, most of them had probably come in to escape the cold, drizzling rain outside. They sat alone in pews next to their knapsacks or grocery bags that contained all their worldly possessions and were either sleeping or staring blankly ahead. The other people seemed to completely ignore them except for two teenagers who were amusing each other by mimicking the snores of a shabbily dressed elderly woman sleeping in their pew. His uncle believed all the homeless were lazy and worthless, whereas a social worker like Lydia would probably insist that many were innocent victims of society. Ryan decided he would gladly pay to watch those two debate that subject.

Thinking about Lydia filled him with a joy he hadn't felt in a long time and he shook his head in amazement that she had actually invited him over. He wished it was evening already and he was knocking at her door with breathless anticipation, but first he had to find a possible witness, or suspect.

Behind the pews he saw a tall African-American man pushing a grocery cart. He stopped next to a man wearing a tattered overcoat and handed him a sandwich wrapped in clear plastic. From the description Ryan had received, he knew this was Bible Bob. He walked over slowly and was frustrated to feel his heart begin to pound away in his chest from sudden anxiety. A good investigator is always relaxed, he told himself as he ground his teeth. *That's why you're not relaxed*, a voice cackled at him, *because you know you'll blow it.*

Ryan studied Bible Bob as he pushed the grocery cart in his direction. He was about 6'6" but probably only weighed 170 pounds. His long, thin arms and legs and hunched-over shoulders made him look like a stick figure that had sprung to life from some hastily drawn sketch. He was bald and the white hair on the sides of his head contrasted with his rich, dark skin. Ryan estimated he was in his fifties. He wore dark pants and a white T-shirt that had the slogan, "Going up!" printed on front along with an arrow that pointed up. A crumpled raincoat was hanging over the handle of the cart.

Bible Bob stopped and smiled at him. "Are you hungry, brother?"

Ryan shook his head. "No thanks. I'm not homeless."

He shrugged. "People that got a home get hungry too sometimes."

Ryan glanced down at the grocery cart which was half filled with sandwiches, apples, and some cartons of orange juice. "Where do you get all this food?"

"Shelters, churches, and a few generous individuals, God bless them."

"You pass it out in train stations everyday?"

"Not just train stations brother, parks, abandoned buildings, street corners, anywhere I can find hungry people. Some of God's children can't think clear and don't know enough to go to shelters for food. So I feed them," he said. "My name's Bob Wills, by the way. But since I give spiritual advice most folks call me Bible Bob." He extended a bony hand with long pencil-like fingers.

"My name's Ryan."

Bob grinned at him and pumped Ryan's hand enthusiastically. "Nice to meet you, Brother Ryan."

"It's very kind of you to help others."

He looked surprised. "Kind? It ain't kind, it's my duty." He turned to one side and raised his voice so everyone nearby could hear. "You see, brothers and sisters, I used to only care about myself and I drank whiskey like a thirsty camel. I was such a bad tempered dude that I had two moods: bad and worse. I finally ended up flat broke and living in the streets and was so miserable and feeling sorry for myself that I could have exploded or something all over a sidewalk."

He paused and smiled at some of the people who were watching him with varied expressions of interest, amusement, or annoyance. "But you know what, brothers and sisters? I'm glad I ended up cold, hungry and lonely, like a penguin stuck by himself on a little iceberg because it made me realize I was goin' down the wrong road. So one day, ten years ago I decided to believe in the Lord Jesus Christ and prayed for Him to forgive me and come into my life. Jesus said, 'Whoever comes to me I will never drive away.' If he didn't boot me into Lake Michigan then there is hope for everybody." He paused again and looked at Ryan expectantly.

Ryan shifted his feet self-consciously, noticing the people watching them. "That's nice."

"It sure is!" Bob said to his audience, his voice booming with delight. "I prayed for guidance. Got a job. Then I got to thinking about all the folks I met when I was living on the streets, how so many of them needed help, physical and spiritual help. I thought to myself, maybe that's why the Lord had let me end up homeless, so's I'd know what it was like and so's I'd want to help the poor. I tell you when that idea came to me it was kind of like a safe falling off the Sears Tower and landing on my head. So I quit my job the next day and began a new one feeding and preaching." He paused and smiled at the people watching him. "I see some of you frowning at me, and that's OK, I understand. I used to make fun of preachers when I didn't believe. I don't know how many people in this world love you. Some of you folks might feel as unloved as a bug in a bowl of soup. But

I gots to tell you that God loves you and He wants to have a relationship with you. He's made it real easy to do, too. Jesus says, 'For God so loved the world that He gave His one and only Son, that whoever believes in Him shall not perish but have eternal life'." He turned back to Ryan and spoke in a lower voice, "Do you believe in the Lord?"

A familiar uncomfortable feeling swept through him. "I'm not sure what to believe," he answered truthfully. "Sometimes I'm convinced there is a God, but I still have questions, like why did He make such an imperfect world?"

Bob nodded at him, his huge brown eyes filled with understanding. "I know just what you mean. Hard world to live in and pure hell for some, but that ain't God's fault. None of us is puppets on a string; He gave us all a free will, to do good or do bad, to believe or not believe. The world's got problems cause of us, not cause of Him."

"Is the train station always this crowded?"

Bob rolled his head back and laughed. "I can tell you didn't seek me out for any spiritual counseling, and that's OK. You can't force Jesus on folks, they gotta want Him. So what can I help you with?"

"Yesterday I talked to a girl named Tina. She said she saw you one night," Ryan paused, watching him carefully, "the night Lucille Johnson was murdered."

Bob nodded solemnly without even flinching. "Yeah, that's true. I remember that night, remember it well. Saw poor, little Tina sleeping in a box like a scared rabbit. Feel so sorry for her. She thinks everybody's out to hurt her, always hidin' somewhere."

"What were you doing in the alley?"

"Lookin' for a woman who knows who the Homeless Slasher is."

Ryan's mouth hung open as he stared at him. "What woman?"

"A woman that lives on the streets and saw the Slasher kill that Burt guy. Says she knows who he is."

"You've talked to her?"

Bob shook his head with regret. "Wish I had. I didn't find her that night. No tellin' where she is now."

"How did you find out about her?"

"I was preaching on a street corner on Roosevelt one night. Afterwards, I got to talking with a few folks about the killings; how something's gotta be done to stop it. A sister came up to us then and shocked our shorts off."

"A nun?"

"No, when I say 'sister' I mean a woman. Young black lady in her twenties. Tall, maybe six feet. Says her name was Yolanda. Couldn't believe what she told us."

"And what was that?"

"Says she met a homeless lady in a soup kitchen that day who knows who the Slasher is. Saw his face when he killed that Burt guy and recognized him."

"Who is he?"

"That's the worst part. She wouldn't tell Yolanda the Slasher's name, too afraid she'd be killed."

"Didn't Yolanda wonder if this woman was lying, joking, or crazy?"

"Yeah, she sure did at first but this woman seemed so sincere. Somehow she convinced Yolanda she was tellin' the truth. That impressed me enough to want to talk to her. Yolanda says the woman told her she'd be spending the night in an empty building somewhere nearby. I decided to go look for her and Yolanda says she'd help so we split up and agreed to meet later. Never found that woman or Yolanda either. She never did meet up with me and that's frustrating cause the woman had told her a couple of places where she hung out and Yolanda was going to tell me later." He paused and frowned. "So if somebody finds Yolanda they can maybe find that woman and then find out who the killer is. So far I ain't had any luck."

"What did the homeless woman look like?"

"Yolanda said she was an older white woman with long gray hair, probably in her fifties. Never told her name." Bob looked at him with curiosity. "You with the police?"

"No. I just want this guy caught."

"Me too, brother. Told the police my story but they said Yolanda probably made it all up. They're wrong though."

"The killer was in the same area that night. Do you remember seeing or hearing anything unusual?"

"Nope. Can't remember anybody particular I saw except Tina." Bob looked past him and Ryan noticed anger in his eyes as he stepped out in front of a couple that was approaching. "Excuse me, folks but I wonder where you is going?"

A huge man in his twenties stopped and glared at him. He was white, and his long, blond hair was tied in a pony tail. He was dressed in an expensive three-piece suit and was as tall as Bible Bob but much heavier and stronger. He had an arm around a young girl in a protective gesture. She had frizzy blond hair with a pale complexion and wore skin tight jeans and a jacket with various patches sewn on it. Ryan estimated she was only fifteen.

The man in the suit sneered at Bob, revealing his crooked teeth. "Get out of my way, Bible Boob. Or you'll be sorry."

Bob ignored him and turned to the young girl. "Excuse me, little sister, but are you going somewhere with this man?"

The girl looked confused. "Well, yes. Travis here is taking me to lunch."

Bob moved closer to her. "Let me tell you something, little sister. You probably just got off the train from Milwaukee or Minnesota. You gots some problems at home so you decided to run away." The girl blinked with surprise. "And you is probably a little scared and lonely just arriving in big old Chicago, so what happens? Travis approaches you, dressed real nice and real polite and offers to take you to lunch. You is hungry and broke so you say OK. Now Travis here will take you to lunch and buy you all you can eat and then you know what? He'll ask if you gotta place to stay and when you say no he'll tell you that you can stay at this extra apartment he has, free of charge. He'll put you up there and wine you and dine you for a couple days and then take advantage of you. And after a few more days he'll start sending some of his customers to visit you in your free apartment for you to entertain."

Travis grabbed Bob by the collar and thrust his face into his. "I warned you preacher man. I told you if you interfered with my business one more time I'd kick your skinny body to pieces."

Bob smiled serenely. "Travis, I keep tellin' you that Jesus loves you very much but He's also very ticked off at you."

Travis pulled back his fist to hit him but Ryan leaped forward and grabbed his wrist. Travis turned to him, nostrils flaring with rage. "Let go of me, fool!"

Ryan glared back at him, tightening his grip. "I'm not letting you hit him."

"Then you're gonna get hurt too!"

Ryan shook his head. "Never underestimate an opponent."

"I'm not! I'll make you bleed a river!"

"Even if you did the cops would be here in minutes and you'd do time on assault charges. And who'll keep track of all your girls while you're locked up?"

Travis shoved Bob away with his other hand and Ryan released his wrist. He pointed at Ryan and scowled. "I'll see you again." He hurried away without a backward glance.

Bob got up from the floor with a grin. "Hallelujah! Blessed are the peacemakers!" He turned to the girl who was still standing there with a stunned expression. "Little sister there's a women's shelter three blocks from here. They'll give you food and shelter. Can I take you there?"

She looked at him with a moment of indecision and finally nodded. "Sure. I guess that'll be fine."

Bob clapped Ryan on the shoulder. "If I can ever help you, Brother Ryan, just ask."

"I will," Ryan said. "Maybe soon."

Chapter Eleven

Ryan didn't notice the car slow down and park across the street, or see the large man get out and silently approach him from behind. He was too busy driving in for lay ups on his neighborhood basketball court. Although it was almost six o'clock there was still adequate light and the cold wind didn't bother him if he kept moving. He liked to shoot baskets alone when he had a lot to think about and one of the reasons he selected an apartment at the intersection of Belmont and Hawthorne was the two paved basketball courts across the street. Also, Franklin Park was far enough away from his hometown of Arlington Heights that he was unlikely to be recognized. He liked the surrounding tree lined streets with the neat rows of small brick ranches occupied by hard working blue collar families. It looked like a neighborhood where you could never feel lonely.

He didn't hear the footsteps behind him as he missed a free throw and shook his head. It was understandable for his shooting to be off with all the thoughts flashing in his mind with dizzying intensity. He had to find an unknown woman who could supposedly identify the Homeless Slasher, but first he had to find some other woman named Yolanda to tell him where the woman liked to stay. And of course he had to consider Bible Bob as a possible suspect despite his seemingly noble lifestyle. In only two hours he would be arriving at Lydia's place, a thought that simultaneously thrilled and frightened him. What if she didn't like him? Who could blame her? He retrieved the ball and this time took a deep breath at the foul line before shooting but it rattled the rim and fell off again anyway.

"Figures," a voice said from behind him. "You can't do anything right."

Ryan turned quickly and saw Kevin Dolan standing there with a disapproving frown. "That's usually true," Ryan said, remembering his last encounter with his uncle and the humiliation he felt when he had left the bar a week ago.

"Are you drinking again?" Kevin asked.

"No. Not at all." Ryan said truthfully. It was amazing to him that he'd resisted the temptation since he started his investigation.

"That's a first."

"Let me guess why you're here. It's to tell me I'm a lazy, neurotic scumbag and you never want to hear from me again."

Kevin shook his head. "No, I don't mind hearing from you again. The rest is true enough, though."

"Thanks."

"You're welcome." Kevin hesitated and looked at him with a serious expression. "Actually I'm here to ask you something. Do you still want to catch the Homeless Slasher?"

"Yes."

"Then I've got a fabulous offer for you. I'll pass on any useful evidence we turn up. It's against regulations of course, but I've broken them before." Kevin paused again. "I'll do it if you promise me one thing."

"What?"

"That after you give up on your knucklehead investigation in a few weeks like I know you will, you'll take one of those jobs I found for you." Kevin raised his eyebrows expectantly. "Well, is it a deal?"

"Yes," Ryan said with a combination of enthusiasm and surprise. "I accept your generous offer but I guarantee you I'm not going to quit. I'm not stopping until I find him."

"Sure, kid. I believe that like I believe in the Tooth Fairy."

"Then why are you doing this?"

"To get you to take a job, for one." Kevin looked at him with concern. "And secondly that little stunt you tried in the bar last week scared me. It scared me a lot."

"I'm sorry."

"You should be. I was so upset I couldn't eat for two days. Your aunt said she never saw me crankier." Kevin turned and spat on the pavement. "Anyway, there is one small piece of evidence we've kept out of the papers. Doesn't amount to much, but there's no sense alerting the killer about it. The night Lucille Johnson was murdered we had the canine unit follow a trail that led out of the alley and down the street. It stopped about six feet from the curb, right about where someone would get into a parked car. We assume he drove away at that point."

"Did you find anybody who remembered the car?"

"No. Who pays attention to parked cars? Besides, it was pretty deserted that night, there weren't many people to ask."

"So the Slasher has some type of vehicle."

"Yeah, big deal, I figured he wasn't walking all over the city anyway but maybe next time we can ask about parked cars and it could lead somewhere. It also seems to kill the possibility that he's one of the homeless, not too many of them have their own wheels."

"I learned something important today," Ryan said, trying to sound modest.

"That you shoot hoops as good as a cadaver?"

"No. There may be a witness."

Kevin's expression hardened. "What are you talking about?"

"There's supposedly some bag lady that saw Burt Wojik get murdered. She claims she knows who the Slasher is."

"You talked to her?"

"No."

"You got a name or a place to find her?"

"Well, no." Ryan hesitated. "I talked to this guy named Bible Bob who talked with some woman named Yolanda who talked to the witness and I don't know how to find either woman."

Kevin laughed so hard his head bobbed up and down like a toy. "Sounds like a real solid lead. There's nothing more important in solving a murder than a third party alleged lunatic witness." He laughed again. "Keep up the good work, kid."

"I figure it's worth pursuing," Ryan said defensively.

"Sure, kid. You'll be the savior of the homeless." Kevin's smile faded. "Actually, it'll be a shame when he gets caught because if he keeps going there won't be any more panhandling bums for us to pick up. Think of all the tax dollars that will be saved if there's no homeless leeching off those soup kitchens. I'm beginning to think the mayor should give the Slasher a medal for cleaning up our fair city."

"Why do you hate the homeless?"

"Because they're all worthless. They shouldn't even be classified as human beings."

"That's your reason?"

"It's one of them." Kevin's eyes narrowed with bitterness. "Remember Don Socia?"

"Yeah, sure. He was your partner. He was killed in action about ten years ago."

Kevin nodded. "Yeah. He felt sorry for some homeless loser sleeping on the sidewalk one cold winter night. Decided to escort him to a shelter but the low life maniac turned on him and killed him with a knife. I was as close to him as I was to your old man."

"Is it fair to hate all of them?"

"I think it is." Kevin shrugged and picked up the basketball and faced the basket that was twenty feet away. "Well, nephew. I hope your investigation will be as easy as this." He casually threw the ball with one hand and it swished through the net.

Chapter Twelve

Lydia was thoroughly disgusted when she realized fear was turning her into a coward. When she had arrived home from work an hour ago her stomach was nauseatingly tight from tension as she wondered if another note would be in her mailbox. Yesterday's note had completed the message, "I WILL GET YOU SOON!" Did that mean there wouldn't be any more or would her anonymous antagonist have more to say? When she walked up her front steps she ignored her mailbox, telling herself she had too much to do before Ryan came over and she'd retrieve the mail later. She knew that was a lie. She was afraid to look at the mail because another ominous note might be there, and that was inexcusable. She was allowing fear to control her again, just as it had years ago when her stepfather had intimidated her and abused her mother. Those painful memories would always haunt her but she'd promised herself that she would never again become a prisoner of fear, or succumb to it in a weak moment. So, she told herself, when you're finished getting ready you will get your mail without any hesitation.

She looked at her reflection in the bedroom mirror and approved of the anger in her eyes which seemed deep enough to overcome any fear. But she frowned as she studied her appearance. She was wearing form fitting jeans and a tight Kelly green sweater that complemented the lustrous red hair that flowed down past her shoulders. The dark red lipstick made her lips look even fuller than usual and the eyeliner and mascara accentuated her bright eyes. She looked like a fashion model primed for a night on the town.

She hurried to the bathroom and scrubbed all the make-up off her face and pulled her long hair back into a braid. She returned to her bedroom and pulled off her jeans and sweater and put on some baggy gray sweatpants and an oversized sweatshirt.

If she looked too attractive it might encourage Ryan to ask her out and then she'd turn him down, which would obviously be embarrassing for both of them. She was grateful he'd rescued her that morning but she had already decided not to see him again after tonight. It just wouldn't be wise because she was undeniably attracted to him and might be tempted into some type of ongoing relationship. At this point in her life she didn't want any romance, she only wanted to lose herself in her career and savor the personal satisfaction of helping others. Anyway, she had fallen in love once, or at least thought so at the time, and it had ended in disaster.

Because her biological father had deserted her as an infant and her stepfather had been so despicable, she found it difficult to trust men at all, much less have a romantic relationship with one. But a few years ago she had met an energetic young attorney who devoted some of his time to representing the poor without charging any legal fees. She had been impressed with his idealistic views and charmed by his sense of humor and relentless pursuit of her. In time she believed she'd finally found a man to trust and share her life with. And it certainly began that way, after moving in with him she had the happiest month of her life. Her Christian grandmother would not have approved of course, she had believed couples should only live together after they were married. She had always warned her that bad choices led to bad consequences but Lydia had no regrets until that unforgettable afternoon when she came home early and found him in bed with another woman. She packed that same night and no amount of pleading or apologizing could dissuade her from moving out. A few weeks later he was killed in a car accident after a long night of drinking. Another memory filled with rage and grief, she thought to herself, I've got too many of those.

She walked out of the bedroom with renewed purpose since she was now ready to get her mail. As she left her apartment and walked down the hall her heartbeats came faster with every step and she had difficulty swallowing. It's just a piece of paper, she said to herself. If it's another threat I'll either take it to the police or throw it away.

She went downstairs and stood in front of her mailbox for a moment taking several deep breaths. When she finally reached in she pulled out a plain, white envelope which again had her name and address typed on it and had no return address. She ripped it open and pulled out the piece of paper that had a new message written in block capital letters which said, "FIND ME OR DIE!" Lydia noticed her hands were trembling.

"I have a prediction," Lydia said with total confidence. "One of us will find the Homeless Slasher tomorrow."

"I hope you're right," Ryan said with considerably less confidence. "But it might take longer."

Lydia smiled and put her laptop down on the coffee table which was covered with maps, newspaper clippings, and notebooks. They had been poring over her accumulated information for two hours now and she was grateful to have something else to think about. When she first read the life threatening note she was overwhelmed by panic but had stubbornly fought it off, determined not to let it torment her. There would be plenty of time later to think calmly and logically about the note and decide when to take it to the police. She was proud to be exhibiting such strong self-control and told herself that maybe she had finally learned to conquer fear.

Lydia leaned back on her couch and looked at Ryan who was sitting next to her with an enigmatic expression. "It'll be easy," she said. "I'll just find that witness tomorrow and then I'll have him."

"An alleged witness. And she might not be easy to find."

"I'm thinking positive," she said. "First thing tomorrow I'll call every shelter in the city and find the woman named Yolanda. Then she'll tell me where this witness likes to hang out and I'll go there and find out from her who the Slasher is and then I'll call the police. It'll be simple."

"Hopefully."

"Definitely." Lydia paused. "You should be proud of yourself."

"I was lucky to find out about the witness and I have a contact in the police department who told me about the car theory."

"I could have told them the Slasher wasn't one of the homeless. They have too much empathy for one another."

"Do you know if Bible Bob has a car?"

"He has a beat-up van. He transports people to shelters." Lydia frowned at him. "You don't consider him a suspect do you?"

"He was in the area the night Lucille Johnson was murdered."

"But he's done so much for the poor and the homeless. He wouldn't hurt anybody. You might as well suspect Santa Claus."

"I'm not saying he is the Slasher, but he fits the profile."

"Whose profile?"

"Well, mine." Ryan noticed Lydia's skeptical gaze and paused self-consciously. "I could be wrong. In fact, I usually am about everything else but the Slasher's motive seems pretty obvious to me. He's making a statement, trying to draw attention to the plight of the homeless which he obviously thinks is a pathetic situation."

"He'd have to be insane to think that way."

"He probably is, but he might not be obviously insane. Ever read about Ted Bundy or Jeffrey Dahmer? They were serial killers but some neighbors and people who worked with them thought they were normal. They couldn't believe they'd murdered all those people. This guy could be like that."

"But how can the Slasher care about the homeless if he kills them?"

"It's a paradox," Ryan said, "but the notes prove his motive. With each victim he leaves a page from a book that's very sympathetic to street people and he underlines a word or phrase like 'job training' or 'more local support.' It gets reported on the news which enables him to speak to the whole world."

Lydia shook her head emphatically. "No. I disagree. I think if someone kills this many people it's because he enjoys doing it. Sadistic pleasure, that's his main motive. He might have a lesser motive, too, such as becoming a famous serial killer or getting revenge or some other reason I haven't thought of yet. But I know he doesn't care about the homeless. I think he's leaving those pages as a clever diversion to disguise his identity. He knows it'll mess up the personality profile the police will create."

"You may be right," Ryan said, deciding that even though he didn't agree with her theory he'd rather not debate it with her. It was hard enough trying to concentrate on what she said because her baggy sweat suit and pulled back hair did not conceal her intimidating beauty. And he kept wondering what her reaction would be when he asked her to go out to dinner with him. On the way over he had practiced various lines but none were any good and he couldn't read what her feelings were towards him. She was very polite but seemed to be holding something back. *She might not even like you. Who could blame her?*

"Don't you agree?" Lydia concluded with enthusiasm.

"Uh, sort of. Yeah." Ryan wondered what he had agreed with. *Don't ask her out,* the voice whispered, *when she says no you'll be humiliated.* "Um, Lydia, do you like Chinese food?"

Lydia bent over a map and pretended she hadn't heard. She had to admit she definitely liked Ryan's polite manners and his wry, self deprecating humor and there was no question she was physically attracted to him but that just confirmed her earlier decision. She should never see him again. If he dropped another hint she'd simply tell him the truth, which was that she had no interest in any relationship and didn't even want to go out for a casual, platonic dinner. She hoped it wouldn't come to that because she didn't want to embarrass him.

She looked up at him with interest. "What do you do for a living?"

Ryan squirmed a little on the couch and almost confessed to being an unemployed ex-policeman. *Brilliant idea, and then she'll ask why you left the force.* "Uh, actually I write plays."

"Really?" Lydia said, impressed. "That must be a difficult way to support yourself."

"Yeah, it is." *Especially when you've never had a play produced. Can't tell her the truth though, she'll never see you again if you tell her who you are.*

"You must be very creative."

"Speaking of creative," Ryan said enthusiastically, hoping his attempt to change the subject didn't sound as contrived as it really was. "If you were the chief of police how would you handle this investigation?"

Lydia shook her head in disgust. "A lot differently. For one thing I'd put every detective in the city on the case."

"And ignore all other homicides?"

"All right, then, most of them. I'd dress half of them up like homeless people and have them live in the streets and shelters. That might be the only way to catch him."

"I'm sure they have some detectives already doing that."

"But not enough. And they probably work in shifts, right?"

"Sure."

"Well, that ruins the best way to catch the Slasher. If he unknowingly targeted an undercover policeman as a victim they could simply pull out their gun when he came at them with his knife and arrest him. But the Slasher picks his victims carefully and probably follows them for days beforehand, so eventually he'd see a detective walk to a car and drive home and know it was a set up."

"But they all have families and personal lives. You can't expect them to stay out there around the clock for weeks at a time. Chances are they wouldn't find out anything, anyway."

"That's what I'd do. Send them out to stay until the murderer's caught."

"You'd be a very unpopular chief of police." A radio was on in her kitchen and Ryan heard an old song come on that he liked to sing along with and laugh at, about some guy who fought the law but the law won. I didn't win when I was the law, Ryan thought, not even close. He sat up with sudden inspiration. "I could go undercover."

"Seriously?"

Ryan noticed her eyes had widened with surprise and genuine respect. He'd do anything to have her continue looking at him that way. "Yes, absolutely. If neither of us catches this guy tomorrow then I'll dress up and live in the streets indefinitely."

"Do you think you could handle the hardship?"

"Sure. What's so hard about being homeless?"

Lydia rolled her eyes. "You'd find out very soon."

"I could handle it," Ryan said confidently, wondering briefly if it would be as easy as he thought. But it didn't matter, because he had decided that this was the ideal time to ask her out, he'd never have a better chance. "I don't like to brag but I'm an expert in the use of chopsticks, and I'd be very happy to give you a free lesson tomorrow night." He saw her stiffen with shock and indignation. "What's wrong?"

"Listen!"

He heard the voice on the radio. "His body was discovered in an abandoned building near Humboldt Park. Police have identified him as Hector Lopez. He's the twenty-fourth victim of the Homeless Slasher."

Ryan realized that he now had a personal grudge against the murderer, not only was he killing innocent people, he had ruined the romantic moment he'd been working up to all evening. He sank back into the couch and heard another, louder voice that drowned out every other sound. *Nothing ever goes right for you. Never has, never will.*

Chapter Thirteen

Lydia slammed the phone down and groaned in frustration. She had been convinced she would learn the identity of the Homeless Slasher. It had sounded so easy last night when she boldly announced her goal to Ryan. All she had to do was call every shelter and soup kitchen in the city until she located the woman named Yolanda. She'd ask her where the witness could be found and go there to get the murderer's name.

But what she hoped would be the most exciting day of her life was turning out to be a dismal failure. During a busy day of serving meals and counseling homeless people she had gradually called the shelters on her list but none of them had any record of a woman named Yolanda. Now that she had failed it was all up to Ryan. After they heard about the Slasher's latest victim on the radio, he suggested they divide up the list of shelters and call each other with any good news and she had readily agreed. Since it was late afternoon now and she hadn't heard from him yet she doubted that he'd been successful either. In fact, she was surprised he hadn't contacted her yet and wondered what could have happened to him. When she remembered that his call would probably be the last time she'd ever get to talk to him she felt another sharp pang of despair but it had to be that way.

She leaned back in her chair and stared up at the familiar cracks and stains on her office ceiling. Not only had she failed to find the witness, but her phone call to the police about the threatening notes had been a waste of time. The policeman she talked to was polite and sounded genuinely concerned but basically told her they couldn't do anything. Tracing the notes was virtually impossible. Whoever was sending them obviously knew her and hopefully was just playing a sick joke on her. But he also said it could be dangerous to assume that and suggested she vary her daily routine, change where she shopped, and perhaps find someone to live with her for a while. He also encouraged her to bring the notes down to the station and she agreed but doubted that would do any good.

Her office door swung open and Augie Rosen walked in carrying a newspaper. "Well, I'm glad to see you're not taking a nap back here."

Lydia sat up straight. "Are we getting busy?"

"Busy? That would be an understatement." He ran his hand through his dark, curly hair. "I'm ready to tear out what's left of my rapidly receding hairline. Half the poor people in Chicago are out there now. When I started this place I never should have settled for such a small building. I should have asked permission to use all of O'Hare as a shelter. Of course I would have stood about as much chance as being chosen Miss America."

Lydia stood up. "I'm sorry, Augie. I'm ready to help now."

He looked at her with a quizzical expression. "You've been playing detective again?"

"Yes, and as usual, getting nowhere. Do you realize Hector Lopez was killed last night only a few miles from here? For all we know we might have driven past the Homeless Slasher on our way home last night."

Augie frowned. "And maybe some police cars did too. I don't think they'll ever catch that guy."

"Well if they don't, I will."

"That's the spirit." Augie held up the newspaper. "Did you happen to read page seven?"

"No. I just read about the murder."

"Well, there was another less publicized murder last night."

Augie handed her the paper and as she quickly skimmed the article she flinched as if she had just stepped into an ice cold shower. It was a brief story about a man who had been murdered behind a bar on Kedzie Boulevard. He had been shot in the back of the head. There were no witnesses and the police had no leads. An arrest warrant for assault and battery had been issued for the victim. His name was Carlos Gonzales.

"How do you feel?" Augie asked gently.

Painfully vivid images instantly appeared in her mind like searing flashes of lightning. She remembered the large, frightened eyes of Maria, little Benito's swollen lip, and Carlos Gonzales's face contorted with rage as he tightened his grip on her throat. Ryan struck down by Carlos and rising to fight back. "I don't know how I should feel," Lydia said.

Augie looked surprised. "I would think you'd be happy. That animal deserved to die after what he did to you. He might have killed you if that Ryan guy hadn't shown up and fought him off."

"I know. But somehow I wish it ended differently for him. If only he could have been miraculously rehabilitated and changed his ways to become a good husband and father."

"That never would have happened. This world is better off without Carlos Gonzales."

Lydia shuddered involuntarily. "I've wasted enough time in here. We've got hungry people to feed."

"That's for sure, a boatload of them."

They walked out of her office and down the narrow hallway. Lydia saw Bible Bob talking to a table of people.

"Preach to us like before," one of the men said to him, "when you talked funny."

Bible Bob smiled at his audience of homeless men, women, and children in the room, some of whom were watching with varying degrees of interest while others ignored him. "You must mean my Gospel poetry. I'll be glad to share a few with you." He cleared his throat. "Eternal life is near! And all you gotta do is hear!"

"Supper's here, too!" Martin called out sarcastically as he came out of the kitchen carrying a coffee pot.

Bible Bob ignored him and clasped his hands. "Jesus is really your only hope. Accept Him now or you'll feel like a dope."

"Why don't you give us all a break and take a night off," Martin said, shaking his head. "If there is a heaven you've already earned your way there."

"You be half right, Brother Martin, there is definitely a heaven," he said with a smile, "but nobody can earn their way there. It says in the scripture, 'For it is by grace you have been saved through faith and this is not from yourselves, it is the gift of God, not by works, so that no one can boast.' See, Brother Martin, salvation is a gift."

"I'm an atheist. I don't agree with anything you say."

"I understand, cause I used to be an atheist. God gives us all our own minds to think what we want. That's why you got to read what Jesus said and decide for yourself."

"I don't have time." Martin grinned. "I'm too busy getting drunk and chasing after loose women." A few men at a nearby table applauded and Martin bowed to them with feigned appreciation.

Bob shook his head at Martin. "Brother Martin would you behave like this in a place of worship?"

"No, but this is a shelter, not a place of worship."

"Ah, but God allows us to worship Him any place. This here shelter's a place so that makes it a worship place." He pointed at him triumphantly. "Gotcha!"

Martin looked at him with disgust. "Your logic is just as ridiculous as your message."

"Thank you."

"That's an insult, not a compliment."

"I know, but I forgives you for it and the good Lord gets real happy when anyone forgives another and He gives that dude a blessing. So by insulting me, Brother Martin, you gave me an opportunity to forgive you and get a blessing." Bob leaned closer to him. "Bet you can't call that ridiculous logic."

"I'd like you to say a prayer for me, Brother Bible Bob."

"Anything."

"Pray that some angels will fly down from heaven and take you to another city far away, to torment social workers there for all eternity."

Lydia walked up to them. "Martin, aren't you too busy to engage in a religious debate?"

Martin's eyes brightened with familiar longing when he saw her. "Yes, I'm too busy planning what we'll do together the first night you go out with me."

"Why don't you go dream about it in the kitchen?"

"Good idea, because my dreams always come true." He grinned at her and walked off towards the kitchen.

"Brother Martin's an unusual dude. Course folks say that about me, too," Bob said with a laugh. "Anyways, Sister Lydia, I brung somebody for you to meet." He gestured to a small African-American man in his twenties who was wearing a green army jacket and glancing around self-consciously. "Brother Byron say hello to Sister Lydia."

"Hello," Byron said with a shy smile.

Lydia shook his hand. "Nice to meet you, Byron. How can I help you?"

Byron looked at Bible Bob. "It's OK, Byron. They's your friends here," Bob put an arm around his shoulder and turned back to Lydia. "Byron here never got enough schooling. He never learned to read, so I told him about your adult reading classes."

"I felt bad about it my whole life," Byron said with downcast eyes. "I want to learn how to read more than anything."

"Then you came to the right place," Lydia said with conviction, "and you shouldn't feel embarrassed, adult illiteracy is surprisingly common. I teach a small group here four days a week, I'd be delighted if you joined us tomorrow afternoon."

Byron looked up at her and nodded. "I'll be here."

Lydia smiled. "I'm glad to hear that. Now, why don't you relax until dinner's ready? I need to talk to Bible Bob about something."

Byron sat down in a nearby folding chair and Lydia took Bob by the arm, steering him over towards the hallway. "I was told you met a woman who knows where a witness can be found." She paused, studying his reaction. "A witness to the homeless murders."

He nodded with a sad expression. "That's true."

"I've called half of the shelters in the city today. None of them have any Yolanda registered."

"I could have saved you the trouble, Lydia. I keep checking around town for her too, and she's nowhere to be found. She must have found a place to live for a while and I'm hoping she'll turn up again cause I ain't having no luck finding that witness and I been asking everywhere."

"Do you think she made up that story about the witness?"

"No, I know she didn't. I could feel it was the truth. Somebody's gonna find this witness and end up catching the Homeless Slasher. I just know it." He leaned closer to her and lowered his voice. "I knew last night's victim, Hector Lopez. Lost his wife to cancer about a year ago and right afterwards he lost his job when a factory closed. Got evicted and had to take to the streets with his six-year-old daughter. Found a shelter down on Wabash to stay at and was out looking for work one day when it happened." He hesitated and shook his head. "His little girl, Juanita, was playing with some other kids chasing each other across the street and she got hit. Hit and run driver. She died three days later. Hector, he be so crazy with grief he just took to wandering the streets. Wouldn't talk at all, if you talk to him he got real scared and ran away. Been about nine months since his daughter died."

"I remember him." Lydia felt a wave of nausea as she visualized Hector lying on the ground with his throat slashed.

"He came in here a few times. When I tried to talk him he'd get up and run out, so the last time I just gave him some food and left him alone to eat in peace."

"I saw him a couple weeks ago. Was coughing real bad and looked sweaty like from a fever. I remember wondering if he had caught his self pneumonia or something. I was worried about him, thought he might not make it through the winter."

"Does it ever make you angry that God allows the Slasher to kill innocent people?"

Bob shook his head sadly. "He gives all of us a free will, to do good or bad. The Slasher, too. This world is God's plan, not ours. Some things we won't understand till heaven but I guarantee God don't approve of what he's doin' and someday He'll see justice is done."

"In the meantime innocent people die because He refuses to do anything to stop it."

"I know you felt that way since your mom was murdered. That was a truly horrible thing but if you turn back to God, He'll comfort you and take away your pain. I know He wants to, you just gotta trust Him."

"No thanks." She suddenly noticed a man was standing beside her and realized she had no idea how long he had been there. He was white and of indeterminate age, wearing a baseball cap pulled low over his forehead, a torn jacket, and faded jeans. His face was smeared with dirt and he stood with his shoulders hunched over and his hands shoved into his pockets.

"If I hear anything 'bout that witness I'll let you know." Bob gently squeezed her hand and walked off towards the front door.

Lydia turned to the man next to her. "Can I help you?"

"Hope so, ma'am," he said with a slight southern accent. "Just got in from Chattanooga and could use me a hot meal."

"We'll be serving dinner soon. What's your name?"

"Uh, Joe." He peered at her curiously. "Haven't we met somewhere before?"

"No, I don't think so."

The man pulled his baseball cap off and grinned at her. "Are you sure?"

"Ryan!" Lydia playfully punched him in the arm. "I didn't recognize you under all that dirt."

"This means my disguise works." He hesitated. "Did you find Yolanda?"

"No, did you?"

He shook his head with discouragement. "No. I knew it wouldn't be easy." He paused, thinking how humiliated he'd be if she could read his mind and discover how attracted he was to her. He stopped smiling and looked at her with a serious expression. "I had a feeling we wouldn't find her today so I figured I'd go undercover for a while just like you suggested."

"I'm very impressed," Lydia said sincerely.

Ryan saw the respect in her eyes and decided that even if he froze off all his extremities in the ensuing days it was worth it have her look at him that way. "I'm starting now. I'm going to spend the night in a shelter down off of Sacramento. Maybe I can learn something about Hector Lopez's murder. Or if I'm real lucky, I'll run into that woman who knows who the Slasher is."

"I hope you do."

Carl walked up to them carrying a tray of food. "Lydia, Augie's asking for you. If you want to hide, do it now."

"I'll be there in a minute."

"Good, make him wait. That's my type of attitude," Carl said with a satisfied smile. "I think you're turning into a cynic like me. That happens to all of us social workers after a few years or else we end up in a padded room."

Augie appeared in front of them twirling a large wooden spoon. "Lydia," he said with a mildly scolding inflection. "You normally don't take any breaks but today you just set the world record for time off. If you're finished now would you mind getting some coffee? We're all out."

"Yes, I'll get some right now," she said. Augie glanced at Ryan without recognizing him and then turned away, walking down the hall after Carl. Lydia looked at Ryan with regret. "I'm sorry; I have to get busy now." She hesitated. "If I can help you please let me know."

"I will." Ryan forced an insincere smile, fighting a feeling of hopeless despair that he would never see her again. *Why should she want to see you? You're not good enough for her.* "Meanwhile I'm off to catch a murderer."

"Good luck." She watched him walk away towards the front entrance, wondering if she had actually seen disappointment on his face when he left her. She turned and walked down the hallway to the storeroom in the back of the building weighed down by a rising tide of depression. Her goal of catching the Homeless Slasher anytime soon seemed like an unattainable fantasy and now she had probably seen Ryan for the last time.

She remembered they had run out of coffee last night and this morning she had picked some up on the way in, so she walked past the storeroom and out the rear door into the parking lot. She hadn't even said goodbye to Ryan properly; hadn't even thanked him again for helping her or told him about Carlos Gonzales's murder. It wasn't his fault she didn't want any romance in her life or that she was attracted to him.

Lydia pulled out her keys as she approached her car and then looked up and saw it. It was placed on her front windshield, held in place by a wiper blade. Her stomach tightened as if she had just slipped on the edge of a roof and was falling from a great height. She moved closer and stared at it with an ominous growing fear. It was another white envelope. There was no return address, and her name was typed on it.

Chapter Fourteen

I asked my wife the other day if she'd consider getting a job. She said she already has one . . . her job is spending all my money." The image of a man wearing a tuxedo flickered erratically on the TV screen in a kaleidoscope of pastels, the unseen audience's laughter gushing forth on cue every time he paused. "My wife belongs in the shopper's hall of fame. When she goes to the mall she has to bring a caddy with her . . . just to carry all her credit cards."

Ryan sat on a battered folding chair in the basement of the church which operated as a men's shelter near the intersection of Sacramento Boulevard and Chicago Avenue. Even though the room was dimly lit, he could still see the stains on the carpet and he still hadn't gotten used to breathing in the damp mildew odor. Glancing around the room he counted twenty-nine men seated around him, all silently staring at the TV and its fuzzy picture with subdued expressions. They had watched several other stand-up comics perform and although Ryan thought some of their lines were funny, he noticed no one in the room had laughed even once. A few of the men had responded with tired smiles a couple of times but that was all. He wondered if being homeless destroyed a person's sense of humor. If so, then he had a definite bond with them because his problems in recent years had nearly destroyed his.

The chair wobbled as he shifted his position in a futile attempt to get comfortable. He wished he had a cold beer, just one. If only it could magically appear in his hand in a cool slippery mug with white froth at the top. He envisioned the first swallow and the familiar salty, tingling taste it would have. Since he would only allow one drink he'd force himself to count to thirty between sips so the pleasure would last as long as possible. Nothing could be more wonderful. Actually, he didn't have to wait around for a miraculous appearance. There was a small neighborhood bar a block away, a crumbling brick building with a window displaying a faded yet enticing poster of a pitcher of beer. It would be so easy to get up right now and walk over and have a drink. No one would stop him, no one would care. He would only drink one beer. One beer shouldn't hurt. It wouldn't necessarily lead to others like it had in the past, this time could be different.

There won't be any leads or clues discovered here, a familiar voice whispered, *you might as well go.* Everything that seemed so promising was quickly sinking into a quagmire of failure. The exciting lead of a possible witness hadn't gone anywhere. Meeting Lydia and becoming infatuated with her only brought the pain of rejection from her obvious indifference when she said goodbye a few hours ago. So, how logical was it to go undercover as a homeless person to impress someone you might never see again? To have one drink and go home to sleep in a comfortable bed in a warm apartment sounded much more logical. It would not mean giving up searching for the Slasher though, because there was nothing else to reach for, nothing at all.

Go get your drink, the voice said loud enough to drown out the comic. *It will help you forget how you've failed as a cop and a playwright and how you know you'll fail at this absurd quest for the Homeless Slasher because a failure like you could never find him. Most of all, it will help you forget the innocent child's eyes that stared at you once in silent accusation and will continue staring forevermore in your mind every time you close your eyes.*

Ryan took a deep breath and rubbed at a dull pain in the back of his head. It wasn't like he hadn't tried; he'd already been at the shelter for a few hours. After seeing Lydia he came over immediately. A thin bald man with brown spots on his head had met him at the door and informed him he was the last one they could accommodate for the night as their limit was thirty men. He then led him down to the lower level of the church to a small kitchen where several volunteer church members were serving spaghetti. They gave him a steaming plate and a cup of coffee and he stared hesitantly at the homeless men who were sitting around the six tables, hunched over their food.

He finally walked over to a table with one empty chair and sat down next to an elderly man who was wearing a red and white Santa Claus cap. The man nodded to him when he sat down and the other four men sitting there ignored him. After tasting the spaghetti he briefly wondered if he should feel guilty for eating food intended for the poor but decided that if he was going to live among the homeless he had no choice but to eat with them.

As he ate, he studied the men in the room, noting that there was an equal amount of whites, blacks, and Hispanics. It surprised him that half of them looked like they were in their twenties or thirties; he expected more of them to be elderly. Most surprising of all though, was their table manners. He had anticipated eating in noisy surroundings with a few drunken winos bickering loudly and greedily shoveling food into their mouths with their hands. But none of them appeared to be drunk, and he noticed they all used their knives, forks, and napkins as properly as most people did who ate in restaurants. The room was extremely quiet with only a few murmurs of conversation. Once a man with a raspy voice complained loudly about his coffee tasting watered down, but no one paid any attention to him.

Towards the end of the meal he asked the men at his table if any of them had known Hector Lopez but unfortunately none of them had. His question sparked a discussion about the Homeless Slasher though, and he was impressed with some of their intelligent ideas about how the police could catch him. He had thought the men would be frightened when he brought up the subject but none of them seemed concerned.

When he mentioned he was scared of being the next victim the elderly man next to him grinned. "Son, he's only killed twenty-four out of thousands of us on the streets," he said. "You got a better chance of dying from pneumonia than you do from his knife."

After the meal some of them went into the bathroom down the hall and took their shirts off, taking turns

114 • Kindness Kills

scrubbing themselves over the sinks. He had expected to be surrounded by unwashed, foul-smelling men but only a few were noticeably offensive. Obviously, most of them used shower and laundry facilities when they had the opportunity at shelters that provided them.

But no one he asked knew anything about Hector Lopez, a woman named Yolanda, or the homeless woman who claimed to know who the Slasher was. His first night undercover was a total failure. He should have expected that.

Ryan turned his attention back to the TV where another comedian was complaining about the rising cost of living. The room was still silent, the men looked bored or depressed, and a few were asleep in their uncomfortable chairs. The bald man came in and turned the TV off. "It's ten o'clock," he announced matter of factly. "Lights out."

The men rose stretching and yawning without any complaints. One of the men who had been asleep started babbling softly with a steady stream of garbled, unintelligible words but no one seemed to notice.

They filed out of the room and turned down the hallway, walking past the kitchen. Ryan was at the back of the crowd and he stopped and looked back at the stairs which led up to the street, which led to that bar and the glass of beer his entire being ached for. He could control himself, he would only drink one.

"Hey, ain't you comin'?"

Ryan turned and saw a thin black man in his twenties watching him with a knowing smile. "I don't think so," Ryan said feeling self-conscious. "I feel like getting a drink."

"Just one drink?" the man said, still smiling.

"Yeah."

"You is lyin', man."

Ryan blinked with surprise. "No I'm not."

"Yeah, you lyin'. Not to me, to yourself. I can see that look in your eyes, I know that look. You got the fever. You ain't gonna settle for one drink, maybe not even one bottle. You gonna drink till you can't walk anymore." He paused triumphantly. "You got problems with the bottle, don't you?"

Ryan nodded reluctantly. "Yeah, I guess I do." He paused. "Have you ever had a bottle problem?"

The man shook his head emphatically. "No way, uh-uh. Not after seein' what it did to my old man. He was drunk every day till he left us for good when I was twelve. Always needed just one drink, my mom called it the fever. He could never hold a job or nothin' and sometimes he got real angry for no good reason. I decided way back then I wasn't gonna catch that fever and I never have. I've never even tasted that stuff."

Ryan visualized himself in the dingy, smoke-filled bar, his ears vibrating from painfully loud music, his mouth too numb to speak, feeling himself slowly slip off his bar stool and crash to the floor to be enveloped by an unending darkness. Maybe he could hold himself to one drink, maybe not. At any rate, he had no chance of finding the Homeless Slasher or impressing Lydia by hanging around some bar. He knew now he wanted to see her again, had to see her again and the best scenario would be to call her with something important he had learned about the case.

Ryan smiled at the man. "Maybe I could do without that drink."

"You be better off, man. Come on, let's go grab us a cot."

They walked down the hall in the direction the others had gone and Ryan noticed the other man had a pronounced limp from one leg being shorter than the other. "My name's Ryan, by the way." he said, offering his hand.

"I'm Isaiah." He shook Ryan's hand firmly. "Been out of work long?"

"A while," Ryan said. It was the truth; he hadn't had a job since he had returned to Chicago.

"I got laid off six months ago and couldn't find nothin' else," Isaiah said as he limped along. "Quitin' high school don't help but after my old man left I had to drop out to bring in some money for my mom and younger sisters. Nobody cares about that when they ask if you graduated though. Anyways, my wife and daughter and me got evicted three months ago."

"Where are they now?"

"They stayin' at a women's shelter where men ain't allowed. At first we stayed together at a family shelter downtown but they got a thirty day limit and after that was up all the other family places were full." Isaiah paused by a doorway. "Listen, Ryan. I hear a warehouse down on Cermak is hiring temporary help. I'm going there first thing tomorrow and you're welcome to come along if you want."

"Thanks." Ryan hesitated. "How come you want to help me? You don't even know me."

"You're livin' on the streets too. We're all a lot better off if we help each other." Isaiah looked at him seriously. "Besides you kinda remind me of my old man, havin' the fever and all. When he was sober, which wasn't too often, he was real nice to us."

They entered a small, windowless room containing thirty cots crammed close together with men sitting or lying on them. They made their way to two vacant ones in a corner. The bald man appeared in the doorway. "OK, you all know the rules," he said in a condescending tone, as if they were unruly children. "No talking and no disturbing others. No leaving the room unless you have to go to the bathroom. If there are any fights or arguments I'll call the police and have you taken away. Is that clear to everyone?" He paused and no one responded. "Good. Have a nice rest. Wake up is at six-thirty. You'll have one hour to eat breakfast and be on your way." He turned off the light and walked away.

Ryan sat down on his cot which creaked loudly in protest and wobbled dangerously as he stretched out on it in a hopeless attempt to get comfortable. A narrow piece of wood was secured across the middle of the cot and every time he moved, it pressed painfully against his back. Isaiah's cot was only two feet away and it was creaking even louder than his. On the other side of him someone sneezed in the dark and Ryan wiped the side of his face in disgust. Annoying, squeaking noises from the other cots filled the air like a discordant symphony.

He heard Isaiah whisper to him in the darkness. "Hey, Ryan. Heard you talking at dinner about them homeless murders."

"So?"

"My wife and daughter and me get together for a little bit every day. Spent this morning in Humboldt Park. A crazy older guy came up to us and says he knew the guy who got his throat cut last night."

"Hector Lopez?"

"Yeah, says he was a friend of his. Said that Hector had told him a few days ago that he talked to the Homeless

Slasher and the Slasher told Hector that he was gonna be his next victim."

Ryan tensed up from a sudden surge of adrenaline. "What else did he tell you?"

"Nothin' much. I figured he made up the whole thing."

"Did he say if Hector told him what the killer looks like?"

"No."

"Or where he was approached?"

"No, nothin' man."

"What does this guy look like?"

"White dude. Maybe fifty. Wore a baseball cap and a tore up orange jacket. Name was Cleo something but he was just a crazy guy talking."

"Yeah, maybe." But maybe not, Ryan told himself.

A raspy, angry voice shouted out in the darkness. "Hey, why don't you stupid morons shut up?"

"OK, sorry." Ryan answered. A loud, incoherent babbling began in the corner of the room.

"See!" The raspy voice shouted again. "Now you got that nut case going!"

Ryan lay still on his cot for a long time. The babbling eventually stopped and no one else talked. But there were frequent coughs and snores and the cots continually creaked from the men shifting their positions. It didn't matter; he was too excited to sleep. Even though the man named Cleo might have made up the story, it was certainly worth pursuing. It could conceivably lead him to the Slasher or give him a reason to contact Lydia. Tomorrow he would hang around Humboldt Park and hopefully find this Cleo. Tonight he would stay awake and think about the case, about Lydia, and how he had made it one more day without a drink. That was a preferable alternative to sleep and the recurring nightmare it brought, which always ended with the innocent lifeless face covered with blood and with him screaming in agony because he couldn't change anything, he couldn't bring her back, couldn't even tell her how sorry he was.

Chapter Fifteen

Ryan sat down on a bench and looked around Humboldt Park, nodding in silent agreement with his thoughts. The grass was neatly mowed and just beginning to yellow with the approach of winter and the tall trees still had a few withered brown or orange leaves. The benches were all painted a fresh coat of green, along with the nearby playground equipment. It surprised him that there were a few ducks floating peacefully in the large distant pond and he wondered why they hadn't migrated south yet. He visualized how beautiful the park would look in the spring when the grass and the leaves were green and the pond was a shimmering deep blue from the sunny sky's reflection. He decided if the park could be magically transported to a quaint New England town or any affluent suburb throughout the country it would be considered a welcome addition.

He glanced behind him at the decaying brick buildings across the street which surrounded the park on all four sides like gloomy prison walls. They were all dilapidated and depressing to look at; some were abandoned with boards nailed over their broken windows. It was ironic, he thought, that a city would take such good care of its parks but allow buildings that people lived in to rot away until they were worthless.

A police car was parked in the middle of the street next to a stalled car that was so rusty it was impossible to guess what type it was. A tow truck maneuvered behind it as a policeman directed, and Ryan watched the flashes of color in the street as various bits of garbage blew past.

He had been sitting on various benches for most of the day watching people drift in and out of the park. Most of them were Hispanic. There were mothers with children, a couple of teenage gangs, and a few homeless people. Even some drug dealers who conducted business openly from their parked cars but there was no one who matched Cleo's description and everyone he asked said they never heard of him. *That figures since nothing ever goes right.*

A few nights ago he had read something in the Bible about being patient until the Lord returns, like a farmer waiting for crops. Hopefully, he thought to himself, I won't have to sit here until spring planting season.

His nose kept running and his back was stiff from the frigid breeze that took away what little warmth the bright sunlight provided. He wished he was wearing his heavy winter coat but it was too expensive-looking for his disguise. Which is probably for the best, he said to himself sarcastically, freezing to death is nobler than drinking your self to death. Being bored to death is nobler too. Is it this monotonous for the homeless? Long dull stretches of time with no place to go and nothing to do?

He envisioned his theater audience again; the rows of seats lined up on the grass all the way back to the basketball courts. The seats were half empty now and those who remained were bundled in heavy fur coats and either sleeping soundly or had their heads turned to watch two men defying the cold to play a game of one-on-one. Who could blame the audience? Ryan decided the basketball players deserved to become the main characters in his fantasy play and he imagined a witty exchange of dialogue for them as they battled each other on the asphalt court. All they needed now was something important to play for, like a wager for their life savings or the right to pursue a girl they both loved.

He was concentrating on his character's motivations so intently that he ignored the person who entered the stage from the left and meandered over towards the basketball players. He finally realized with annoyance he would have to come up with a reason for this new character's entrance. He was a middle-aged man wearing a baseball cap and a torn orange parka. Ryan jumped up as if he'd been stung by a wasp. It was Cleo.

Ryan crunched on leaves as he ran across the grass. This could either be nothing or a vital turning point, he said to himself. *And if it is important you'll find a way to blow it.* He ran up behind the man who was now watching the basketball players. "Cleo?"

He turned around, a small white man in his fifties wearing a Mickey Mouse baseball cap that was pulled down to where his huge, childlike eyes blinked at him nervously. His nose was flat and wide like a boxer's who had lost too many fights.

"You are Cleo, aren't you?" Ryan asked.

"Yes." Cleo's eyes widened even further.

"I've been looking for you all day."

Cleo's mouth dropped open with a low moan. He took a step backward and then suddenly began running away with surprising speed.

Ryan sprinted after him. "Hey, where are you going? I just want to talk to you!"

Cleo glanced back and screamed like a wounded animal as Ryan gained on him. Ryan caught up to him as they reached the parking lot and he grabbed onto Cleo's shoulder but he twisted away from his grip and tripped, landing on the pavement with a grunt.

"Are you OK?" Ryan reached out to help him up but Cleo pushed him away and scrambled to his feet, gasping for breath.

Cleo pointed at him in silent terror as he took a few tentative backward steps. "Run!" he shouted. "Everybody run!" The people standing in the parking lot were all staring at them, even a drug dealer had gotten out of his car to investigate. "Now! Run now!" He gestured wildly to the onlookers and his eyes brightened with hope as he noticed the policeman across the street with the tow truck. "Get the policeman! Hurry! He's here!" He pointed at Ryan. "He killed my friend! He's the Homeless Slasher!"

Ryan shook his head in disbelief. "I'm not the Slasher!"

"Yes you are!" Cleo took another backward step. "You're gonna kill me with your knife!"

"What knife? I don't have any knife!"

"Yes you do. It's in your coat pocket. I see it! Help! Police!"

Ryan looked down at the bulge in his coat pocket and reached in and pulled out a banana. "You mean this?"

Cleo nodded at him in stunned silence.

Ryan held the banana up higher. "Relax everybody," he said to the curious onlookers. "It's only fruit. He thought I was going to stab him with it." He paused lamely. "I wasn't, of course."

Cleo peered at the banana suspiciously. "How do I know it's not a knife covered up with a banana peel?"

"Incredible." Ryan tossed the banana to him. "Open it up. Eat it if you want to."

Cleo peeled the banana and sighed with relief before taking a huge bite out of it. "Good," he mumbled with his mouth full.

"Help yourself," Ryan said sarcastically. "I'll just hyperventilate while you chow down. You must be a former Olympic sprinter."

"I run fast," he said as he chewed, "when I'm scared."

Ryan noticed with relief that everyone who had watched Cleo shouting at him now completely ignored them. "Why did you think I was the Slasher?"

"Saw your knife, I mean banana."

"Do you think the Slasher wants to kill you?"

"He killed my friend, Hector." He shrugged. "I think he be comin' for me next."

"Why do you think that?"

"I dunno, just think so." He swallowed the last part of the banana. "Thanks for the dinner." He shuffled away, carrying the banana peel.

"Hey, where are you going?" Ryan hurried after him.

"To feed squirrels." Cleo held up the banana peel.

"Will squirrels eat that?"

Cleo frowned. "Hope so. If they really hungry maybe."

"Well, anyway, do you mind if I come along?"

"No. I gots no one to talk to now that Hector is gone."

They walked across the grass to a cluster of tall, barren trees and as they passed his theater audience Ryan saw most of them were awake now and watching him with interest instead of the basketball players. "Do you like squirrels Cleo?"

"Yeah. They never do mean things like some people do."

"I've noticed that too."

They stopped under the trees and Cleo carefully separated the banana peel into three equal pieces and set each of them under a different tree. "Gotta be fair, else their feelin's get hurt." He straightened up and looked up at the trees. "Dinner time, guys!"

"How long did you know Hector?"

"Not real long, but he was my best friend. We talked all the time."

"About what?"

"I guess I talked mostly and Hector kinda listened. He seemed to listen real good. When he did say stuff it was all about how his wife and daughter died and how lonely he was and then he'd cough a lot." A gray squirrel appeared on a branch near the top of the tree and looked down at them as his tail twitched nervously. "Gotta treat for you little buddy! Come on down!" The squirrel scampered back into his hole in the tree trunk. "Hey, where you goin'?" Cleo sounded hurt. "Maybe he's gonna tell the others."

"Did he ever talk to you about the Homeless Slasher?"

"Yeah." Cleo shuddered. "It was spooky."

"What did he say about him?"

"Hector says he come to visit him one night."

"When?"

"I dunno. A week ago, I guess."

"Where did the Slasher visit him?"

Cleo pointed to an abandoned building across the street. "Hector, he lived over there." He pointed to his left. "I live down that way. Gotta bigger place all to myself."

"Did Hector refer to the Slasher as he or she?"

"Um." He paused. "He, always he."

"So what did he say to Hector?"

"Um, let's see. Different stuff, like about Hector's wife and daughter and his cough."

"Hector's cough?"

"Yeah, he's all the time coughin' and sweatin'. So this Slasher guy he tell Hector he ain't gonna live through the winter anyway so he's better off goin' quick."

"I assume Hector was scared when he told you this?"

Cleo shook his head. "No, but I was. Hector, he just says he don't want to live no more anyways. Says he wants to be with his wife and daughter again but he can't kill himself or he might not get into heaven."

"So he didn't go to the police?"

"I guess not."

"Did you think about telling the police?"

Cleo looked down at the ground. "No. I figure Hector maybe jokin' with me. Or if he wasn't and I tell the police, maybe the Slasher guy get mad and come after me and I'm real scared to die, don't want to die, not now, not never. So I didn't tell anyone." He looked up again, eyes misty with tears. "But now I wish I told the police or somebody."

"What else did Hector say about him?"

"I dunno. Don't remember nothin' else."

"Did he say what this guy looks like?"

"No, didn't say."

"Did he say what his name was?"

"Uh-uh."

"How about his age or if he'd ever seen him before?"

"No, none of that stuff."

"What did you ask Hector about him?'

"Nothin'."

"Why not? Weren't you curious?"

"It was too scary. I was afraid I might get spooky dreams." Cleo glanced up at the top of the trees. "You think maybe they don't like me?"

Ryan exhaled in frustration, realizing the most likely explanation was that Cleo made up the entire story. Why would the Slasher tell someone ahead of time that he was going to kill them? Maybe there'd be little risk of getting caught if he knew that person wanted to die, but why take the chance? Why not kill Hector immediately?

"Did anybody else live in that building with Hector?"

"Sometimes. Last week a couple of mean guys stayed there. Slept downstairs somewhere. I come looking for Hector one day and they push me down and take my three dollars away. Why they have to do that?"

"Were those mean guys still there the night the Slasher talked to Hector?"

"I dunno. Maybe."

Ryan walked over to a tree and leaned against the trunk. He decided it would be logical for the Slasher to postpone killing Hector if there were other people in the building. They might hear the sounds of a struggle, investigate, and see him leaving. He wouldn't risk that, he was too careful. That was why there were no witnesses or just one if Bible Bob's story about the homeless woman was true. "Did you tell the police everything you've told me?"

"Um, let me think." Cleo clasped his hands over his hat with a serious expression. "A nice policeman talk to me in the park yesterday and I says how I knew Hector and would miss him very much but I dunno who killed him. Then I says two mean guys took my money and hurt me last week and I ask him if he'd go catch 'em and get my three dollars back and he says 'Sure, OK' and walks away."

Ryan stared wistfully at the abandoned building Cleo had pointed out and wished he could check out the murder site for clues but he knew it would still be cordoned off by the police. He'd have to settle for whatever information his uncle could pass along. "Can you remember anything else Hector said about the Homeless Slasher?"

"No."

Ryan stepped away from the tree. "Thanks for talking with me, Cleo. I'm going now."

"Don't you wanna see the squirrels eat?"

"No thanks."

"But it was your banana."

"You can watch for me."

"Wait!" Cleo hurried after him with a desperate look. "Don't you wanna talk to me some more?"

Ryan kept walking. "Sorry. I've got to go."

"I have no friends now that Hector died. Will you be my friend?"

Ryan paused, turning to look at his frightened, child-like face. "I don't have any friends either." Ryan swallowed hard. "Truthfully, you're better off not having any friends than having me for one."

"After the squirrels eat we can watch the basketball players."

Ryan turned and walked away, plowing through a small pile of leaves.

"Do you like to sing?" Cleo called after him. "We could sing some songs or go around saying hello to everybody in the park."

Ryan shoved his hands in his pocket and walked faster.

"I could show you where I live!"

Ryan kept walking.

"Wait a second!" Cleo called. "I could show you my picture of the Homeless Slasher!"

Ryan stopped, flinching as if he'd been struck by a searing bolt of lightning. He turned around and stared at him. "What picture?"

"The one Hector gave me the same night he told me his story." Cleo hesitated. "It's in my room. You wanna see it?"

Chapter Sixteen

Are you being honest with me?" Officer Howell looked up from the notes lying on his desk and leaned back in his chair, studying her with obvious interest. "I've got a feeling you're holding something back."

Lydia straightened up in her chair and folded her arms across her chest. "I've told you everything I know about the notes."

"I don't mean about these. I mean about who's sending them."

"I don't know who's sending them. That's why I'm here."

Officer Howell shook his head slowly and ran his hand through his curly blond hair. "I think you know. Or at least have a pretty good idea. That's the way it usually is with this kind of stuff."

"I've told you the truth."

"Maybe. Maybe not."

Lydia felt her face redden with anger and she deliberately looked away, gazing at the photos hanging on the wall of his tiny office and quickly realizing that most of them were pictures of Officer Howell himself. In a way he was right, she did suspect her stepfather might be sending the notes. It was logical to think that after the horrible things he had done to her mother but she had no proof and didn't even know if he was living in Chicago, and she had already decided that Officer Howell was definitely the last person she would ever tell about her past.

She looked directly at him again, trying to control her anger. "Will you check the notes for fingerprints?"

"Sure," he said. "But if he doesn't have a criminal record his prints won't help any, and if he was smart enough to use gloves and seal the envelope with a sponge then we've got absolutely nothing."

"You'll test them, though?"

"Yeah, I guess," he said reluctantly. "We can trace the phone calls to your apartment in case he starts calling you, but there's not a lot we can do without any suspects."

"So what you're saying is you don't take this seriously and you're not going to bother offering me any protection."

"I wouldn't put it that way," Officer Howell shrugged, "but this is probably nothing to worry about. So far he's only sent you a few harmless notes which could be some type of joke and this one he left on your car yesterday is pretty vague. 'YOUR TIME IS RUNNING OUT.' Who knows what that means?"

"I'd rather not find out. And I don't think 'I WILL GET YOU SOON' or, 'FIND ME OR DIE' are vague at all."

Lydia watched him lean forward, flashing his snow white teeth with an insincere smile. She sensed he was about to ask her out. Ever since she had sat down in his office he had let her know he was interested through the brazen way he looked at her, even though she hadn't offered any encouragement. She had to admit he was extremely good looking, a tall, athletically built man in his thirties with bright blue eyes and a strong jaw and could probably be a male model for a jeans ad. None of that impressed her though; in her opinion physical appearance was mostly a matter of heredity not something someone earned. Good looks had nothing to do with how kind or intelligent someone was so they were, therefore, totally irrelevant to a person's true worth. She suddenly thought of Ryan and visualized his brown eyes staring at her with mysterious pain and was surprised at her disappointment when she wondered if she'd ever see him again.

"Ms. Dupree, can I ask you something?"

"What?"

"Do you have a boyfriend?"

"Why do you ask?"

"Well if you do and you were having some problems then that might explain all this."

"I don't have a boyfriend."

Officer Howell looked both surprised and pleased. "Well, how about an ex-boyfriend? Someone you broke up with recently?"

"No."

"No?" He raised his eyebrows and grinned at her. "You have had a boyfriend sometime in your life, haven't you?"

"Yes. There was one I broke up with a couple of years ago. He's dead now."

"Oh. I'm sorry," he said without any trace of sympathy. He paused for a few seconds and then snapped his fingers with enthusiasm. "Hey, I've got a great idea. I know this fantastic Italian restaurant on Addison. How about if I take you to dinner there tonight and we can talk this over in a more relaxing atmosphere?"

"No thank you," she said sharply. "I came here to get help, not get hit on."

"Oh." His mouth dropped open and he blinked at her in amazement. "Well, you don't have to get testy."

Lydia decided that his reaction proved he didn't get turned down for a date very often. "Do you have any advice for me or are we finished?"

"Yeah, I have some advice," he said, eyes narrowing with annoyance. "Why don't you tell me the truth? You had a boyfriend and you broke up with him recently, didn't you?"

"No."

"You're probably seeing some other guy now so he's ticked off and sending you these notes."

"You're wrong."

"Until you give us his name there's nothing we can do."

"That's all you have to tell me?"

"For now, yes. I wouldn't worry about this too much. Nothing's happened to you yet."

"Thanks for nothing!" She got up out of her chair.

He shrugged. "I'll let you know if we find any prints on the notes."

Lydia walked out of his office and passed a row of desks where other policemen were talking on phones. She hurried out the front door and went down the cement steps, too aggravated to even notice the cold, light rain that was falling. Instead of being doubted and leered at she could have spent the last hour helping people back at the shelter. She quickly approached her car which was parked on the side of the street, wedged into a long line of other cars. She took her keys out of her purse and exhaled loudly when she saw the plain, white envelope on the windshield that was held in place by a wiper blade. She looked around and only saw an elderly couple walking on the sidewalk in the distance. She studied the office and apartment buildings that lined both sides of the street, searching accusingly for a face watching her from one of the windows but didn't see anybody.

Finally, she grabbed the soggy envelope and tore it open as her heart began fluttering. She took out the piece of paper that was inside and unfolded it and read the message that was printed in block letters. It said, "THEY CAN'T PROTECT YOU FROM ME!"

Chapter Seventeen

S o what does he look like?" Ryan asked as he followed Cleo down the garbage strewn alley.

"Who?" Cleo asked with a confused expression.

"The Homeless Slasher."

"Um, I dunno."

"You said you have a picture of him in your room."

"Oh, yeah. I forgot for a second."

"Well, what does he look like?"

Cleo thought for a moment. "Skinny. He's real skinny." He stopped in front of the open doorway of a huge abandoned brick building and gestured proudly. "Here we be!"

Cleo stepped over the threshold into the large dingy room and as Ryan followed he inhaled a musty odor. The ground floor was a large open area with rusty metal shelves lining the far wall. Broken crates and boards were scattered around along with some moldy looking cardboard boxes. Even in the dim light he saw that a thick gray dust covered everything and a spider web was draped over one corner like a delicate silver curtain.

"Is this where you sleep, Cleo?"

"No, my room's upstairs. It's nicer than here."

They walked towards the wooden stairs in the corner and Ryan almost tripped over a two by four. "Don't you ever sleep in shelters?"

"Nope. Used to live in a hospital though." He started up the stairs which creaked so loudly it sounded like the squeals of a wounded cat.

"What kind of hospital did you live in?"

"A spooky one," Cleo said as they both continued upstairs. "Hated it there. They keep makin' me take medicine all the time and it was so scary, people yellin' and screamin' a lot. Sometimes people died there. I was scared I would, too. There was this woman who used to bother me. Big woman, maybe seven feet tall. All the time botherin' me, comin' up to me askin' me to feel a bullet hole in her head and I always say to her I don't wanna feel no bullet hole so please leave me alone but she follows me everywhere and keeps askin' so one day I bust out a window and run away. Too bad, cause the food was good there but I had to go or I'd have died and now I'd be walkin' around like a dead guy."

They reached the top of the stairs and Cleo led him down a dark, narrow hallway with rotting floor boards. Ryan pictured them falling through and landing in a giant, sticky web with thousands of frenzied black widows crawling around on it, delighted to have them for dinner.

They passed several dark, open doorways. "There's lots of room here if you wanna move in," Cleo said hopefully.

"No thanks. I'll stick to shelters."

Cleo paused at the doorway at the end of the hallway. "It's real quiet here and nobody hurts you. We can go to the park everyday."

"Let's take a look at that picture."

"OK," Cleo said with obvious disappointment. They went into a small room cluttered with cardboard boxes and wooden crates. Cold air streamed through a large open window and the late afternoon's sunlight clearly exposed the dust that was everywhere. Cleo pointed proudly to a pile of torn blankets in a corner. "That's where I sleep."

"A cot in a shelter would be more comfortable."

"Oh, no. I'm real comfortable here and nobody bothers you."

"If you say so," Ryan said skeptically as he glanced around. "Well, how about showing me that photo."

"Photo?" Cleo looked puzzled.

"The picture of the Slasher."

"Oh, that. It ain't a photo. It's a drawing."

"A drawing? You said it was a picture!"

"It is. A picture Hector drawed on a box."

"A box?"

"Yeah. Must be around here somewheres."

"Terrific." Ryan chewed softly on his lower lip and glanced up in frustration, noticing the rusty stains on the ceiling. He should have known the picture wouldn't be a close up of the Slasher with the killer's name and address stamped on his forehead. *No, that would be too easy and nothing is ever easy, especially for a perpetual failure.*

Cleo moved various boxes around in the center of the room. "Picture, picture, picture." He paused and looked around, scratching his ear thoughtfully.

"Cleo, are you sure there really is a drawing?"

"Ah hah!" Cleo grinned and pointed triumphantly at a lone box that sagged against the wall in the far corner. "It was too spooky to look at so I put it over there." He hurried over and turned it around with a solemn expression.

Ryan quickly walked over and knelt down in front of it, feeling his heart leaping erratically in his chest. It was a large cardboard box with a crude drawing on its side that had been sketched with a black magic marker and although it was a little faint in spots, it left an unmistakable image. It showed a stick figure person holding a huge knife in his right hand and waving with his other hand. The face showed two dots for eyes and had a broad smile drawn underneath. Written above it were the words, "One that takes." Near the bottom of the box the name "Hector" had been written.

"Cleo did you draw this?"

"No."

Ryan put his hand over Hector's name. "How do you spell Hector?"

"Um. 'H A K', something. No, wait. 'H A C K', something."

"OK, never mind." Ryan took his hand away and pointed at the words. "'One that takes.' Do you know what that means?"

"Um, no."

"Did Hector tell you why he wrote it?"

"I dunno. I don't remember."

"What did he say about this drawing?"

"He just drawed it a few days ago after the Slasher talked to him. Says for me to come look at the Slasher so I do and I hear myself start moanin' and my hands get shaky so I took it and put it over here and Hector he says he's sorry for scarin' me and won't talk about him no more."

"Are you sure he never said anything about these words he wrote?"

"Yeah." Cleo began pacing. "I'm scared the Slasher guy's gonna come for me next, and I don't wanna die cause they just bury you underground all alone and then maybe you get taken somewheres worse than a hospital." He paused. "Are you scared to die?"

"Some days, yes." Ryan stood up and walked over to the open window where the cold air flowed unchallenged into the room and filled it with incessant rustling noises. He looked out and saw the side of a similar brick building just twenty feet away with its windows boarded up as if it actually contained something of value that had to be protected. In the alley below there was an overturned dumpster and bits of paper and garbage bounced along the ground towards the street, like a polluted stream feeding a large river. "Why don't you board up this window? It's freezing in here."

Cleo shrugged. "You can see the park. I love the park."

Ryan stuck his head out the window, and in the distance beyond the alley he saw the top of a few trees in Humboldt Park. He pulled his head back in and turned around. "Did you spend last winter here?"

"Nope. Moved in this summer. You like it here?"

"Cleo, you won't survive the winter if you stay here."

"Will too."

"No, you won't. You'll freeze to death some night."

"I can get more blankets."

"That won't help much."

Cleo's lips quivered slightly. "I'll burn some boxes. I'll get nice and warm."

"And end up burning down this whole building and yourself along with it."

"This is my home now."

"This isn't any home. Not for a human being at least." Ryan moved closer and affectionately patted him on the shoulder. "Why don't you come with me? I'll find a nice shelter for you."

Cleo stepped back and tears welled up in his eyes. "No! I don't like them places."

"They've got to be better than this."

"People will do mean things to me there then they'll send me back to some hospital again and I don't wanna go, not never, never, never!"

"Cleo, if you stay here this winter you'll die."

"No!" Cleo threw himself down on his bed of torn blankets and buried his face into one, sobbing like a small child.

Ryan considered his options. He could keep trying to convince him to leave but it seemed highly unlikely he'd be successful. He could physically overpower Cleo and drag him to a shelter, but who would stop him from eventually escaping and returning here? And if he took him to court and tried to have him committed he'd probably lose since Cleo was not a threat to others. "OK, Cleo." He crouched down next to him. "I can't make you stay in a shelter, but I hope you'll consider it for your own good. Will you?" He waited in vain for an answer and finally stood up and walked to the door. "Thanks for showing me the picture," he said, pausing to see that Cleo's face was still buried in the blankets. "You're a good guy, Cleo. Take care of yourself."

Ryan walked down the hallway wondering why his stomach felt queasy. He had discovered a cryptic but potentially important clue that the Chicago Police Department knew nothing about and now he had a perfect excuse to call

Lydia and hopefully see her again. This is a lucky break, he said to himself, I should be ecstatically tap dancing down the hallway.

Ryan quickly descended the creaky stairs. He didn't know what to do to help Cleo. He would ask Lydia, it would be another good reason to call her, and she'd know how to get him into a shelter. He reached the bottom of the stairs and hurried towards the entrance doorway that was shining with an amber glow from the fading sunlight. A mental image of Cleo lying face down on tattered blankets was still stuck in his mind and he willed it to disappear.

Chapter Eighteen

One that takes," Lydia repeated thoughtfully. "It might be a clue that the Slasher is some type of thief or burglar."

"Or it just means that the Slasher takes lives but we already know that, so it doesn't really help us." Ryan shrugged. "Maybe the police will decipher it. They seemed pretty excited when I called them about it a few hours ago."

"The possibilities are endless. If we can figure out what Hectors' drawing means it could lead us to the Slasher. We should go over there now and look at it together."

Ryan shook his head. "The police have taken it away by now. My uncle's one of the detectives assigned to the case and he said he was going over there immediately."

Lydia exhaled in frustration and leaned against the back of the plastic booth they were sitting in. She studied Ryan's enigmatic expression for a moment as he watched her from across the narrow table that separated them. She glanced around the coffee shop, it was after nine o'clock at night and the only other customer was an elderly man sitting at the counter. A lone waitress stood by the cash register wistfully staring out the window at all the cars passing through Logan Square. Lydia looked back at Ryan and smiled. "I'm glad you called me and I'm very impressed that you discovered this clue. Have you ever considered becoming a detective instead of a playwright?"

Ryan winced and felt his cheeks redden. "I've just been lucky so far. Besides, I haven't discovered anything substantial yet. I know there may be a witness, but I have no idea where she is. I know the Slasher told Hector in advance he was going to kill him but that really doesn't lead me anywhere and if no one can figure out what that drawing means then it's totally worthless."

"I believe something you've learned will eventually solve this case, and besides, you should be proud of yourself. You've already discovered more than the Chicago Police Department has in over a year." Lydia paused, realizing she was so impressed with Ryan's investigation that she now wanted to be part of it. She almost asked him outright if he'd be willing to accept her as a partner but stopped herself and took a sip of coffee instead. What if her attraction and admiration for him gradually weakened her resolve and tempted her into a romantic relationship? She didn't want that to happen. But wasn't it worth the risk to help find the murderer? "So what's next?" she asked, leaning forward on the table.

"I'm going to keep working undercover as one of the homeless. I think I'll hang around the Loop for a few days and look for that alleged witness and for that Yolanda woman who talked to her."

"I'll keep calling all the shelters to see if anyone named Yolanda signs in." Lydia set her coffee mug down on the table. "I have a strong feeling about you, Ryan. I think you just might be the one to catch this killer."

"I wish I were that confident."

"I know you can do it." She looked directly into his eyes and smiled. "With the help of a determined, dedicated female partner."

"And where do I find one of those?"

"Right here. As of this moment, I officially volunteer."

He stared at her, fighting back a surge of elation because he wasn't sure she was serious. "You want to work together?"

"Absolutely! I'll be terrific, a non-smoking, non-complaining, work-around-the-clock partner. What more could you ask for?"

Ryan envisioned a dizzying series of images, meeting with Lydia at restaurants, driving places together, talking about the case at her apartment. He envisioned the affection in her eyes as she confessed her undeniable attraction for him and as he reached for her with ecstatic longing the front page of a newspaper appeared, blocking out the scene entirely. It was the usual page with the large headline that had his picture under it. The pleasant images stopped abruptly. "You don't know me very well," he finally said.

"I know you probably saved my life by rescuing me. I know you're an idealistic person who's on his way to finding a serial killer. What else do I need to know?"

Ryan swallowed hard as a sudden wave of nausea tightened his throat. He knew he could fool her for a while, pretending to be someone he was not, but eventually she'd learn the truth. *Oh yeah, sooner or later she'll find out, you can count on that and then you'll get to see that incomparably pretty face contorted with horror and disgust. Then she'll despise you all the more for trying to hide the truth from her.* "There's a lot to know about me," he said hesitantly. "Too much."

"Sure. Besides being a great detective you're a talented playwright."

"I've never had a play produced. Not even one." He shook his head, amazed that his words came out so easily. "I lied to impress you. I have written a few plays but they're all worthless."

Lydia's eyes widened slightly and she was silent for a moment. "I bet they're very good, even if they haven't been produced."

"That's not all I lied about." Ryan slumped down into the back of the booth, feeling as if he was slowly sinking into a dark, bottomless abyss. *It's hopeless, tell her now. Get it over with.* "My name's not Ryan Johnson like I told you and the police at your shelter. It's Ryan Dolan." He waited expectantly, surprised there was no flash of recognition in her eyes.

"So?" She waited with a genuinely puzzled expression.

His heart was beating so hard that his inner ears were vibrating and it seemed like a hot wind was blowing into his face with an increasingly angry force. "Don't you remember that name? About five years ago I was the major news story in Chicago for a while."

"I don't remember." She clenched her hands together to combat her growing tension and deliberately composed her face into a calm expression.

"Then I'll tell you the whole story. You'd find out eventually anyway." He paused, scanning her face, memorizing every detail of her beauty before he told her. "I'm a murderer."

She shook her head, eyebrows raised. "No."

"It's true. Actually, I have a lot in common with the Homeless Slasher. We've both murdered innocent victims." He paused again, his voice sounding weak and sickly to his own ears. *Just go on. Get it over with.* "It's ironic, though, because I never dreamed I'd end up this way. You see, it's a Dolan family tradition to become a cop. My grandfather, my uncles, my cousins, all ended up as one of Chicago's finest. My father was, too. When I was ten he was killed trying to stop a liquor store holdup. That didn't discourage me though; I wanted to become a policeman more than ever but not to avenge my father's death. It just seemed to me this world is so full of chaos and violence that the law is the only thing keeping us from destroying ourselves. If everyone lived within the law we'd have that perfect world so many of us long for. I've always hoped we'll reach that Utopian level someday, but until we do, enforcing the law is absolutely necessary. Do I sound like a fascist?"

"No, idealistic."

"Good." He forced a quick smile but she kept staring at him seriously. "So anyway, I majored in Criminal Justice at Eastern Illinois. After I graduated I went to the police academy and when I got out of there I was assigned to a West Town precinct. It's a tough area so there's plenty to keep you busy; robberies, drug deals, rapes, anything and everything." His voice cracked a little and he paused to take a sip of coffee. "I'd only been working there for a year and a half and my partner and I were stuck with the graveyard shift this one unforgettable time. It was seven in the morning and we were almost done when we got a call that a fight had broken out on a street nearby. It was a neighborhood with rows of identical dilapidated apartment houses. When we pulled up we saw two guys yelling and shoving each other with a few people watching. Suddenly, one of them pulled a gun out and shot the other guy and took off running. I told my partner to call for back up and I jumped out of the car and ran after him. He went into the nearest apartment building so I followed.

"I had my gun out when I went in the front entrance and an elderly woman in the hallway screamed at me not to shoot her and pointed to a door. I opened it and saw some stairs that led to the basement and I went down them very slowly. I could actually hear my heart pounding and I wondered if the other guy could too. When you don't know if you'll live or die the surge of adrenaline that charges through you is incredible. There was enough morning light coming through some dusty windows that I could see pretty well, and when I finally got to the bottom of the stairs I heard a noise from behind this huge furnace in the middle of the basement. I knew he was obviously hiding behind it, waiting for me. I yelled out for him to throw down his gun and give up but he didn't answer. I should have waited for my partner but I was so pumped up I didn't think, I just reacted and held out my gun and ran over to the furnace and pushed up against it. Of course I heard noise from the other side as he maneuvered around to get a shot at me. I was about to start sliding around the furnace when he ran out the other side. I whirled around, my gun exploded, and I saw a body tumble down onto the cement floor. I walked over and couldn't believe what I saw. It was a little girl wearing pink pajamas and holding a doll in her hands. She was lying there with the top of her head blown off."

He looked down at his hands. He had been concentrating so hard on keeping his voice calm he had forgotten about them and they were shaking uncontrollably. She reached over and put her hands on top of his. "It's OK, Ryan."

"It turns out the guy had already gone out the back door of the basement. My partner cut him off and he surrendered. The guy he shot only had a minor flesh wound. The little girl I shot was five years old. Her name was Lisa Thomas. They said she loved to play with her dolls in the basement and had a cardboard box she used for a doll house. When I looked up from the pool of blood she was lying in that was the first thing I noticed, a big cardboard box in a corner with crayon markings on it, windows and doors and stuff. I just kept staring at that doll house until they came for me."

They were both silent for a moment, staring down at their entwined hands with numb expressions. "Ryan, that's one of the saddest stories I've ever heard," Lydia said, looking up and choosing her words carefully. "But it was an accident. It could have happened to any policeman. You have to find a way to forgive yourself."

He cleared his throat and looked up at her, noticing the undisguised pity on her face and he wondered if she looked at pathetic homeless people that way. "The papers weren't as understanding as you are. They said I was the epitome of the incompetent Chicago policeman. Lisa was black and a few wondered if the shooting was racially motivated. The Mayor ordered a special investigation which finally concluded that I wasn't a racist, just a fool who made an incredibly stupid, tragic mistake. The department sent me to a shrink for a 'fitness for duty' exam and of course he flunked me saying I was extremely traumatized. That ended my brief career in law enforcement. I drew disability checks for a while and since then I've just taken temporary jobs when I'm running out of cash."

"And you've never put this behind you."

"I can't," he said, surprised that she didn't understand. "Lisa's still with me. She'd be ten years old. I keep visualizing what she'd look like now and certain times of day I wonder what she'd be doing at that exact moment, if she'd be happily playing with friends or learning something in school or at home with her mother." He shook his head. "My uncle says I'm the world champion head-case."

Lydia frowned. "I think I've met your uncle. Is he a detective named Kevin Dolan?"

"Yeah."

"He came into our shelter once asking about the homeless murders and making crude comments. He didn't seem like the sympathetic type."

Ryan released his hands and took another sip of coffee. Lydia rubbed at her forehead which ached from the tension that was pounding away like hurricane driven waves battering a defenseless shore. "Ryan, everyone makes mistakes, and plenty of us have unbearably painful memories."

Ryan shook his head. "No offense, but you could never understand. Someone like you couldn't have any tragic mistakes or memories to forget."

"Is that right?" she asked with obvious bitterness.

"I guess so," he said, confused by her tone and the strong emotion shining in her eyes. "I mean, you're so giving, so sure of yourself and what you want out of life. You're probably the most well-adjusted person I've ever met."

"I don't consider myself well-adjusted. I have tragic memories too." She hesitated for a moment and then looked directly at him. "When I was twelve my mom remarried. My stepfather was a drunk and he beat her. Sometimes I was afraid or angry, but mostly I was hopeful because there was someone who could protect us, someone I believed in and talked to everyday."

"Are you talking about God?"

"Yes. I became a Christian when I was a little girl; I probably had as much faith back then as Bible Bob does now. Technically, I still am a Christian; they say you can't lose your salvation. I bet you didn't know that?"

Ryan shifted uncomfortably. "No, I didn't."

"A lot of good salvation does. It doesn't prevent tragedies. My stepfather got mad at me one night for no reason and ended up breaking my mother's neck. The police never found him. He left me a note saying my turn was coming. I had prayed for months that God would protect us, I guess He was too busy to listen."

"I'm sorry to hear about your mother."

"It's not your fault, but it is somebody's fault. I know God gives everyone a free will, the choice to do right or wrong. Too many people choose to do wrong, that's why this world has so many problems. But He also promises to answer prayers. He could have prevented my mother's death if He wanted to." She paused and looked at the window; pellets of rain were beading up on the glass. "Murder, crime, disease, and so much pain. Why does our Creator, who allegedly loves us, allow such terrible things to happen?"

"I'm no expert and I'm not a Christian but I've been reading the Bible lately. It seems like bad things happen sometimes to God's people. I mean, John the Baptist got his head cut off, Paul was thrown in prison and of course Jesus, His own son, was crucified." Ryan frowned. "There are only two reasons I can think of for a loving God to allow these things to happen. First, He must have a plan to eventually bring justice to this world, on Judgment Day I guess. Secondly, He knows the future and knows how wonderful heaven is. Maybe the bad things that happen here pale in comparison to spending eternity in paradise with Him."

Lydia stared at him for a long moment. "That's probably the best answer I've ever heard. Are you sure you're not a Christian?"

"Yes."

"Why?"

"Because I don't believe God will forgive me for killing that little girl, and I don't believe I deserve forgiveness."

"Sounds like we both have a problem with forgiveness. I won't forgive God and you don't think He'll forgive you." She took a deep breath and leaned forward. "Does this mean we can be partners now?"

Chapter Nineteen

Augie Rosen stuck his head into the stove. "We either need a new element in here or a new stove. If we need a stove we need more donations." His voice sounded muffled and far away to Lydia. "Should be easy, right?" he asked without waiting for an answer. "Except nobody wants to hear about our problems feeding the homeless. They're more concerned with going on vacation or buying more things. Sometimes I could scream." He accidentally banged his head inside the stove and screamed in frustration.

"Did you hear me, Augie?" Lydia asked patiently. "I'll be back in fifteen minutes. If he calls tell him to call me on my cell phone."

As she spoke the kitchen door swung open and Martin entered with a stack of dirty dishes. "If who calls? Don't tell me I have a rival for your affection?" He put the dishes down and grabbed a fork and waved it around as if it were a sword. "I'll challenge him to a duel. Tell me who he is so

I can jab him to death," he looked at the fork with feigned seriousness, "or feed him to death."

"Never mind who he is," Lydia said.

"Martin, do you realize what this means?" Augie's voice echoed from inside the stove. "Lydia's got a boyfriend," he sang off key, "Lydia's got a boyfriend."

Carl came through the kitchen door. "Hey, can you guys cut this concert short? I have more homeless folks out there then I know what to do with."

"This is more important," Augie said. "Lydia's got a boyfriend."

"That's cool," Carl said with mock seriousness. "Anybody I know?"

"She won't tell us," Martin said with an exaggerated sigh.

Lydia felt her cheeks redden as she walked towards the kitchen door.

"Where are you going," Martin asked, "to buy him a present?"

"I'm teaching my reading class this afternoon. I left all my material at home."

"Lydia's in love." Augie sang from inside the stove. "Lydia's in love."

Her hand was on the door when the phone rang and Martin picked up the receiver. "Helping Hand," he said, his eyes widening as he listened. "You want to speak to Lydia? I'm sorry she's leaving with me right now; we're going to Vegas to get married. Can I take a message?"

Lydia grabbed the phone from him. "Hello?"

"Hi." Ryan's voice answered her.

"I'm glad you called," Lydia said, turning in towards the corner, conscious of the others listening to her with interest. "I think I came up with a good lead."

"Great. What is it?"

"I called some shelters this morning and none of them had anyone named Yolanda signed in but one social worker told me she heard a tall, African-American woman referred to as Yolanda, even though she signed in under a different name."

"What name did she sign in as?"

"Oprah Winfrey."

Ryan chuckled softly. "That's what I call an obvious alias."

"But why wouldn't she use her real name?"

"I don't know, but it's worth finding out. Who knows, maybe this is the Yolanda who talked to the witness. Where is this place?"

"It's a woman's shelter downtown on Jackson Boulevard."

"Good, that's not too far from where I am. I'll head right over there. Looks like our partnership is already getting results, thanks to you."

"I don't think I deserve any credit so far. The social worker's name is Jeanie. Let me know if you find out anything."

"OK." He hesitated. "I really enjoyed talking with you last night. I'm glad I told you about shooting that poor little girl. I thought you'd condemn me for it but I'm relieved you didn't. It made me feel a lot better."

"Last night made me feel a lot better, too." Lydia turned around and Martin grinned at her lasciviously. Augie had pulled his head out of the stove and was on all fours on the floor staring up at her impassively. Carl shook his head at her. She covered the receiver with her hand. "Don't you guys have anything better to do?"

"No!" Martin wiggled his eyebrows suggestively. "This is getting real interesting. I want to hear about last night."

She snorted with disgust and turned away from them again. "Good luck," she said to Ryan.

"You don't need luck if you're good," Ryan said, "and together, I think we're very good. I'll talk to you later."

"Bye." She hung up the phone wishing she had said more to him. She glanced back at Martin who had his arms folded and a stern expression on his face.

"All right. Who is my rival?" Martin asked. "A politician? Rock star? Movie star? Who?"

"I'll be back in fifteen minutes," she said. Augie nodded at her and put his head back inside the stove.

Martin playfully gripped his own hair and pretended to pull on it. "I must know. Please tell me!"

She hurried out of the kitchen, glancing at the men and women quietly eating at the tables, wishing she could announce she'd found homes for all of them and see the despair instantly vanish from their faces. Someday it could happen, she told herself, everything's possible.

As she walked down the hallway towards the building's rear exit she suddenly felt as out of breath as if she'd just finished running a marathon. Every time she went to her car she expected to find another note. When Ryan had walked her to the car last night there hadn't been one, and there wasn't one in her mailbox when she arrived home but that didn't mean the threats would stop. If another one was waiting for her now she was determined to read it without any fear, in fact she almost hoped one would be there because she was ready for it. Last night she decided not to be a helpless victim any more while her stepfather tormented her. She had spent hours devising a plan of attack and the next time she received an ominous message she'd put that plan into effect. If he was responsible for the notes then she'd soon be dealing with him on her own terms.

She opened the door and stepped into the parking lot, squinting at her car in the bright afternoon sunlight and willing her heart to stop pounding away with its savage intensity. I don't fear him anymore, she told herself.

She quickly approached her car and didn't see anything on her windshield but checked under the wiper blades to be sure. There was no note. She got into her car, chiding herself for her shortness of breath and rapid pulse which were physical manifestations of the fear she had vowed to banish forever.

She drove around the building and turned north on California Avenue. She remembered it was the middle of the afternoon and the mail had probably arrived. But it shouldn't upset her if another note was in her mailbox. It couldn't hurt her; it was just words on a piece of paper. She decided to think of something pleasant while she drove and Ryan's face appeared in her mind, sad and vulnerable, as he had looked last night at the coffee shop. She was glad he told her about his tragic past and was impressed by the remorse he felt over the little girl's accidental death. Didn't that prove that he was a caring, compassionate man? And in time, maybe even with her help, he could let go of his burden of guilt and lead a normal life again.

After they had finished talking he walked her to her car and said goodnight. For an awkward moment she thought he was going to kiss her but he smiled instead and said he'd call her. Strangely enough, she had felt disappointed, an inexcusable reaction for someone who did not want any romance in her life.

She frowned as she pulled into the driveway of her apartment building, feeling out of breath again as if she were sprinting up a flight of stairs. It didn't matter if there was a note in the mailbox, it wouldn't frighten her at all and she'd simply implement her plan to capture him. She got out of her car and wondered if she had enough time to check her mailbox since her reading class would begin soon. No, it would be an act of cowardice if she postponed looking.

She walked up the front steps to the building, staring so intently at her mailbox which was next to the door that she stumbled over a package that had been placed on the top step. She fumbled in her purse for her key and swallowed involuntarily as she opened her mailbox. There was a plain white envelope inside. She quickly pulled it out and turned it over and saw it was only a bill from the phone company. She chuckled to herself, realizing it was the first time in her life she was happy to receive a bill.

As Lydia turned towards the front door her eyes were drawn to the package she had tripped over. It was a medium sized cardboard box, a cube about two feet high and wide. Her name and address were written on it in ink with block letters, just as all the notes had been. She crouched down and carefully looked at the sides of the box. There were no markings to indicate it had been delivered by the post office or any parcel service, which meant the box had been delivered personally. She grabbed the box and lifted it up, surprised at how light it was. She shook it and its contents shifted slightly. Something was inside. She realized she had two choices. She could go behind her apartment building and unceremoniously drop the unopened box into a garbage can or she could open it. She didn't want to open it, her stomach was churning in a queasy protest at that thought, but she refused to behave like a coward.

She moved determinedly to the front door and opened it with her key while awkwardly balancing the box on her hip. She carried it through the small foyer and headed up the stairs lecturing herself that she had nothing to fear from a cardboard box. She glanced at it again with a forced smile, at least it wasn't ticking.

Lydia entered her apartment telling herself that this time she was out of breath from the stairs, not from fear. She went into her kitchen and set the box on a table and turned on a bright overhead light. She got a knife from a drawer and stood over the box for a moment, her eyes closed while she slowly inhaled and exhaled. She sliced into the top of the box with the knife, cutting across its entire length and then pulling its flaps apart and peering in cautiously.

She screamed with surprise and disgust at what she saw. A small white kitten was lying on its back in the box, its fur caked with dried blood, its head flung back and attached by only a few slivers of red flesh from where its throat had been brutally slashed.

Lydia stepped back, her hands shaking uncontrollably. She pulled a hand up to her mouth and bit into her knuckles to stifle another scream. It was time to find him, definitely time.

Chapter Twenty

His imaginary friends were still watching him and he sensed their increasing frustration. Ryan kept walking on the sidewalk along Wacker Drive visualizing hundreds of people sitting in miraculous chairs from the thirtieth century that were floating just above the city skyline in brazen defiance of gravity. They were peering down at him with high-powered binoculars and hearing everything with their high-tech listening devices, a jaded and demanding audience from the future squirming impatiently in their seats as they wondered if he would ever do something interesting. There certainly is a lot of pressure being a leading man; Ryan told himself, I'm glad I write plays instead of acting in them.

He wondered if other playwrights ever imagined invisible audiences watching them, not to actually believe in like an aberrant delusion, but simply to make their lives more enjoyable. Probably only failed playwrights did that. Nonetheless, Ryan was glad he did because it always made lonely, painful moments more bearable if he pretended others were observing him with genuine concern. During bouts of excessive drinking or deep depression in recent years he had been unable to sustain his fantasy of being on stage and that seemed to make things worse. He had a strong feeling that if he didn't make any progress today they would abandon his mind again.

At least the audience had a spectacular view of an elaborate set with towering buildings that stretched for miles on an immense stage. It was undoubtedly the largest cast ever assembled with thousands of actors crowding the sidewalks or riding by in an unending stream of cars and buses. The actors were all consummate professionals, staying in character by ignoring him completely as he passed them dressed in his shabby homeless disguise. This greatly surprised Ryan because he had always assumed people reacted with either pity or contempt when they passed a homeless person, not complete indifference. For the first time in his life he felt invisible. He even experimented by staring directly at various people as they passed him and when their gaze locked onto his for a brief second they always looked away quickly. He politely asked one well-dressed man what time it was but the man refused to answer, clenching his jaw as he strode past.

You'll never find the woman named Yolanda, a familiar voice whispered to him, *and that also means you'll never find the alleged witness she talked to.* Ryan shook his head and continued walking; trying to remember the encouraging slogans he'd heard on his positive thinking tapes. The social worker he talked with had described the woman as being a tall African-American. She also had a little girl with her and had been staying at the shelter for a week. The shelter turned everyone out in the morning and let them back in for the evening meal and then gave them a cot to sleep on.

Since there was no guarantee she would return that night Ryan decided to search the surrounding area instead of waiting around. *With your luck she won't come back tonight and Lydia will realize what a failure you are.*

He swallowed hard, remembering how Lydia had looked at him last night with sincere understanding when he confessed his tragic past. It was amazing that she hadn't condemned him for killing an innocent child. Even though it had been an accident, he could never exonerate himself for what he had done, it was unforgivable. It also impressed him that she had grown up to lead such an exemplary idealistic life after enduring such a horrifying childhood. Ryan forcibly ground his teeth as he thought of her stepfather. How could he live with himself after murdering Lydia's mother?

When he had walked Lydia to her car he came perilously close to making a fool of himself. As she said goodnight he thought he saw genuine affection in her eyes and he felt an overpowering urge to embrace her and kiss her passionately. Fortunately, he resisted that absurd impulse and had simply smiled, saying he would call her in the morning. He wondered now how he could have considered doing such an idiotic thing when it was obvious she was far too bright and beautiful to ever be attracted to him. So even though his feelings for her were unbearably powerful, he would have to be content with just being her partner. At least he'd be able to see her often and call her anytime he wanted; that would have to be enough. *It's more than a worthless person like you deserves, Ryan old buddy.*

He turned onto a bridge and stared up at the Merchandise Mart that towered over him like some huge fortress overlooking the Chicago River to protect against pirate attacks that would never come. Along the edge of the roof hundreds of audience members were venting their frustration by shredding their programs and leaning forward in their chairs to throw the pieces at him, showering the air above the street with a veritable paper snowstorm. Most of the paper drifted harmlessly to the ground around him or clung to the elevated tracks that ran along the right side of the building. Ryan reached the end of the bridge and continued walking towards Wells Street which was shaded by the elevated tracks.

A tall African-American woman wearing a tattered overcoat was standing at the building's side entrance and a little girl was sitting nearby on a cement step. As Ryan approached he noticed the little girl was about the same size Lisa Thomas had been when he had shot her and a sickening, bloody image of Lisa's face flashed in his mind. He stopped next to a row of newspaper boxes and watched the woman as some men dressed in expensive suits walked out of the revolving door.

"Excuse me, Gentlemen," she said in a polite but frustrated tone. "Can you spare some money for a homeless woman and child?" The men ignored her as they filed past and she stepped in front of the last one. "Sir, do you have a few dollars to spare?"

He shook his head and grinned as he stepped around her. "Sorry, my ex-wife took it all."

A black man wearing a three-piece suit and carrying a briefcase walked out of the revolving door and down the steps. "Excuse me, Sir," she said, hurrying after him. "Can you help me and my daughter?"

He paused and looked at her skeptically. "And what would you do with the money?"

"I'm trying to raise enough to get us an apartment."

"There are shelters for the homeless you know."

"Yeah, I know all about them. The one we're staying at now has roaches as big as my thumb and they only allow you to stay there for thirty days."

He shrugged as he reached into his pocket and handed her a few coins. "Make sure you don't buy a beer with this."

As he walked away she looked at the coins in her palm and then glared after him. "You can't buy beer with three cents!" She sat down on the cement steps next to her daughter and glanced back at the revolving door with obvious bitterness.

Ryan approached them and the woman watched him with open suspicion. He glanced down at the little girl and noticed the sleeves of her over-sized coat hung down over her hands. Her hair was neatly braided and she stared up at him with huge brown eyes. Ryan estimated she was about six years old, an age Lisa had never reached thanks to him. He forced himself to look away from her and smiled at her mother. "Having much luck?"

The woman exhaled sharply. "Oh, sure." she said sarcastically. "I'm just sittin' here gettin' as rich as a lottery winner."

Ryan nodded sympathetically. "Seems like a good place. People going in and out of here have jobs and money."

"Except all their money goes home with them." She stood up as a stylishly dressed woman came out of the revolving door. "Excuse me, ma'am. Would you be willing to help a homeless woman and her child?" She shook her head with disgust as the other woman ignored her and kept walking. "Thanks for acknowledging our presence!"

"How long have you been out here?" he asked her.

She was as tall as he was, in her twenties, and her eyes radiated anger and hurt. "You mean panhandling or homeless?"

"Both I guess."

"We been panhandling since nine, that's when our shelter kicks us out till supper. As for livin' on the streets it's been over a month now."

"Rent troubles?"

She snorted in derision. "Man troubles. My man got heavy into drugs and started dealin'. I got scared for my little girl and me to be around him so we left."

"Has he been looking for you?"

"Him? Be real! He probably didn't even notice we're gone yet. But just to be sure I been signing in as Oprah Winfrey at shelters." She patted her stomach which was covered up by her overcoat. "In a few months I'll be havin' another little one. I'm not gonna raise my kids in a drug store."

"Your real name is Yolanda, isn't it?"

She paused for a moment. "Maybe, maybe not. Who are you?"

"My name's Ryan. Bible Bob told me about you and I've been looking for you."

"Why?"

"You told him you found a witness, someone who claims to know who the Homeless Slasher is."

"Yeah, that's true enough." She glanced at his worn clothes. "You must be an undercover cop. I didn't bother to go tell you guys. Figured you'd think me and her was crazy."

"I'm not a cop. My partner and I are working on our own."

"Nobody's ever gonna catch that guy. He's too smart and nobody cares about the people he's killin'."

"My partner and I care," he paused, "and if there really is a witness somebody's going to find her. Who is she?"

"Said her name was Sally. A tired-lookin' white bag lady. Probably in her fifties. Just saw her that one day at that Salvation Army soup kitchen."

"What did she tell you?"

"She said she saw the Homeless Slasher kill someone in an alley."

"That would have been Burt Wojik."

"Anyways she was sittin' behind some boxes or somethin' so the killer didn't see her, but she saw him. She says she knows him."

Ryan took a deep breath, hoping to slow down the sudden surge in his heart rate. "Did she tell you his name?"

"No. I asked her who he was and then she kinda looked sad and said she couldn't tell anyone cause they told her not to."

"They? Who's they?"

"The voices." Yolanda rolled her eyes.

"Voices?"

"Yeah, the voices that are talkin' to her all the time and tellin' her what to do."

"She hears voices?" Yolanda nodded and Ryan grimaced as if he'd been punched in the stomach. "That figures. I should have known." He tossed his hands up in the air in frustration. "I've been wasting my time tracking a crazy person."

"Oh, she be kinda crazy all right but I still believe her story. I bet she really knows who that killer is."

"Why do you believe her?"

"After I talked to her a while I took my little girl to the bathroom, but I forgot and left my purse next to that woman and it had about a hundred dollars in it. It was after lunch and the place was emptied out and she was sittin' by the front door. She could have run out with it and nobody'd have known a thing but when we come back she was still sittin' there huggin' that purse and protectin' it for me and when I counted up all the money later it was still there." She paused, glancing briefly at a man who came out of the building. "Lots of people would have run off with my purse but this lady didn't. That tells me she's an honest person, so what she says must be true."

"Maybe."

"That's not the only reason I believe her. She says the killer approached her that same day as the murder, tellin' her the voices were speakin' through him and that she had to go to that alley before midnight." Yolanda shrugged. "Makes sense to me that a smart killer might trick people like that to kinda set up his victims. Maybe he planned to kill her there, too."

"It does make some sense. Did she say where she was when the killer approached her that day?"

Yolanda shook her head. "No, and I didn't think to ask. She didn't tell me nothin' else neither, kept sayin' the voices wouldn't let her tell no one who he is."

"Did she always refer to him as 'he'?"

"Yeah."

"Did she ever describe what he looked like?"

"Nope."

"Did she ever mention when she first met him or whether he's homeless, or has a job, or anything else?"

"No, she didn't say anythin' else about him and I haven't seen her since then."

"OK, how about herself? Did she mention any places where she stays?"

Yolanda crinkled her eyebrows. "Let's see. She says she don't like stayin' in shelters. She did say she got stiff sleepin' in Grant Park the night before." She paused. "Libraries. Says she likes spendin' her days there cause they're nice and quiet."

Her little girl came over and tugged on her sleeve. "Mama, I'm hungry."

"OK, darlin', we be goin' back for supper real soon."

Ryan reached into his pocket and pulled out a candy bar he'd been saving. He crouched down in front of her, forcing himself to look at her directly. "Would you like this?" The little girl nodded and he handed her the candy bar.

"Hey, girl, what do you say to the nice man?" Yolanda said.

"Thank you," the little girl mumbled shyly.

Ryan turned away from her, trying to block out the bloody scene from the past that was flashing away in his mind again like an out of control neon sign. "Are you getting any financial aid yet?"

"Some of it starts up this month but it's only half of what we need to rent a place of our own." Yolanda patted her stomach again. "And if I find a job I got nobody to look after my little girl or the baby when it comes."

"Well, I want to thank you for talking to me." He glanced down at the little girl who was happily eating the candy bar. "I wish you and your children all the luck in the world."

Yolanda nodded at him. "Thanks. We'll do the best we can."

He pulled out his wallet and took out a twenty-dollar bill and handed it to her. "Here. It's all I have on me."

She looked up at him with surprise. "Thank you for your kindness."

Ryan walked back towards the front of the building and as he approached the corner he heard Yolanda ask someone else for money. He turned and saw a well-dressed man shaking a finger in her face. "You should be ashamed of yourself; using a child as a sympathy ploy."

Yolanda turned away from him and sat down on the steps in discouragement. Ryan looked up at his audience that was still sitting in their chairs along the edge of the roof, some were frowning at the man's comment but he was disappointed to see that at least half of them were applauding in agreement.

Chapter Twenty-one

I know she'll show up eventually," Lydia said with typical confidence. "We just have to be patient."

"I agree." Ryan hesitated. "But what if she is mentally ill?"

"Even if she is, it doesn't mean she can't help us. All we need from her is a name." She rubbed her hand on the steam covered window and peered at the distant darkness of Grant Park. She wished the cold drizzle would stop so they could continue searching for the witness. She felt guilty that she had agreed to take a break from the rain; they certainly wouldn't discover the Homeless Slasher's identity sitting in a parked car.

Ryan yawned, shifted his position, and wondered why his car had to have such lumpy, uncomfortable seats. He glanced over at Lydia and fought back an absurd impulse to tell her how beautiful she looked. Even though it was two o'clock in the morning and she had wet hair and no make-up on, she was still the most attractive woman he had ever seen. *Great idea, Ryan. Tell her that and watch her laugh or retch.* "How many of the homeless have mental problems?"

"Some studies estimate as many as one-third."

"Why aren't these people in institutions?"

"That's a good question." Lydia frowned. "The way the laws are a person can't be institutionalized against their will unless they're considered a danger to others or themselves. Usually, only those who are dangerous to others ever get committed. The rest, the helpless ones, are left to roam the streets like stray dogs or cats. I believe in some cities homeless animals are cared for better than homeless human beings."

"It doesn't seem fair." Ryan stretched and glanced at his watch again. "In a few minutes we can take a quick walk through the park again. She should have arrived hours ago if she was going to spend the night here."

"I know, but it's worth a try. If we do find her tonight we'll give the name to the police and the murders will stop."

"That sounds good, but we can't count on her showing up tonight. Maybe you should go home and get some sleep. I'll call you if I find her."

"No thanks. I'm more than willing to endure sleepless nights to catch this guy." Besides, she thought to herself, there was no guarantee she would be able to sleep, the image of the slain kitten might unmercifully torment her when she closed her eyes. A sinking sensation gripped her stomach whenever she wondered if another sick surprise was waiting on the front steps for her. She turned to Ryan who was studying her with an inscrutable expression. "I need to ask you something. When you were a policeman did you ever learn much about stalking?"

"A little. Why?"

She began talking slowly at first, then the words rushed out faster and faster as she described the ominous notes that had arrived in the mail or were left on her car, of her unsatisfactory conversations with the police, and finally of the bloody kitten she had received only twelve hours ago.

"I know it's my stepfather." She paused, taking several deep breaths to regain control. "So this afternoon I decided to fight back. Instead of going to the police again I went to a private detective agency. I didn't tell the investigator anything about what's been happening to me. I just gave him my stepfather's name and told him when he lived in Cleveland, and that I think he's in Chicago now. Although he's not listed in the phone book because I already checked. I said I wanted him found as soon as possible. He said it probably wouldn't take long."

"It depends. If he's living here and using his real name they could find him tomorrow. If he's using an assumed name it'll take longer." Ryan swallowed hard, anger burning his insides like steel-melting flames. The thought of Lydia being harmed was unbearable to consider. "Maybe I can find him for you? I can start tomorrow."

Lydia shook her head adamantly. "We're on the verge of catching the Homeless Slasher. That's more important."

"Not to me."

"Then I'll offer you a non-negotiable deal. When we find the Slasher then you can look for my stepfather."

"I don't like your deal."

"Too bad. We're equal partners, right?"

"Right."

"So we both have to agree on any plan of action, right?"

"Yeah."

"Then I'll keep voting against your looking for my stepfather until after we find this murderer."

Ryan exhaled loudly. "You should have been a lawyer."

She laughed. "I take it you agree to my terms?"

"Yes, I reluctantly agree but I'm very concerned. Whoever's threatening you could mean exactly what he says."

"I know," she said quietly. "That's the problem."

"There's one thing I don't understand, though. Why are you so convinced your stepfather is doing this?"

"You can call it intuition or whatever you want; I just have a strong feeling about it. I know he's doing it."

"But in your line of work you meet a lot of people, some of whom have mental problems. It could easily be someone else."

"After he murdered my mother he left me a note saying my turn was coming." She shivered. "He's a sick person."

"I'm sure he is, but I'm not convinced he's the one threatening you now." They were silent for a moment and he stared ahead at his fogged-over windshield which lit up with bright grayish light whenever a car approached. "What are you going to do when you find him?"

"Confront him." Lydia was surprised at the sharp anger in her voice. "I'll tell him a hired detective will follow him twenty-four hours a day and if he comes near me he'll be arrested."

"Then I vote to be there when you confront him. I don't want anything bad happening to my partner."

"All right," she said, forcing a smile. "I vote for you to be there, too."

"Good."

"You can have a front row seat; it'll probably be the fight of the century."

The rain outside had changed to sleet and was making soft tapping noises on the roof. He turned the key in the ignition again and warm air pushed straight out of the vents towards his face, making him feel instantly drowsy. He glanced over at Lydia and wondered if he should tell her why he was so concerned for her safety. It was because he cared so much, too much in fact. He would rather be sitting in his beat-up car with her than be lounging on a tropical island beach with any other woman in the world, but he knew she couldn't possibly feel the same about him. *So why tell her your feelings? She'll either laugh or toss her cookies out the window. That's probably true,* he admitted to his inner voice, *but wouldn't it be wonderful if she said she wasn't totally repulsed by me?*

He looked at her through the dim light, wishing he could reach out for her hand. That would be certain disaster but would it hurt to drop a few hints about his feelings?

"Lydia." He cleared his throat. "I really like your eyes." He felt his stomach heave. He liked her eyes? What a clumsy, inane statement to make. "Um, I mean, well that's not what I mean."

Another car approached, illuminating his car's interior with its headlights and he saw she was leaning her head against the window, her eyes tightly shut and her mouth slightly open, breathing with the tranquil rhythm of sleep. A lucky break, he said to himself. *Ryan the lovesick loser almost made a fool out of himself.*

He exhaled loudly and noticed that he now felt wide awake from making his clumsy overture. He decided he might as well go on a brief search for the homeless woman, maybe she had finally shown up and Lydia should be perfectly safe if he stayed near the park entrance and kept his car in sight the entire time. He opened his door and got out into the steadily falling sleet, closing the door as quietly

174 • Kindness Kills

as he could. He peered in the window and saw that Lydia hadn't even stirred.

He put his hands in his pockets as he crossed Michigan Avenue and headed towards Buckingham Fountain, suddenly feeling so optimistic that it bordered on unbridled euphoria. Everything was coming together. The detective agency would locate Lydia's stepfather and then he'd make sure she wasn't threatened by him again. They'd keep checking out Grant Park and various libraries until they found the witness and learned the killer's identity. It wouldn't take long, just a few more hours, a couple of days at the most. He visualized Lydia hugging him in celebration, but harsh laughter pierced his thoughts and the image melted away. *It won't happen that way*, the voice sneered, *you'll blow it somehow. You always do.*

Chapter Twenty-two

S ally Malloy wondered if the answer was ever going to come. She had been sitting in the hard wooden chair for two hours with her eyes tightly closed and her fingers gripping the edge of the table expectantly but nothing happened. They remained stubbornly silent.

She finally opened her eyes and stared at the surrounding bookshelves, marveling again at the seemingly infinite rainbow of colors that the books provided. She looked at the people at other tables who were all quietly reading or writing and smiled to herself. Of all the libraries she frequented, this particular one was her favorite because it was so peaceful. The only noises were the soft, serene sound of pages being turned and people talking in barely audible whispers with only an occasional cough or sneeze to disturb the tranquil setting. It was an ideal place to receive messages.

She sighed, frustrated that they were waiting so long to respond. What if another innocent person was killed in the meantime? It had been weeks since she saw the Homeless

Slasher murder Burt. Shortly afterwards they had threatened her, as she knew they would, telling her with sadistic delight that she was forbidden to reveal the killer's identity to anyone and if she disobeyed them, she would die. She had reluctantly obeyed their warning and it shamed her deeply to realize how selfish and cowardly she was. Actually, she had told a few other homeless people that she knew who the Slasher was but refrained from giving out his name and then she had heard the tragic news that another homeless person had been killed, someone named Hector Lopez.

Now she couldn't keep her secret any longer; she couldn't live with her guilt as other helpless victims lost their lives. So a couple of hours earlier she had fervently pleaded with them to allow her to tell the police his name or if they preferred, she was willing to stop him herself. She knew where to find him and she had it all planned out. Obviously the murderer would kill her if she told him in person to stop, so she would simply leave him an unsigned note saying she knew he was the Homeless Slasher and that if he killed again she would turn him in. As long as no one saw her leave the note she would be perfectly safe.

A woman and a little girl walked past her table and Sally noticed how similar they looked with their hair pulled back in the same type of braid. Sally smiled and waved at the little girl who smiled back shyly. "She's precious." Sally said to the woman. "You're very lucky to have such a friendly daughter."

Sally's smile faded, remembering it had been more than a week since she had greeted others. Normally, every day she would go to a busy street corner somewhere in the city and spend a few hours saying nice things to the people who passed by. She would say "hello" first and then try to compliment each person in some way. She might tell a woman that her outfit looked pretty or a young man that he looked very honest and should have a bright future. If she saw a couple walking hand in hand she would say that she hoped they would always stay in love and be happy. To many of them she would simply say that she hoped their day would be wonderful and that all their dreams would someday come true. Occasionally, a few coins or dollars would be thrust at her, but she always politely refused them.

Once a tall man in a three-piece suit stopped and watched her for a while, finally asking her what she was trying to accomplish. She explained she was simply trying to be nice to other people in hopes of making them a little happier. It was actually the only thing she could do to help others because she had no money or worthwhile skills. She truly believed the world would be a better place if everyone was more friendly and encouraging to each other. She even hoped her example on street corners might inspire others to be nicer to their fellow human beings and maybe even start a chain reaction of goodwill across the entire country.

The man had listened impassively to her explanation and when she finished he threw his head back and laughed loudly. "You are a crazy old broad," he said scornfully. "They should lock you up and throw away the key."

She blinked at him with surprise for a few seconds until her anger exploded within her and she swung her knapsack at the man's knees with enough force that he almost fell over. A policeman across the street saw her and rushed over and took her by the arm to his patrol car where he gave her a stern lecture before he finally let her go. His talk was unnecessary though, she regretted her reaction the instant she swung her knapsack. It seemed like her temper flared out of control far too often, which she knew shouldn't happen to someone concerned with people being nicer to each other. It was hypocritical and set a bad example for others. She wished she had ignored the man's insult and continued greeting others until they called her away.

They usually spoke to her several times a day, ordering her to go somewhere on a special mission without explaining why and always demanding she do something illogical when she got there. She was too frightened to disobey them anymore because whenever she had in the past they always punished her by making her sick or causing something bad to happen to her. On several occasions they had threatened to kill her if she ignored their commands. Several years ago when she had been going to a clinic the doctors had assured her the voices she heard weren't real and were only symptoms of her illness. The medication they prescribed for her had made them go away for a while but eventually they returned, screaming at her in a series of uncontrollable rages that they would kill her if she kept taking her medicine. She knew they would follow through on their threats and so she stopped taking her medication and never went back to the clinic. It was just as well, she never had much faith in doctors. All of the ones she talked to refused to believe there were evil spirits who existed just beyond human comprehension and tried to influence our behavior, when she knew intimately that it was true. It amused her that doctors always seemed so confident in their own abilities and opinions when none of them ever really saved anyone from death. The credit they received for saving lives through surgery or treatments was pathetically inaccurate because all their patients eventually died anyway. At best, they only postponed the inevitable and never actually saved anyone so why should she listen to them?

Her thoughts were interrupted by an incessant tapping on her shoulder. She looked up to see a thin, middle-aged woman standing over her with her lips pressed together tightly. "I'm sorry, but you have to leave now."

Sally squinted up at her. "Why? It's not closing time yet, is it?"

"No. But I think you've stayed here long enough."

"What are you, a bouncer?"

The woman's forehead crinkled ominously. "I'm a librarian and I want you to go."

Sally took a deep breath and told herself she had to remain nice and pleasant. Can't unleash the anger, she thought, can't let it out no matter how unfriendly this woman gets. "You know what?" Sally said with a sincere smile. "I like that sweater you're wearing, it's very pretty. It compliments your lovely blue eyes."

The woman glared at her. "Did you understand what I said?"

"Please, I have to stay." Sally gripped the table hard, hoping she could keep controlling her temper. "I'm waiting for an important message. It could save a lot of lives."

"I'll call the police and have you removed."

Sally stood up; her rage and humiliation made her legs feel shaky. "But, can't you see?" she said as meekly as she could. "I'm not bothering anyone."

The woman wrinkled her nose. "You're bothering everyone just by being here. You sometimes mumble to yourself which distracts others, your unsightly clothes need washing, and you need a bath!"

Sally winced as if she'd been slapped and tried to remember when she had taken her last shower. It must have been at that shelter on Wabash because they had been out of soap in the shower room and a woman waiting her turn had broken down and begun sobbing. How long ago had that been? Was it two days or two weeks?

"Are you leaving or not?" The woman folded her arms impatiently. "This is a library not a hotel. Why don't you go to a homeless shelter where you belong?"

"Because they kick you out after breakfast until dinner time, for one." Sally said, feeling her voice rise. "But I try to never stay at any cause they're not very pleasant. If you ever visited one you'd know what I mean."

"I've heard enough. I'm calling the police and telling them you're causing a disturbance." The woman walked away toward the front desk with rapid strides.

"How about if I read a book until my answer comes?" Sally walked over to the nearest bookcase and scanned the titles on a shelf. She reached for a book and pulled it out.

The librarian's voice boomed at her from across the room. "Don't touch any books!"

"Why not?"

"You're filthy!"

Sally inhaled sharply, as if she'd received a blow to her stomach. "At least my mind's not filthy!" she shouted back.

"Get out of here!"

"Not until I've touched all the books I want to!" Sally threw down the book she was holding and ran her hand across the entire row of books on a shelf. "See? Look at me!"

She looked back at the librarian who was speaking into a phone. "Hello, we have a disturbance here and we need your help."

Sally ran behind the bookcase, hearing an angry rushing sound like the first winds of a hurricane. She took hold of a shelf and crouched down quickly, then pushed back up using her lower body like a weight lifter would as the bookcase slowly leaned forward and fell over and its books poured out of the shelves. It landed with a tremendous thud as if a giant oak tree had been blown down in a raging storm, coming to rest in the middle of the large room. Twenty people stared at her from around the room, their mouths hanging open and faces expressing shock or revulsion. Sally shook her fist at them. "This is supposed to be a public library and I'm part of the public too!"

She grabbed her knapsack off the table and sprinted out the front door, almost colliding with a man who was coming in. She hurried down the steps and ran down the sidewalk, her arms and legs pumping desperately as she dodged people. She ran for two blocks and turned down an alley without slowing her pace, even though she was gasping for air with desperate moans. She knew a patrol car would be looking for her in a few minutes and she had to get as far away from the library as possible.

She crossed two streets before she felt it was safe enough to walk. Her lungs were burning with pain but she realized her desperate run had taken away her rage, and that was certainly for the best. Anger never solved anything, it only made things worse. She wished she hadn't pushed the bookcase over. That had been a senseless, shameful act. No matter how much that librarian had provoked her she should have controlled her temper. Who knows, maybe if she had continued saying complimentary things the librarian might have relented and allowed her to stay and everyone who witnessed their encounter might have been inspired to be nicer to others as well. Too late now, she thought, you set a bad example but you can learn from it this time and never let it happen again.

As she trudged along the sidewalk she decided she'd write a letter of apology to the librarian and mail it to her, it was the least she could do. Maybe then she could return to that library branch someday and the woman would come up and apologize for being so rude and making her feel worthless and unwanted. Sally smiled as she walked, thinking of what she would write in her letter when she heard a soft, hoarse whisper. She stopped and listened, not even breathing as she strained to hear her long awaited answer. After a moment she jumped up and down and shook her fist in the air. "Yes!" she shouted with unbridled joy. They had finally answered her and they had given her permission to leave an anonymous note for the Homeless Slasher, warning him not to kill again!

Chapter Twenty-three

Ryan walked across the dirt infield of the baseball field and glanced around at the surrounding darkness of Grant Park, wishing a four-poster bed with a canopy would magically appear for him to collapse onto. He paused at the pitcher's mound and saw his theater audience sitting in comfortable chairs that were lined up in neat rows across the outfield. Even in the dim light he could see they were all asleep, some snoring quite loudly.

"Wake up everybody!" he shouted at them. "Don't I deserve a round of applause for trying so hard?"

A few shifted positions in their seats but none of them opened their eyes. *You can't blame them. Anyone would rather sleep than watch you.*

He had gone without sleep the night before while they searched in vain for the elusive homeless woman and all day he had visited numerous libraries but failed to find her. One library had offered some hope though, a woman matching her description had pushed over a bookcase an hour before he got there, which could mean he was getting close. *But close doesn't count, does it, Ryan my man? If you never find her then that means you failed once again, just like you did as a policeman and a playwright and anything else you try. If you ever become a Christian you'll fail at that, too.*

Ryan jogged off the infield and slowed to a walk as he approached the tall trees towering over him in the dark like giant sentries, their branches rattling in the wind like sabers in their scabbards. He wished Lydia was with him, he felt empty inside without her. They would be together at this very moment if he hadn't stupidly agreed with her idea to split up for the night, with him remaining in Grant Park while she checked out various shelters. He couldn't believe he'd consented because now he wasn't just lonely, he was worried too. A sick, dangerous person was harassing her and she was driving around the city at night all alone. The thought of any harm coming to her made him dizzy with anger. What had he been thinking of?

He came out of the trees and headed towards Buckingham Fountain as two teenagers wearing gang jackets approached from the opposite direction. One of them gestured to him. "Hey, rich dude! I like your fancy threads." Both teenagers laughed and walked past him. Ryan looked down at the worn clothes he had selected for his disguise and wondered if homeless people were insulted often. As he came up to the huge circular fountain he noticed a woman was sitting on a nearby bench with a large knapsack next to her. His heart vibrated excitedly in his chest as he stopped in front of her and forced a smile. "It's a nice night, isn't it?"

She looked up at him and smiled back, she was a white woman in her fifties with shoulder length gray hair that flowed out from under a gray wool cap. Her overcoat was faded and torn in a few spots. "Yes, it is nice out," she said, her voice as soft and high pitched as an adolescent girl's.

"My name's Ryan. What's yours?"

"Sally. Sally Malloy."

"It's nice to meet you, Sally." He hoped he sounded casual; it was a struggle to keep the excitement out of his voice.

"Well, thank you for saying so, Ryan." She smiled again and brushed some of her hair away from her eyes. "I can see you're a very polite young man. Most people aren't real polite these days, they just ignore each other. I think that's so sad."

Ryan nodded. "Me too. Good manners are important."

"It's not just manners. People need to be nicer to each other. If everybody treated each other like they want to be treated the world would be a much better place."

"That's true."

"That's what my job is. I go around saying nice things to people so they'll feel better about themselves, and of course I hope that my example inspires them to be nicer to others."

"That's very commendable."

"Thank you. I can tell you're a very kind, young man." She studied his face for a few seconds. "And you're very handsome, too, with a very honest face. Anyone would be lucky to have you for a friend."

"Well." Ryan shifted his feet self-consciously. "I don't know about that."

"I do." She paused, looking at him with a sympathetic expression. "Are you homeless too?"

Ryan hesitated. "Uh, yes. Kind of."

"It's nothing to be ashamed of," she said with a wave of her hand. "And don't get discouraged like some people do. You're a nice young man and things will turn around for you. If you keep trying I know you'll find a job and a place to live."

"I hope so."

She gestured at the bench. "Why don't you sit down here and we'll talk."

"Thanks. I'd love to." He sat down a few feet away and noticed she had large, childlike blue eyes that were staring at him with naive trust. "How long have you been homeless, Sally?"

She wrinkled her forehead. "Let's see, it's been years now. My husband left me and that made me very sad. Soon after, I began hearing voices but I tried to ignore them. I couldn't find a job so I ran out of money, and without any relatives I had nowhere to go. A doctor gave me medicine to keep the voices away but they came back and ordered me not to take it again and they've been tormenting me ever since." She paused and shook her head. "Enough about me. Let's talk about something more interesting. Something you'd like to talk about."

"OK." Ryan took a deep breath. "How about discussing the Homeless Slasher?" He noticed that she flinched. "Is that all right with you?"

"Well," she hesitated, "maybe."

"I think it's a tragedy that he's killed so many innocent people. Don't you?"

"Yes, it is," she said reluctantly.

"Wouldn't it be wonderful if he were caught?" He spoke slowly, carefully choosing his words. "If he was in prison he couldn't kill anyone."

"Yes."

He leaned closer and lowered his voice. "Can I tell you a secret, Sally?"

"Sure."

"I'm here for a reason. I'm looking for someone. A woman who sleeps here often. A nice lady who saw Burt Wojik get murdered and she knows who the Homeless Slasher is." He paused and licked his lips. "Are you that woman, Sally?"

Her eyes widened and she stood up quickly and grabbed her knapsack and began walking away. Ryan jumped up and hurried after her. "Hey, where are you going?"

"I'm very sorry, Ryan," she said in obvious distress, her legs moving forward with short, quick strides. "You're a wonderful young man but I can't talk to you any more."

"Why not?"

"Because I'm the woman you're looking for. I saw poor Burt get murdered and I know who did it."

"Who is he?"

"That's the problem. I can't tell you."

"Who can you tell?"

"No one."

"Why?"

She stopped and looked up at him, biting her lower lip for a few seconds. "Because they won't let me."

"Who's 'they?'"

"The voices."

"You mean the voices you hear?"

"Yes." Sally sighed. "I hear from them almost every day. They give me orders and I have to obey them or be punished."

"When they speak to you are there ever any other people around?"

"Sometimes."

"Do any of those other people hear these voices, too?"

"No." Sally shook her head sadly. "I know what you're going to say, that it's all in my mind and I must be crazy. That's what everybody else thinks, including doctors."

"I wouldn't say you're crazy."

"No, but you're thinking it. You figure I must be imagining those voices and I don't blame you. Years ago I would have thought the same thing about someone else." She smiled at him. "But haven't you ever wondered if there are other intelligent beings alive besides us? Maybe what some would call angels or spirits? They can easily observe us but we can't see them because they're just beyond the reach of our minds and senses."

"I guess it is possible."

"It's more than possible. It's true."

"What do these angels sound like when they talk to you?"

"They're not angels." Sally shuddered. "They're spirits; evil spirits. There are a lot of them, and they usually talk to me in hoarse whispers. If I don't do what they tell me they make me get sick, or get robbed, or something else horrible."

"Why won't they let you tell anyone who the murderer is?"

"They want more helpless people to suffer and die. They delight in human misery." Her voice broke and she rubbed at her eyes. "There must be a few others they talk to. I'm not sure why they chose me. Maybe they don't want me teaching people to be nice to each other and that's why they torment me, but I do know what they told me after I saw Burt get killed. They said if I tell anyone who the murderer is they'll kill me and kill the person I tell. That's why I can't say anything."

"But you can tell me. I'm not scared of any voices or spirits."

"That's very brave of you but I don't want you to die, you're a good person."

"I won't die. I can take care of myself."

"Have a nice life Ryan, and please be good to others." She turned away and began walking again towards the trees looming ahead in darkness.

Ryan quickly caught up to her. "You don't have to say goodbye to me because I'm not going anywhere. I'm staying with you from now on. Wherever you go I will too."

Sally continued walking and stared at him in amazement. "Why?"

"I'm hoping you'll eventually change your mind and tell me who the Slasher is."

"I can't, they'll kill us both."

"Then maybe they'll change their minds and let you tell me."

"No, they never will." She shivered. "They're probably mad at me right now for talking to you."

"You don't have to worry, Sally. I'll protect you from them, I promise."

She glanced at him, smiling sadly. "Thanks for saying so, but you're wrong. You're just a man; you can't protect me from them."

"You just watch me."

"All right, suit yourself." She shrugged. "It would be nice to have company for a change. You're welcome to stay in my guest house."

"Where is this house?" Ryan looked around skeptically as they approached the tall trees.

"Follow me." Sally stepped into the woods, maneuvering around the maze of tree trunks. Ryan followed and immediately smacked his forehead on a low hanging branch. She called back to him, "Don't forget to duck!"

"Yeah, right." Ryan rubbed at his forehead and crouched down like a gorilla as he followed after her.

After a moment he heard her cheerfully call out in the darkness. "Ryan! Here we are!"

He pushed a branch out of the way and stepped into a tiny clearing in the midst of the huge trees. Two large cardboard boxes were leaning against different tree trunks. Both boxes were soggy and lopsided. "This is it?"

"Yes, they're not really houses but they're home to me." She pointed to one of them. "This one's yours unless you'd rather have the other one."

"No, this one will be just fine." He bent over and peered into the box's impenetrable inner darkness, wondering if a rat or snake was concealed in it.

Sally pulled a blanket out of her knapsack and carefully spread it out on the bottom of her box. "It's not very cold tonight so we should be comfortable."

"Definitely."

"The police won't bother us as long as we don't start a fire. I'm really sleepy, how about you?"

"Actually I'm wide awake. I was hoping we could talk some more."

"I can't tell you who he is."

"I know that and I respect your decision." He paused, trying to come up with a strategy. Why did everything have to be so hard, he thought, why couldn't she just blurt out his name? What am I doing wrong? "Is it OK if I ask you something else?"

"Like what?"

"Tell me what happened in the alley when Burt was killed. You don't have to mention a name, just tell me what you saw." He paused. "Please."

"Well, I suppose I could do that. I was sitting behind some crates and the murderer came up to Burt from behind and cut his throat with a knife." She shook her head. "It was so horrible, I felt sad for Burt and scared for myself all at the same time."

"Why were you in that alley?"

"I thought the voices wanted me to go there. I know now it was just a trick, though."

"What kind of trick?"

"A certain person, I can't tell you his name, talked to me that day and told me he had an important message for me." She paused, licking her lips. "This person said the voices had spoken to him and told him to give me their orders. They said I was supposed to go to an alley near Western Avenue and I had to be there at one o'clock in the morning or they'd come after me and kill me. When I got there I saw that certain person kill Burt. After the murder the voices said he'd lied to me, that they hadn't spoken to him, but they warned me not to tell anyone who he was."

"The certain person who talked to you is the Homeless Slasher, right?"

"Yes."

Ryan frowned. "I wonder why he wanted you to see him kill Burt."

"I think he wanted to kill me but Burt was there, so he killed him instead."

"Maybe," Ryan considered her theory for a moment, "or maybe he wanted to kill both of you. He could have tricked Burt into showing up there, too."

"Yes, he might have done that."

Ryan glanced up at the night sky wishing the black curtain of clouds would move so he could see Sally's face in the moonlight. "Where were you when he told you to go to that alley?"

"I'm sorry. I better not tell you."

"Why not?"

"What if you guess who he is? Then we'll both be killed."

"I won't be able to guess who he is, I'm sure I don't even know him."

"Just in case, I won't tell you where he approached me."

Ryan ground his teeth. "Terrific."

"But you don't have to worry. He's not going kill any more people. I put an end to that today."

"What do you mean?"

Sally chuckled softly. "That's for me to know and you to find out." She bent down and crawled into her box. "Time for bed. I'm too sleepy to talk."

Ryan crouched at the open end of her box. "But our conversation is just getting interesting."

"Goodnight, Ryan."

"I've got a great idea, I'll do most of the talking and you can just answer yes or no, OK?"

"No."

"That's perfect; just keep answering yes or no just like that." Ryan ground his teeth for a few seconds. "I know you don't want to tell me the Slasher's identity and I respect that but I do notice you keep referring to him as 'he.' So, obviously he's a man, right?" He waited in vain for a response. "That doesn't give away who he is because there are a million men around Chicago. Knowing that doesn't hurt anything." Ryan swallowed. "So is the Slasher a man?"

"Yes," she answered softly.

"Thank you." Ryan's heart began rattling away in his chest and he hoped he could maintain a casual tone of voice. "I still have no idea who he is." He paused. "What race is he?"

"I don't think I should tell you that."

"Sure you can. There's a huge population of every race in this city. I still wouldn't know who he is, but I'm real curious about it. What color skin does he have? White? Black? What? Please tell me, I'm dying to know."

After a moment of silence she cleared her throat. "He's the same race as Jackie Robinson."

"Jackie Robinson? You mean the baseball player?" Ryan resisted the urge to jump up and pump his fists in the air in triumph. "He was the first African-American to play major league baseball. So the Slasher is African-American?"

"Maybe. Maybe not." She yawned. "I said he's the same race as Jackie Robinson. Only I know what that really means."

"OK, Sally. Thank you for telling me, I really appreciate it and it doesn't give anything away." Ryan cracked his knuckles and exhaled loudly. "There's one other thing I'm real curious about, and it wouldn't give anything away, either. I've been wondering what part of town he lives in. Where should someone go if they wanted to find him?"

She waited a long time before answering. "Think of Malibu Beach and the end of summer."

"Malibu Beach? That's out by Los Angeles isn't it? Are you saying this guy doesn't even live in Chicago? Or is he moving to California this summer? Or did he used to live there?"

"I've said all I'm going to say," she said wearily.

"One more question, please."

"I'm sorry." Her voice was almost a whisper. "Too sleepy."

"Just one more thing. Can you tell me what he does for a living?" He waited a full minute, sweating despite the cool air. "Does he have a job?"

"Yes." Her voice was barely audible. "He's supposed to be good."

"Good? In what way?" He waited again but she didn't reply. "Sally?" He leaned forward and heard the faint echo of her rhythmic breathing from inside the box. One of her feet was protruding from the entrance and he grabbed hold of her damp shoe and gently shook it. "Come on, Sally, let's talk a little more."

She didn't respond so he let go and stood up and began pacing around the small clearing, too energized to feel tired.

He thought about the cryptic information she had given him, wishing it was more specific. It doesn't really matter, he thought, tomorrow I'll somehow get the killer's name from her, and what she said tonight will be irrelevant. When I give the police his name they can place him under surveillance or get a search warrant to find evidence in his home. Or I can follow him myself and stop him when he tries to kill his next victim. That sounds very tempting. Why share the glory with the police?

He finally stopped pacing in front of the box and decided he might as well sit down to think. He crawled into his box that reeked of moldy cardboard and lay down, leaning his head against the back of it and hoping a spider wouldn't suddenly drop down onto his face. He wondered how many people around the country were sleeping in boxes or abandoned buildings and how they coped with the indignity and hardship on a regular basis. Well, he didn't have time to ponder that, he had a murderer to catch. In the morning he'd call Lydia. He visualized the excitement in her voice when he told her he'd found the witness and a euphoric happiness overwhelmed him as it always did whenever he thought of her.

But he knew he shouldn't dwell on Lydia now, pleasurable as that was, he needed a plan to trick Sally into giving him the name. That's all he needed, just a name. As he considered various strategies he felt a curious floating sensation and was stunned to find himself standing in the familiar musty-smelling basement staring again at the bloody, lifeless form of Lisa Thomas. He heard the stairs rattling as someone ran down them frantically and a few seconds later he was pushed out of the way by a woman wearing a faded robe. She dropped to her knees and pulled her daughter's lifeless body to her chest, rocking back and forth as she hugged her tightly and wailed uncontrollably. Ryan tried to speak, he desperately wanted to tell the woman how sorry he was but somehow he couldn't get his tongue to move so he just stood there in helpless silence as the woman began shuddering with violent, spine-shivering sobs.

His neck ached as if he'd been bludgeoned by a baseball bat and he sat up and rubbed it vigorously as his head brushed against something above him. He reached up and felt damp cardboard and realized he must have fallen asleep despite the discomforts of the box. He scrambled out and hurried over to Sally's box. "Sally?" He reached inside and found it was empty. He got up and looked around the small clearing seeing only the tall trees that stood over him in the darkness like mute witnesses of his incompetence. She was gone.

He began to run, bumping into tree trunks and crashing through branches that clawed at his face and clothes. He finally burst out of the trees, his arms and legs pumping wildly as he sprinted across the dew covered grass, his mouth wide open and gasping for air. He knew what awaited him up ahead as soon as he saw the flashing lights but he kept running just as hard, as if he could somehow get there in time. The police car was parked on a path that led to Buckingham Fountain, its blinking lights erratically illuminating the surrounding area like frames from an old silent movie reel, the static from the police radio was the only sound in the night air. Two policemen were standing there talking to several homeless people. As he drew closer he saw Sally and forced himself to continue on.

He finally stopped about ten yards from the policemen, moaning with every breath he took. Sally was lying on her back on the ground and the grass near her head was darkened with her blood. Her throat had been slashed and her open eyes were staring up with terror.

Ryan began running again, ignoring the policeman who called after him, his legs moving so fast now that he felt numb and weightless as if he'd rise up off the ground any second. He ran out the park entrance and turned south on Michigan Avenue, sprinting down the middle of the street oblivious to the oncoming headlights and distant sirens. His arms and legs moved up and down even faster carrying him along at a speed he never would have thought possible, but nevertheless it wasn't fast enough because he couldn't outrun the voice and the words that thundered at him with malicious delight. *You're a failure, Ryan! And always will be! Just like I told you!*

Chapter Twenty-four

Lydia refused to admit she was scared until she noticed her hands were shaking. She was holding a rolled up magazine and both hands vibrated slightly as if she were gripping some type of drill. At this precise moment when she was about to learn her stepfather's whereabouts she wanted to feel relieved. Sometimes, she told herself, fear makes me a captive when I least expect it. But there is no excuse for feeling this way. I'm going to stop him from terrorizing me; so there's absolutely no reason to feel so weak and nervous.

She got up out of the waiting room chair and approached the secretary who was writing something at her desk. "Excuse me. Could you see if Mr. Dorner is off the phone yet?"

The secretary, a middle-aged woman with rust-colored hair and pink framed glasses, shook her head sympathetically. "I'm sorry; he's still on the line. He should be off any second."

A door opened and Lydia was frustrated as a haggard man in a wrinkled suit walked out instead of the investigator she was waiting for.

The man yawned loudly, looking as if he hadn't slept in days. "Well, the bodies keep piling up," he said to the secretary.

"What bodies?"

"Homeless ones." He rubbed at his eyes. "Last night the Homeless Slasher sent another one to that great soup kitchen in the sky. It was just on the news."

"Where did it happen?" Lydia asked, feeling a sickening premonition of disaster.

"Grant Park." He yawned again. "It was some bag lady. He got her near the fountain. Actually it was thoughtful of him not to dump her body in the fountain or they'd have to drain it and clean it." He started to laugh but stopped when he saw her expression.

Lydia stared at him, her mouth hanging open helplessly. Ryan was supposed to have spent the night in Grant Park and he hadn't called her or responded to the messages she left on his cell phone. In fact, when the private investigator called her at work and asked her to come to his office she had gone to the phone expecting it to be Ryan. What happened to him? "Was anyone else killed there?" she asked.

"No."

"What time did it happen?"

"I think they said the body was discovered around four in the morning."

"Was her name Sally?"

"I don't know. They're probably withholding her name until they can find any relatives."

Lydia leaned against the secretary's desk, taking a deep breath and brushing her hair back with her hands.

"Are you all right?" the secretary asked her.

"Yes, I'm just worried about a friend," Lydia said, straightening up again. "I have to leave now."

Lydia turned saw a dark-haired man in his forties watching her with a concerned expression. "Lydia, I'm Greg Dorner. Are you OK?"

"Yes, I'm fine."

"Good. I have the information you wanted. Can you spare a few more minutes before you go?"

She hesitated. "All right. But only a few minutes, I have to find someone."

He gestured to his office and she walked in and sat down in a comfortable leather chair in front of his desk as he closed the door behind them. "Before I begin I'd like to ask you something but you don't have to answer." He sat down in his chair and drummed his fingers on a manila folder lying on his desk. "Was Bobby Joe Miller a friend or relative of yours?"

"No, not by my definition."

Greg Dorner nodded solemnly. "All right then. I'll be brief." He flipped open the manila folder and scanned the piece of paper inside for a few seconds. "Bobby Joe Miller lived in Cleveland, Ohio until ten years ago when he was convicted of murder. He shot someone outside a bar after a fight." He paused and glanced up, studying her for a few seconds. "He was sent to Lucasville, Ohio. Five years ago he was killed there in a prison riot."

Lydia felt as if the room around her had been transformed into a carousel, surrounding her and spinning out of control with ever increasing speed and blinding lightning like flashes of color. Relief and unbridled joy overwhelmed her, practically lifting her up out of her seat. The nightmare was over, she thought, he could never hurt her or anyone else again. An evil man had met a well deserved violent end. This proved justice triumphed sometimes in an imperfect world. Yes, it can!

She either stood or actually floated up out of the chair from an incredible surge of ecstasy. Was it hypocritical of her to feel happy over another person's death; she who lived to help others? Wouldn't it have been a far better ending if he would have realized how wrong he was and repented, living out the rest of his life doing good deeds for his fellow human beings? That would have been better, she decided, but if he didn't change his ways then dying in prison was the next best thing.

Suddenly though, she painfully collapsed back into her chair with a moan as a revelation occurred to her, screaming within her mind with piercing agony. Her stepfather hadn't threatened her with ominous notes and a mutilated kitten; he could never harm her again, but someone else wanted to and she had no idea who it was.

Lydia knew that if her tormentor was following her now he could harm her without any fear of being seen. The sun was setting after a chilly day and Montrose Beach was deserted, there'd be no chance of anyone coming to her rescue.

She almost wished he would appear before her, at least then she'd know who he was. If he does show up here, she thought, he'll be sorry. She visualized a faceless man materializing before her and she casually walked up to him and gave a sudden push that sent him sprawling into Lake Michigan. She looked out at the water, growing darker by the minute in the fading light, its murky waves incessantly rippling into shore. He'd be so stunned by its frigid temperature that she could easily get away, laughing mockingly at him as she ran.

She continued walking along the ledge of dark gray rocks as it curved along the shore. The tightly packed rocks were lined up in neat shelves, the bottom ledge licked by the lake's waves and the top one was level with a large grassy area. The ledges stretched ahead for miles, like steps custom made for a family of giants to climb up when they emerged dripping wet from the cold water. Ahead on the distant horizon the rocks seemed to connect to the towering buildings of the Loop where a seemingly infinite number of windows glowed as amber specks of light. She glanced to her right at the marina, carefully tucked away in a small cove that was a safe distance from the lake. It was empty now since all the boats had been removed for winter. When she looked back she saw someone waiting.

The person was forty yards ahead sitting with his knees drawn up to his chin and staring intently out at the lake. When she was close enough to recognize him she called out his name but he didn't turn his head even though he must have heard her. She came up quietly and sat down next to him on the cold shelf of rock while Ryan kept staring out at the water as if he were hypnotized by its undulating surface. "I've been worried about you, Ryan. I thought you might be out on the rocks. The other night you said you liked to come here sometimes to think."

After a long moment of silence he cleared his throat. "She's dead," he said with a voice drained of emotion.

"I know." She flinched as she spoke, thinking her words sounded hollow and inadequate. "The police haven't released her name yet, but somehow I knew it was the woman we were looking for."

"Her name was Sally Malloy." Ryan swallowed hard. "Her goal in life was to be nice to others in hope that some would emulate her. A simple but noble goal isn't it?"

"Yes. Very noble."

"She can't be nice to anyone now, thanks to me," he said bitterly. "I'm quitting this thing. You'll have to find another partner."

"I don't want another partner."

"I quit." His voice rose slightly. "Don't you understand? I blew everything. Just like I always do."

Lydia paused. "Tell me what happened."

"She knew who the Homeless Slasher was but wouldn't tell me his name no matter what approach I took. She finally fell asleep but I wasn't discouraged at all, I was ecstatic that I had found her. I figured in the morning I'd somehow convince her to tell me who he is." He shook his head and bit into his lower lip. "The worst part is I really liked her. Most people would classify her as a mental case but I think she was a caring, idealistic person. If she were still alive I'd do my best to get her off the streets and help her live comfortably. I really would."

"I believe you."

"But I can't now, because I fell asleep. When I woke up she was gone and a few minutes later I found her body. The police should arrest me for her murder. I killed her with my typical incompetence. Just like I did years ago with that little girl."

"No."

He looked at her, his reddened eyes wide with disbelief. "Sure I did. If I hadn't fallen asleep I would have gone with Sally when she left and the Slasher couldn't have hurt her."

"Maybe not. He might have killed both of you."

"No. He'd have backed off, he's very careful. He wouldn't have known if I was carrying a gun or not."

"Do you think he knew that Sally saw him kill Burt?"

"He must have. She said she'd done something to warn him to stop the killings. Maybe she left him a note and he saw her do it. Whatever she did, it made him realize she was a witness."

They were silent for a few minutes, staring out at the fading patches of light quivering on the lake's surface like an immense patchwork quilt floating on the water. "They said he left another page from that book," Lydia said. "He circled the word 'nice.'"

"Nice?" Ryan frowned with disgust. "She was certainly that. This guy knew her well. He knew she heard voices so he told her they wanted her in a certain alley one night, the same alley where he killed Burt Wojik. He probably planned to kill both of them there."

"Did she say anything else about him?"

"Yeah, a few things. I asked what his job is and she said he's supposed to be good."

"That's very important. Something that could lead us to the killer."

"Maybe, except it's too vague. Did she mean he's supposed to be good in a moral sense, or skillful at whatever he does?"

"It still might help us later on. What else did she say?"

"That he's a man. I asked where I could find him and she said I should think of Malibu Beach and the end of summer."

Lydia shook her head. "I don't understand."

"Who could? The only important thing I learned is that he's probably black."

"She told you that?"

"Well, not exactly. She said he's the same race as Jackie Robinson."

Lydia blinked at him. "Who's he?"

"He was the first black to play major league baseball."

"Oh. I don't follow sports." She paused. "How do you know that's the Jackie Robinson she meant?"

"Who else could she mean?"

"I don't know. Maybe she knows someone else with that name. Or maybe she was deliberately trying to fool you since she obviously didn't want to give away his identity."

"You could be right." Ryan shrugged. "So I guess that means we can't even be sure of what race he is. That figures."

"Regardless of what race he is you still learned something about his job and where to find him. If we figure out what she was talking about we can find the killer."

"You mean you can find him. I'm quitting, remember?" He stood up and began walking slowly along the ledge towards the distant skyline where the buildings were now speckled with brighter yellow lights.

Lydia got up and quickly followed, resisting an illogical impulse to crouch down in frustration and scratch her nails across the rocks as one might do on a classroom blackboard. "You can't quit. I need your help, and I still think you're a great investigator."

"Such a great investigator that a sweet, defenseless woman lost her life because of me."

"Does that really bother you?"

"Of course it does."

"No, I don't believe you. I don't think it bothers you at all that Sally was murdered."

He stopped and turned. "What do you mean?" he asked, his voice rising indignantly.

Lydia met his angry gaze. "If you really liked her you'd be upset and angry that someone killed her."

"I am upset and angry."

"No, you're not. If you were you'd want to see her murderer captured."

"I do want that."

"No, if you really want him found you wouldn't quit. You'd keep searching for him even if it meant talking to every homeless person in Chicago or spending the rest of your life out on the streets. You wouldn't give up no matter what. Because the memory of Sally lying on the ground with her throat ripped open wouldn't let you."

Ryan swallowed hard. "You just don't understand," he said softly. "I want her murderer found but I know I can't find him. I'm a failure at everything I've ever tried."

"You're only a failure if you don't try."

"If you knew me better you wouldn't say that."

"I know you well enough to want you for my partner. I think you're a special person, Ryan, I really do, and I need your help in finding this guy."

"We can't find him now, I blew it."

"How about giving it a little more time? A month, a week, a few days even?"

"It'd be a waste of time."

"Then do it for my sake, or more importantly, for Sally's sake." She paused. "She wouldn't want this guy killing other innocent people, but he will unless someone stops him."

He hesitated a moment, the pressure building in his mind like a tiny wave on the lake increasing in size and momentum until it was a massive tidal wave, pushing him in a direction he did not want to go. "OK," he finally said, "for you and for her. I'll try for a little while."

"Yes!" Lydia excitedly pumped her fist in the air.

"But only for thirty days. If we don't find him by then I'm quitting for good."

"If we figure out all the clues you've found we can catch him in a week."

"Don't count on it."

"I am counting on it; I know we're going to catch this guy. And I gratefully accept your thirty-day offer." She extended her hand to him. "I'm proud to have you for my partner."

"You shouldn't be, but I'll give it my best shot." He reached out for her hand and shook it, surprised at how soft and slender it was.

"Together we can't fail."

Ryan was vaguely aware that she said something else but he didn't even listen because he was staring at her so intently, reiterating to himself that she was the most attractive woman he had ever met; not only because of her physical beauty. She was so unselfish and had such an irrepressible positive attitude. He had never met anyone who was even remotely similar to her. He felt as if he were floating, completely disconnected from his own body as he stood with her on the ledge and was able to watch them both from above as if in a dream. He saw himself put his hands behind her head and pull her towards him, pressing his mouth on her lips which were parted in surprise. He immediately realized with shock and delight that he wasn't imagining it, he really was kissing her and even more amazing she wasn't resisting, she actually put her arms around him and kissed him in return.

Lydia's mind was blank, her sense of time and place totally lost as she responded to Ryan with an enthusiasm that overwhelmed her. She kissed him with increasing ardor for what may have been a few seconds or a blissful eternity, it didn't matter. It was wonderful until painful images from the past began flashing away in her mind, her stepfather screaming at her mother, her ex-boyfriend in bed with another woman. She opened her eyes with a shiver as if a bucket of ice water had been unceremoniously dumped on her head. She saw Ryan's dark brown eyes looking at her with emotion and suddenly her mind was working again, reminding her that she didn't want romance in her life now and wasn't sure she could ever trust any man.

She pushed away from him and staggered backwards a few steps, gasping for breath. "Ryan, I can't do this," she stammered. "If this is what you want we shouldn't see each other again." She saw his expression change to hurt and confusion and then she quickly turned away, scrambling up the rocks and hurrying away across the grass.

Ryan wanted to shout after her that he loved her, that he'd be happy to marry her this very night to prove it, he truly would, but instead he choked on his words as he watched her walk away into the enveloping darkness. It wouldn't do any good; her feelings for him couldn't possibly be the same. His chest vibrated from his pounding heart and nausea gripped his stomach as he realized the magnitude of his actions. Lydia was only interested in catching the Homeless Slasher, and he had acted like they were a young couple in love.

He slid down numbly onto the ledge as a loud voice screamed at him with delight. *Way to go*, the voice shrieked; *now you ruined everything with Lydia, just like you ruin everything else.* He bowed his head and covered his ears in a desperate attempt to block out the scornful torrent of words that filled his mind like a poisonous flood.

BOOK TWO: HUNTERS AND PREY

Chapter
Twenty-five

Tell me the truth about the last three weeks," Lydia asked, leaning forward over their table in the coffee shop. "Do you think we're any closer to finding the Slasher?"

"No," Ryan said with frustration. "I could spend the rest of my life hanging around homeless shelters and not learn anything." He wanted to tell her he'd thought about her constantly since he last saw her three weeks ago. He also wished he could go back to that night on the ledges to stop himself from kissing her and embarrassing them both, but he didn't have enough courage. He never had enough, never would.

"That's what I thought," Lydia said confidently. "You're too negative. You need to convince yourself you're going to find him or you never will."

"You're probably right," he said, barely listening, remembering that after she'd run away from him that night he had gone back to his apartment, numb with the sickening realization that he'd just destroyed any chance of ever

214 • Kindness Kills

having a relationship with her. He was amazed when his phone rang a short time later and he heard her voice, sounding perfectly normal as if nothing had happened, reminding him to keep calling her with daily progress reports. He had eagerly agreed and returned to living in the streets the next day even though he no longer believed he had any chance of ever finding the Homeless Slasher. He continued to call her every day but she never mentioned that night on the ledges.

"It's worked for me." Lydia paused and took a sip of coffee. "I decided I wanted to be a social worker so I worked my way through college and became one. Now my goal is to open my own shelter and someday have a chain across the country. I know if I continue to believe in my dream and keep working hard it will happen someday. I know it will."

"I believe you."

"Then why don't you believe you'll catch the Slasher?" Lydia smiled, and rolled her eyes. "Wait, don't tell me, let me guess. Because you always fail, right?"

He paused with surprise and then laughed. "You got it."

"That is so pathetic!" Lydia believed Ryan was a good person with unique abilities but she wished she could change his negative opinion of himself. She also wished she hadn't become so attached to him. The last three weeks had been a miserable experience because their phone conversations were always too brief and she longed to see him and ask how he really felt about her. But instead she had decided to act as if that embarrassing night on the ledges had never happened, even though she'd never forget the passionate feelings he'd brought out of her. "I want you to do something for me."

"Anything." Ryan felt a sudden surge of hope and immediately visualized her asking him to kiss her again. He then quickly shook his head with disgust that he would even think of something so impossible.

"Ryan, I want you to promise me something."

"OK."

"But only if you really mean it. I want you to promise you'll set a goal to catch the Slasher within a specified period of time," she paused, "and then you have to convince yourself you will catch him before your deadline is up."

Ryan considered it for a moment. "All right. I'll do it. I have one more week left on the month I committed to, so that will be my goal."

Her mouth dropped open. "A week? That's all?"

"Absolutely," he said, surprising himself that he actually meant what he said. "Maybe it'll be fun to be optimistic for a change," he lowered his eyes, "but if I don't catch him by the end of this week I'm going to quit." He looked up and instantly regretted his words when he saw the disappointment in her eyes. "But hopefully that won't happen," he quickly added, "because I'm going to catch him this week. I know I am."

She smiled. "Now that's the right attitude."

He's mine, he's mine, he's all mine. For six consecutive days he'd told himself that, ever since he'd promised Lydia he would change his attitude. He kept visualizing himself standing before a large crowd with a veritable forest of cameras and microphones pointing at him, the reporters straining to hear every word he spoke while Lydia stood nearby smiling at him with undisguised admiration.

For the past six nights he'd read some of the Bible, focusing on positive statements, such as Jesus telling His followers to ask and receive, seek and find, or if you had faith as big as a mustard seed you could move a mountain. The only problem was he doubted God would ever want to help him. He didn't deserve God's help or mercy. The promises in the Bible could not possibly apply to him.

As he continued walking down the crowded sidewalk on Michigan Avenue, a row of theater seats seemed to appear in front of him, lined up along the storefronts for several blocks. Most of the seats were empty but the small audience that was there rose and began shouting and taunting him with various insults. They began throwing things, but he ignored them and kept walking through a blizzard of popcorn and theater programs. It didn't matter what they thought because an hour ago at breakfast he'd met someone who told him how to find the Homeless Slasher.

When he crossed a street he heard banjo music and triumphantly thrust his fist into the air. He saw Shakin' Macon half a block away, strumming on his banjo for a dozen people who had stopped to watch him. He looked exactly as the elderly man at breakfast had described him, a small black man in his thirties wearing a straw hat and overalls.

As Ryan approached, Shakin' Macon finished his tune with a flourish and the people applauded. He reached into his pocket and pulled out some leaflets which he quickly passed out to his audience. "Don't take drugs," he said in a deep, booming voice. "Don't even try 'em. It ain't cool to be a fool. Drugs have killed or ruined everyone I know and almost killed me, too."

Ryan accepted the piece of paper that Shakin' Macon handed him and glanced down at it, noting it listed the many dangers of drug abuse.

"I'm homeless now cause I got hooked," Shakin' Macon said to all of them. "It can happen to you too. So don't try the view or you'll soon be blue."

The small crowd moved away and Shakin' Macon looked at Ryan quizzically. "Got any questions?"

"My name's Ryan. I'm looking for some information."

"Just gave you some. Best you'll ever get."

"I mean about a person." He hesitated. "I was told you know who the Homeless Slasher is."

Shakin' Macon laughed and waved a hand at him. "Well, I don't know nothin' for sure. But I did meet this dude at a temporary shelter a couple of nights ago who told me he's the Slasher."

"What's his name?"

"Named Darius. An African-American, around thirty I guess. About average height with a bushy beard."

"What exactly did he tell you?"

"Nothin' much. Just says to me after the lights went off that he's gettin' more famous everyday, so's I ask why and he says cause he's the Homeless Slasher. I asked him why he's killin' all those folks and he just laughs and says he likes it, then he rolls over and goes to sleep."

"Where is this shelter?"

"It's just a temporary one. The basement of some carpet store on LaSalle."

"Thanks for your help." Ryan turned to go.

"But hey man, wait a sec'. I don't believe nothin' that dude told me. He was just some fool feedin' me some jive, he' ain't no Slasher. I guarantee you that."

"He's the Slasher," Ryan said optimistically. "He's got to be. Because tonight's the last night I'll ever look for him."

Chapter
Twenty-six

Lydia opened her desk drawer, saw the blood, and immediately wished her stepfather was still alive. If he hadn't died in prison then at least she'd know he was the one harassing her, and she'd have someone to be angry with. Anger, not fear, was what caused her to grind her teeth as she looked into the drawer.

In the last week her rage had increased every time her unknown tormentor contacted her. She had felt a cold righteous anger the day she received a note in the mail demanding that she disrobe at midnight in front of her window with the shades pulled up and the lights on. She hadn't done so of course, but when midnight arrived and passed and the police who were hidden outside reported that no one had come to look at her window, her anger heated up. He obviously knew they'd be waiting for him, one of the policemen told her with a grin, and he must have a sick sense of humor.

A few days later she felt even angrier when an envelope arrived containing a handful of worms and a note that said,

"YOU'LL BE UNDERGROUND WITH THESE SOON!" She yelled out in frustration when the latest note arrived a few days ago which said, "MEET ME FOR A ROMANTIC RENDEZVOUS AT THE TOP OF THE SEARS TOWER TO-MORROW AT NOON WITHOUT POLICE." She went to the Sears Tower the next day with some plainclothes policeman already stationed there. She roamed around the crowded observation floor for hours, ignoring the spectacular view of the city provided by the huge windows, staring instead with suspicion and apprehension at any man who was there alone. At four o'clock the policemen came up to her and told her it was time to give up and she went home feeling almost feverish with rage, the same way she felt now.

Lydia grabbed the handle of the desk drawer and slowly pulled it open, peering in cautiously at the bloody rag lying on top of some papers. Of course she wouldn't know until the police tested it that it was real blood and not some kind of dye but she was certain it was. And if so, whose blood was it? She looked at the rag more closely and noticed a heart printed on it, realizing with a moan that it was her own T-shirt, a special one that her deceased ex-boyfriend had once given her on Valentine's Day. It had been hanging in her closet in her apartment the last time she had seen it. This meant the person who did this had somehow gotten into her apartment and brought it to her office. The blood soaked T-shirt was bunched up as if it was wrapped around something and she grabbed a pen from the top of her desk and used it to cautiously push the edge back. A small piece of paper was underneath covered with dried blood droplets and someone had written, "YOU'VE BETRAYED ME FOR THE LAST TIME!"

Her office door burst open and she jumped up and screamed. Martin Sanders paused in the doorway with a startled expression. "I didn't know I was that scary looking."

"You're not," Lydia said, taking several deep breaths.

"Good, I'll take that as a compliment." He walked over to her desk. "Are you going to tell me what's wrong?"

"That." She pointed at the drawer.

Martin looked into the drawer and grimaced. "What is it?"

"I could be wrong," Lydia swallowed hard, "but I think that's blood all over the T-shirt."

Martin went to the doorway and shouted for Augie and Carl and then turned to her with a concerned expression. "Who would do this?"

"I wish I knew."

Augie Rosen hurried into the office wearing an apron splashed with tomato sauce. "Don't you two know you're never supposed to interrupt a master chef when he's working?"

Carl walked in with a frown. "I hope this is important."

Martin gestured towards the drawer. "You guys won't believe what's in there."

Augie walked over and looked in and grunted in disgust.

Carl came over and glanced at it. "That looks like blood."

Augie shook his head with a worried expression. "What's that note mean, Lydia?"

Lydia related the entire story to them beginning with the first threatening note she'd received and everything else that had transpired up until she had opened her drawer a few moments ago. After she had finished they all silently stared at her with genuine concern.

"The main problem," Martin finally said, "is that you still don't have a suspect."

"Not unless you're doing this, Martin," she said wearily.

"No way." Martin said emphatically. "I want a relationship with you, I won't deny that, but I would never terrorize you or anyone else like this."

"I believe you, Martin," she said, moving away from her desk, not wanting to look at what was in the drawer anymore. "You're not a good enough actor to fool me."

"When was the last time you opened this drawer?" Augie asked her gently.

"This was the first time today." Lydia shrugged. "I may have opened it yesterday but I don't remember. Then again, I might not have opened it for a few days."

"OK." Augie nodded as if that confirmed something. "That means the psycho who's doing this was here sometime in the last couple of days. Have any of you noticed anyone who looked suspicious or who was carrying something that could have concealed this?"

"No," Lydia said, frustrated.

"There have been a couple of hundred people here the last few days," Carl said. "Half of them look dangerous or unstable."

"That's certainly true," Martin said. "And any one of them could easily have carried this in their knapsack or pockets."

"And we leave the back door unlocked during open hours," Lydia said. "Someone could have snuck in that way and left without being seen."

"Sounds like it won't be easy to catch this guy." Augie said. "Lydia, you should have told us what was going on."

"It's my problem. I wanted to handle it myself."

"But we're your friends, we'd be glad to help anyway we can," Augie said, "and since the police have been totally useless I'm surprised you didn't confide in us long ago.

"I considered it."

"Well it's not too late. We can start helping you right now." Augie began pacing in a small circle in front of her desk. "You should never go anywhere by yourself and you shouldn't be alone in your apartment. We can take turns being with you, right guys?"

Carl nodded. "Absolutely."

"You can count on us, Lydia," Martin said sincerely.

"We'll take turns staying at your apartment every night." Augie paused and looked at Martin with a grin. "Although we may need a chaperone when Martin's there."

"Very funny," Martin said, not amused.

"And," Augie said, "I know you have other friends who'll gladly volunteer their help too."

Lydia shook her head. "Thanks anyway, guys, but I'm turning you down."

They all stared at her. "You're kidding," Martin finally said, "aren't you?"

"No, I'm not."

"But, Lydia," Augie said with sincerity, "I want to help protect you. We all do."

"I'll be fine."

"How do you know that? Some maniac is threatening you and giving you dead kittens and bloody shirts. What if he decides to do something more drastic next time?"

"He won't," Lydia said, feeling the anger return. "I've come to the conclusion that he doesn't have the courage.

He didn't show up at the Sears Tower or that night he asked me to undress in my window. He's all talk."

"But what if you're wrong?" Martin asked.

"Then I'm in big trouble and if I am wrong any friend who's with me could be harmed too. I wouldn't want that on my conscience." She clenched her jaw tightly. "I'm convinced he's a harmless coward."

Augie raised his eyebrows. "You're not scared of this guy?"

"No," Lydia said emphatically. "That's exactly what he wants and I'm not going to give in. I have to admit I was scared at first but I've overcome it. Now I'm so angry at him that I think I'll tear his face off if he ever approaches me. There was a time when I was young I lived in constant fear of my stepfather. I assure you I'll never let anyone make me feel that way again."

"But what if this guy follows through on his threats?" Augie asked with concern.

"I've got a few ideas on how to catch him," Lydia said, moving to the phone, "but right now I'm calling the police again."

Lydia finally sat back down at her desk, grateful the police had finished talking with her and taken away the bloody T-shirt to run tests on it. If she were still twelve and naively trusting God she'd be praying desperately now, but she would never ask Him for help again. She picked up the phone and began methodically calling a list of shelters and soup kitchens that Sally Malloy had frequented, something she had done sporadically since Sally's murder. Ryan thought the Homeless Slasher might be African-American because Sally had said he was the same race as Jackie Robinson, but she still wasn't convinced Sally had been referring to the baseball player.

The fifth number she called gave her the answer she had hoped for. A social worker at a soup kitchen told her a man named Jackie Robinson had registered for meals the last few days. She didn't remember what he looked like but said he might show up for lunch or dinner today. Lydia thanked her and hung up the phone and picked up her purse, telling herself with euphoric excitement that today she was going to learn something important about the Homeless Slasher.

Chapter
Twenty-seven

He hated being thirteen. He hated it with immeasurable passion. Leonard, the tall freckle-faced bully, had rudely snatched the knitted cap from his head and held it high in the air, taunting him to try to take it back. A small crowd had gathered on the snow covered asphalt outside the gloomy brick building known as Arlington Heights Junior High, and most of the guys watching were grinning with relief that Leonard hadn't chosen them to torment. It was ironic that Leonard called it a stupid looking hat because he thought so himself and had argued vociferously with his mother that very morning that none of the tough guys at school ever wore hats no matter how cold it got. But when he'd finally noticed the sorrow in her eyes that seemed to be there so often now, he'd quickly given in and put it on. Since he despised the hat it shouldn't really matter to him what Leonard did to it, except that it was his personal property and by taking it and ridiculing it in front of his classmates, Leonard was actually demeaning him.

He jumped forward and grabbed for the hat but it was just out of his reach and Leonard flicked his wrist, sending the hat sailing into a nearby garbage dumpster next to the building. Young Ryan Dolan's cheeks reddened with humiliation as he hurried over and saw his hat sitting on some garbage at the bottom of the nearly empty dumpster. As he leaned over the edge and reached for it, he was shoved hard from behind and fell into the dumpster with a loud clatter. He heard raucous laughter as he struggled to his feet amid crushed cartons and rotting food. He grabbed the side of the dumpster and swung one leg over but Leonard suddenly appeared and shoved him back down and this time his head slammed hard against the metal bottom.

"Let's keep him in there!" Leonard yelled gleefully.

He got up quickly and saw Leonard and his followers had surrounded the dumpster and were peering over the sides like a hungry wolf pack he had read about in a recent novel. They began jeering and spitting at him and when he tried to climb out he was violently pushed down by a sea of hands. He tried leaping out different sides but was always thrown back.

It was when he remembered his father that everything fell apart for him. His father had been a highly respected policeman who was killed in the line of duty only a few years before. He'd often talked with him about various police procedures in all kinds of situations, but no matter how hard he tried Ryan couldn't seem to remember him ever explaining what to do if he was outnumbered and trapped in a garbage can. And now of course, he could never again ask him for advice.

Ryan slid down into a corner and burst into tears, sobbing uncontrollably with deep heaving gasps, oblivious of the scornful laughter of his tormentors who leaned over the sides to mock him. He continued crying even after they slammed down the lid of the dumpster over him, enveloping him in rancid-smelling darkness as they pummeled away outside on the metal sides with a deafening rattle. He sat there crying after the bell rang and they all hurried away. By the time he finally stopped and climbed out his first period English class was almost over.

He knew men and boys are never supposed to cry in front of their peers, so he wasn't surprised when he was branded with the nickname Cryin' Ryan and teased unmercifully for years afterwards. Even making all-league safety on the football team his senior year didn't erase the shame from his memory.

Ryan hadn't thought of that painful incident for many years but it had returned with nauseating clarity as he watched a man named Winston curl up defensively into a ball in the corner of the room.

Winston was a withered looking elderly black man who was missing most of his teeth and wearing a loose fitting coat that was several sizes too large. Earlier he had quietly told Ryan how he'd once been a fireman and saved a man from a fire. Two men in their twenties were standing over Winston, one was a tall white man with long dirty blonde hair and the other was a short, muscular Hispanic wearing large earrings.

"Come on, Winston," the tall one named Mick said impatiently. "We know you have a ten-dollar bill. You pulled it out a while ago when you were tellin' those worthless fireman stories."

The shorter, muscular one shook his head. "You better give it to us quick old man or you gonna get hurt."

"Please go away," Winston muttered, fearfully clutching a torn knapsack.

Ryan sighed with frustration as he sat on his mat on the cement floor. Lydia had warned him about this type of place. It was the basement of a run-down carpet store on LaSalle that the owner had opened as a temporary shelter for homeless men. Because of the cold weather the regular shelters were filled up and turning people away. The naked light bulb hanging from the ceiling cast just enough light so that the grime on the walls was depressingly visible. Earlier he had heard scratching noises from inside the wall behind him and with every breath he inhaled an eclectic odor of dust, sweat, and unwashed clothing. But this was where Shakin' Macon had met Darius, the man who claimed to be the Homeless Slasher.

Twenty men were scattered around the floor but none of them matched the description of Darius. A few were sleeping, but most were stoically watching the confrontation taking place before them.

Mick prodded Winston with his foot. "Hand it over loser."

Ryan desperately wanted to tell them to leave Winston alone but if he did he knew there'd be a fight and he'd be kicked out of the shelter. He couldn't let that happen because if the Homeless Slasher showed up later he wouldn't be here to talk with him.

"You better do what Mick says." The shorter, muscular one kicked Winston hard in the ribs. "Give us the money!"

But Ryan knew that there was another reason. He was afraid that if he got kicked out he'd go looking for a bottle. Lately his craving for a drink had increased every day and he frequently fantasized about drinking until he passed out with mind numbing pleasure. Just one time couldn't hurt. That is, unless he couldn't stop again.

"We mean it, old man!" The shorter, muscular one stomped on Winston's ankle.

Ryan wished he could wipe the smug, vicious expressions off the faces of the two men who were picking on Winston. Maybe, he told himself, it's better to sit here and believe everything will work out fine. Just visualize a positive outcome and it will all come true. Those two guys won't hurt Winston, he'll either give them the money and be left alone or else they'll give up and walk away any second now. One way or the other it will be settled peacefully just like I'm picturing in my mind. Then Darius will arrive and brag about being the Slasher and my investigation will be over and there will be no more uncomfortable nights spent in shelters and Lydia will be very impressed with me.

"Hey loser." Mick bent over Winston. "Rico here, he don't mind breakin' no bones. Not at all. Fact is he kinda enjoys it, so if I were you I'd give us the money."

Ryan closed his eyes and visualized the two men giving up and walking away from Winston.

"I say we take the money," Rico said, "and then I break his bones anyway."

Ryan forced himself to imagine them apologizing and leaving the basement.

"Rico, I definitely like your style." Mick angrily grabbed Winston by his coat collar and pulled him to his feet. "Search him."

Rico reached into one of Winston's pockets and grimaced as he removed a rotting rust-colored apple. "Man, you're disgusting!" He scowled malevolently at Winston and threw the apple into a corner where it splattered against a wall.

Mick grabbed Winston roughly and held him in a headlock.

"Please," Winston gasped. "Let me go."

Rico reached into another pocket and took out a ten-dollar bill and triumphantly raised it over his head. "Yes! Victory!"

"That's my money," Winston stammered.

Mick grinned and tightened his grip. "See if he's got anything else worth taking."

"OK, but he better not have no more rotten food or I'll punch his ears off." Rico put his hand in one of Winston's pockets and withdrew half of a peanut butter sandwich. "Uh, that's sickening!" He threw down the sandwich as Mick released Winston. "You got my hands dirty!" Rico glared at Winston and then slapped him hard across the face. "I guess I'll just have to wipe my hands off on your face." He slapped him harder and Winston fell back against Mick with a groan. Rico slapped him a third time and blood trickled out of his mouth.

Ryan stood up, surprised to find his anger had melted away his fatigue. "Let him go," he said firmly to the two men, "and give him back his money."

Mick and Rico looked at each other and laughed. "Hey Rico, it looks like Winston here has a friend. As bad as he smells I didn't think he had any!"

They laughed again and as Ryan walked over he felt his eyelid begin to twitch involuntarily. "Give it back."

Rico nodded at him sincerely. "OK, man. We don't want no trouble. You can have it." He held out the ten-dollar bill and when Ryan reached for it Rico quickly lashed out with his other hand, crashing his fist into Ryan's temple and knocking him to the floor.

Ryan rolled over and saw Rico standing over him, grinning proudly. "I used to be in Golden Gloves. I was pretty good."

"Search him for money," Mick said.

Rico looked at Ryan expectantly. "You gonna give me your money, right?"

"I'll give you everything I have," Ryan said in a meek tone. He slowly pushed himself up from the floor and when he stood up he suddenly kicked Rico in the stomach, causing him to bend over with a surprised grunt. Ryan quickly put his hands on the back of Rico's head and rammed his knee into his nose with a sickening crunch. Rico fell to the floor and the ten-dollar bill fluttered out of his hand.

Mick shoved Winston aside and glared at Ryan. "You're gonna get it now."

The door from above swung open and a huge man carrying a baseball bat hurried down the stairs. He glanced at Rico, who was sitting up and trying to slow down the blood streaming from his broken nose. Ryan kept watching Mick as they moved in a small circle with their fists clenched, maneuvering for a good opening.

"Hold it right there!" The man yelled. "You three get out of here now!"

"No way!" Mick pointed at Ryan. "He started it!"

"Get out of here now," the huge man waved his baseball bat menacingly, "or I bust your heads open and call the police!"

Mick spat on the floor and looked at Rico. "Let's blow this hole." Rico followed him up the stairs holding a blood covered hand over his nose.

The man with the baseball bat glared at Ryan. "That means you, too."

Ryan bent over and picked up the ten-dollar bill and carried it over to Winston. "From now on keep it hidden."

Winston nodded gratefully as he accepted the money from him. "Thanks much. You're a real good man."

Ryan turned away and walked up the stairs while the man with the baseball bat followed close behind.

"I'm sick of being a babysitter," the huge man said with disgust. "I don't know why the owner lets homeless scum like you stay here at night." They walked through the darkened showroom, past numerous racks of carpet samples. "If it were up to me," the man said, "you would all freeze to death in the streets. You're all homeless cause you're lazy, every single one of you. You're totally worthless human beings."

Ryan paused at the front door. "My uncle believes that too, but you're both wrong."

"Get out of here," the man said threateningly.

Ryan stepped out of the store onto the sidewalk and took a deep breath of the cold night air. He estimated the temperature was in the thirties and steadily dropping. *It's an ideal night to spend in the streets. The last night you'll look for the Slasher.*

He walked down the sidewalk past darkened storefronts figuring that as long as he kept moving he'd stay warmer. The streetlights shined down on the night blackened sidewalk creating small circles of light. The street was deserted, although he heard a shuffling noise behind him as he passed an alley.

Ryan turned and saw a shadowy form rush out of the dark alley into the white glare from a nearby streetlight. It was Rico. His face was smeared with blood and he held a knife in his hand.

"Hey, hero!" He heard a voice behind him. He glanced back and saw Mick step out of a hidden doorway with a knife in his hand. He approached Ryan with a malicious grin. "We got some unfinished business."

Chapter Twenty-eight

Ryan's first instinct was to run out into the street but he changed his mind when he noticed they were both leaning that way expectantly and would obviously cut him off.

"You gonna pay for bustin' my nose," Rico said bitterly.

"That's right hero," Mick said, edging closer and holding his knife out threateningly. "It's too bad we pawned our pieces yesterday. If we still had them we'd have already blown your head off."

"Yeah, so now we gonna have to use these." Rico waved his knife back and forth as he moved closer. "That means you gonna die real slow."

"I hope you like to bleed," Mick said.

Ryan's heart was throbbing violently and his throat tightened as if he were being strangled. He reached for his wristwatch and pressed a button and it immediately emitted a loud beep.

"What was that?" Mick asked.

"It's a signal." Ryan struggled to keep his voice calm. "I'm an undercover policeman. I've just called for backup."

Rico snorted in disgust. "You lie! You ain't called nobody."

"Nice try!" Mick lunged at him and swung the knife up towards his face. Ryan ducked under his arm and spun away, backing up against a brick wall. Rico and Mick quickly moved in front of him, blocking any path of escape. "Now you're gonna learn," Mick said, "what it feels like to die."

A beam of light flashed at them from across the street and Ryan saw it came from an alley entrance.

"Don't move!" An authoritative voice boomed from a loudspeaker. "You're under arrest! Drop your weapons and put your hands up now!"

Mick and Rico glanced at the light and then looked at each other with stunned expressions. "He was tellin' the truth! He is a cop!" Mick said, amazed. They both sprinted to the nearby alley and ran down it, the sound of their footsteps quickly fading away. A tall figure emerged from the shadows across the street pushing a shopping cart and continuing to aim a flashlight in his direction. Ryan recognized Bible Bob as he crossed the street.

"Are you all right, Brother?" Bible Bob asked as he approached.

"Yes."

Bob parked his shopping cart at the curb and held up his loudspeaker, chuckling softly. "I usually use this for preaching on street corners. The Lord done inspired me to a different kind of use tonight."

"Thanks. You just saved my life." Ryan reached out and shook his hand.

"Glad to help, and I'm glad they run off cause I don't think they'd have let me make a citizen's arrest and take them to the police." He chuckled again and looked at Ryan with a quizzical expression. "Don't I know you from some-wheres, Brother?"

"We met at Union Station last month."

"That's right, I remember you now!" Bob grinned. "You helped me save a little girl from that pimp. I don't remember your name, though."

"Ryan."

"Well it's good to see you again, Brother Ryan. I hope everything's going OK for you."

"Not really."

"Sorry to hear that. Maybe things will get better?"

"Maybe."

"Say, wasn't you working on that Homeless Slasher case?"

"Yeah, you could say that."

"Havin' any luck?" Bible Bob asked hopefully.

"Not much."

"Well I know somebody's gonna catch that guy real soon. I been prayin' about it as hard as I can." Bob smiled know-ingly. "In fact, it might even be me that gets him."

"What do you mean?"

"I was out at Garfield Park and someone there told me about some guy comin' around talkin' to the homeless and asking weird stuff."

"Like what?"

"Like how long they been livin' in the streets and if they go to shelters at night and if they sick or not. And weirdest of all, if they're happy or not."

"That doesn't mean whoever's asking that is the Slasher."

"Right, but he could be. How many people go around asking that kind of stuff?"

"Not many."

"So that's why it's worth checkin' out."

"Yeah, maybe."

"No maybes about it. I been going to Garfield Park the last couple of days asking everyone if they seen or talked to this guy directly. I'm gonna find him."

"Good luck." Ryan thought of how pleasant it would be to have a bottle in his hands and take a few sips to keep warm.

Bob looked at him curiously. "Whatcha doin' in this part of town tonight, Brother Ryan?"

"Believe it or not I was hoping to meet the Slasher."

Bob's eyes bulged out. "What? Are you jivin' me?"

"No. I got a lead about a guy who told someone else he was the Slasher. I just came from a temporary shelter up the street but he wasn't there."

"You know this guy's name?"

"His first name's Darius. He's a black guy, average height and around thirty. Has a beard. That's all I know."

He shook his head. "I don't know no Darius."

"Then I guess this isn't my lucky night." Ryan shoved his hands into his coat pockets and hunched his shoulders against a sudden chilly wind that descended from the narrow strip of dark night sky between the tall buildings. It would be so easy to go buy a bottle somewhere. No one ever deserved one more.

"You know," Bob said thoughtfully. "I just came from a vacant lot where a bunch of street folks is sharin' some bottles. If this Darius hangs around this part of town he could be one of them."

"Maybe." Ryan hesitated for a moment. "Can you take me there?"

"Be real glad to." Bob pushed his grocery cart next to a newspaper box. "I'll just park this here. Anybody who's hungry can help their selves."

They crossed the street and went into a dark alley. Ryan kept stepping on various types of trash and walked faster than usual to keep up with Bible Bob's long strides. *It's not over as long as you hope,* he told himself. *Might as well believe the Slasher will be there and this will be the breakthrough. Unless,* a familiar voice whispered, *you mess up as usual.*

They came out of the alley and crossed another street. Bob was humming some hymn and Ryan glanced at him. "I've been reading the Bible a lot lately."

"That's cool. Are you a Christian yet?"

Ryan shook his head. "I don't deserve forgiveness. I've done a lot of things that are wrong and I took an innocent life."

"So you're sayin' you ain't perfect?"

"That's right."

"Well join the club! Ain't none of us perfect. The scripture says 'There is no one righteous' and 'All have sinned and fallen short of the glory of God.' Notice it doesn't say some have sinned. It doesn't say most have sinned. It says all have sinned. That means me, and you, and six billion other people in this world."

"Yeah, but . . ."

"But nothing. You ever hear of the Apostle Paul? Before he believed in Jesus he participated in the arrests and murders of Christians. He called himself the worst of all sinners, but God forgave him as an example for the rest of us. Jesus took your punishment for you, on the cross. He is the atoning sacrifice. All you gots to do is accept it. Like a gift."

The alley ended and they crossed a street and walked onto a vacant lot that was surrounded by tall buildings. A few scraggly weeds were scattered around the acre of frozen dirt. An orange fire was burning in a trash can and a dozen people were standing around it or sitting on some nearby crates. As they got closer Ryan noticed two of them were women. All the people wore clothes that had obviously been given out by a shelter, their coats and pants were either too tight or baggy and some of the colors clashed.

A white-haired man groaned loudly as they approached. "Go away, Bible Bobby. We already told you we don't want no savin' tonight."

"Unless you brung a bottle," another one called out, "then we'll listen to you." Several of them laughed.

"We're sinners, Mr. Preacher Man," one of the women said. "Ain't no use talkin' to us."

"Jesus said, 'People who are well do not need a doctor,'" Bob said enthusiastically, "'but only those who are sick.'"

"We're sick all right," the white-haired man said. "Sick of hearin' you. Why can't you leave us hopeless sinners in peace?"

"Cause they ain't no such thing as a hopeless sinner." Bob moved next to the flaming trash can. "Like I was just tellin' Brother Ryan here, God wants to forgive us."

"But I got a long list of sins," someone said and a few of them laughed.

"So did I," Bob said. "I used to be an atheist, so I understand how you feel. It's a fact though, that Jesus died on the cross so we could be forgiven." He glanced at Ryan. "Brother Ryan please listen to this carefully." He turned back to the others. "I just want you all to know what to do if you want to be put right with God. It's real easy. It says in the scripture, if you confess with your mouth 'Jesus is Lord', and believe in your heart that God raised Him from the dead, you will be saved."

The white-haired man moaned. "Any more of this and I'll puke my liver out."

"It's that simple," Bob said to Ryan. "You just gots to pray to Jesus that you believe in Him, ask for forgiveness, and ask Him to come into your life. You can do it anytime you want to."

A tall, thin man stood up shaking his head. "We heard enough of you already, Bible beater. Why don't you get lost before we use you for firewood."

They cheered and applauded and Bob smiled at them. "All right, maybe I'll leave you folks alone if you'll tell me somethin' about a guy named Darius."

"I'm Darius." The man sat on a crate behind the others, barely visible in the darkness beyond the flickering light. "Whattya want with me, fool?"

"Just a little talk," Bob said, "with me and my friend here."

"I ain't talkin' with you, preacher boy," the man said, "or none of your friends neither."

Bob turned to the others. "Well then ladies and gentlemen, I'm sorry to say you won't be gettin' rid of me for a long time. If Darius ain't gonna come talk with us then I'm just gonna stand here preaching all night tellin' you how Jesus is standin' and knocking at the door of your heart, and He wants to come in and have fellowship with you."

"I've heard enough," the white-haired man said. "I say Darius goes with the Bible guy or we don't share any more booze with him."

The others nodded and murmured in agreement and Darius jumped to his feet in the dim light. "What you people sayin'? I ain't gonna go talk with this fool!"

"Then you ain't gonna party with us," the white-haired man said with a chuckle.

"No booze," some of them chanted, "no booze, no booze."

"You people is crazy, too," Darius said with disgust. He moved closer to the fire and Ryan saw that he was a bearded black man of average height, in his thirties, wearing a torn coat and a red head band. "I'll talk to this mindless sucker for two minutes but I'm takin' one of the bottles with me." He grabbed a bottle out of the tall man's hands.

"You better not bring it back empty," the tall man warned him.

"I'll think about it," Darius said sarcastically.

"Thank you, Brother Darius," Bob said gratefully.

"I ain't yo' brother." Darius scowled at him. "Let's walk."

They followed him across the barren field, their shoes crunching on the hard ground and Ryan debated what approach to use. If Darius really was the Homeless Slasher he'd have to be extremely careful in questioning him.

"We want to ask you some questions," Bob said to Darius.

"Uh, let me handle this," Ryan said.

"It's OK Brother Ryan, I don't mind helpin'," Bob said.

"Twenty dollars," Darius said, stopping at the edge of the lot and taking a big swallow from his bottle. "I want twenty dollars to talk."

"Why?" Ryan asked.

"Cause I need money, fool," Darius said. "Give me some green paper or I ain't sayin' nothin'."

"OK." Ryan impatiently thrust his hand into his pocket and pulled out his wallet and handed a twenty-dollar bill to Darius. "Can we talk now?"

"Sure." Darius grinned as he put the money in his pocket.

Ryan swallowed hard. "I appreciate you talking to us. I have a friend who . . ."

"What Brother Ryan is trying to say," Bob interrupted, "is that he's been told you're tellin' folks you're the Homeless Slasher."

Ryan's mouth dropped open. "Wait a minute."

"It's OK, you don't have to thank me. I'm on a roll." He nodded at Ryan and turned back to Darius with a stern expression. "Now are you the one killin' poor folks or not?"

"Subtle." Ryan threw his hands up in the air. "Real subtle."

Darius stared back defiantly at Bob. "That's right, preacher man. I'm him. I'm the Slasher."

Bob stiffened. "Why are you doing it?"

"Whattya think?'

"I don't know, that's why I'm asking."

Darius moved closer. "Maybe I don't like other homeless people . . . or maybe I just like cuttin' throats."

"That's sick."

Darius grabbed Bob by the collar. "Who you callin' sick?"

Ryan quickly separated them. "OK, Darius, no need to get physical."

"It ain't sick to kill," Darius said. "People been killin' each other since the beginning of time."

"That don't make it right," Bob said.

"Shut your mouth!"

"OK, OK." Ryan said. "Darius, are you being straight with us? Are you really the Slasher?"

"That's right."

"Then if you don't mind my asking," Ryan said carefully, "why are you telling people?"

"Cause I'm real proud of myself."

"But aren't you afraid the police will hear about you?"

"No way, I'll cut all their throats, too."

The tall man from the fire approached Darius from behind. "Are you lyin' again about being that Slasher dude?"

"It ain't no lie." Darius told him. "I'm the main man of death on the streets."

"You are, huh?" The tall man chuckled. "Then who was killing all those homeless people when you were in jail for the last six months?"

"I did it myself. I snuck out every night."

The tall man turned to Ryan. "He just got out a couple of weeks ago." He suddenly grabbed the bottle from Darius. "I want some of this before you drink it all."

"No way, not till I'm done with it." Darius ripped the bottle out of the tall man's hand and sprinted away.

"Get back here!" The tall man ran into the darkness after him and quickly faded from view.

Ryan stepped into the street and began walking away. "Good night, Bible Bob and good luck."

"Hey, you wanna come with me?" Bob called after him. "I told you someone's asking folks strange questions out at Garfield Park. I'm going out there now to spend the night and tomorrow I'll be asking about that suspicious guy."

Ryan paused near the entrance to an alley and turned. "No thanks, I'm giving up. I'll never play detective again."

"Think about what I said. God really wants to forgive you."

"I'll think about it after I get myself a bottle."

Bob looked at him with compassion. "I'll pray for you, Brother Ryan."

"It's a waste of time to pray for me."

Chapter
Twenty-nine

Lydia leaned into the open window of the police car. "The person I'm looking for is in that rusty van parked up the street. When I'm done talking to him I'll drive back to my apartment."

Officer Bill Groth nodded at her from behind the steering wheel. "We'll keep an eye on you and follow you home." His partner, Officer Michael Dadosky, sat on the passenger side with his eyes closed and his head lying back on top of the seat.

"I'm sorry for the hassle," Lydia said apologetically.

"That's OK," Officer Groth said. "It's our job to protect people, right, Dadosky?" He elbowed him in the ribs and Dadosky woke up with a startled grunt and glared around indignantly.

"Well, thanks anyway." Lydia turned away and walked down the sidewalk towards the van that a social worker from the nearby soup kitchen had pointed out to her. The van belonged to a man named Jackie Robinson. When Sally

Malloy had told Ryan the Homeless Slasher was the same race as Jackie Robinson he had assumed she meant the major league's first African-American player. Lydia wasn't comfortable with that theory because Sally had been so reluctant to give him any information the night she was murdered. Sally had frequently used the nearby soup kitchen which meant the man inside the van may have known her. If so, then he might be the one she'd referred to as being the same race as the Slasher.

She glanced back uneasily at the police car parked at the curb. That morning they had offered her around-the-clock protection after viewing the bloody T-shirt in her desk drawer and she had reluctantly agreed. She still had mixed emotions about her decision because even though the individual harassing her was obviously disturbed, he still hadn't attempted to harm her physically. One of the policeman believed the blood probably came from an animal, not a human being, although they couldn't be certain until they tested it. She was glad she still felt anger, not fear, whenever she thought about her situation.

In frustration, last night she had actually opened the Bible her grandmother had given her before she died. She hadn't opened it since she was twelve. She read a few Psalms that talked of God's protection for His loved ones and then she read how Jesus saved a woman's life when she was caught committing adultery. A self-righteous crowd wanted to stone her to death, but Jesus simply told them that any one who had never committed a sin could throw the first stone. The crowd all left one by one. Lydia was impressed but couldn't help wondering why her mother couldn't have been protected from being murdered, it just wasn't fair.

The gray van was covered with dust, and rust had eaten large chunks out of the sides. A man and woman sat in the front seat and watched her approach. The social worker had been right, they were white.

She walked up to the driver's side and the man rolled down the window. "Hello, my name's Lydia Dupree. I'm a social worker at The Helping Hand shelter. Are you Jackie Robinson?"

The man nodded slowly, he appeared to be around forty with a thin face, extremely pale complexion, and long blond hair. "Yes," he said cautiously.

Lydia noticed his wife sitting in the passenger seat, a petite woman with long dark hair who looked exhausted. "I was wondering if I could talk to you," Lydia said to him, "about a homeless woman who sometimes ate here at the soup kitchen, a woman named Sally Malloy. Did you know her?"

Mr. Robinson nodded again. "Sure, we know Sally real good. She's always been real nice to all of us. Keeps tellin' me I'll find another job if I keep tryin'."

"Did she ever talk to you about the Homeless Slasher?"

He paused for a few seconds. "Well, yeah. I guess she has talked about him a little. I think she's scared of him."

"Can you remember anything specific she ever said about him?"

He shook his head. "No. Can't really remember."

"I do." His wife spoke in a soft voice. "One time a few weeks ago we were having dinner at the soup kitchen here and some people started arguing about the Slasher and two men got into a fight." She looked at her husband. "Remember?"

"Oh, yeah. Now I do," he said. "Two guys were arguing about what color the Slasher is and started pushin' each other so I jumped between them and tried to separate them. Before I know it Sally's there too, helpin' me push them apart and yellin' that they gotta be nicer to each other. A couple of social workers ran over and the guys cooled off and Sally says to one of the guys that he was right. That the Homeless Slasher is a white guy. So I asked her how come she knows that and she says it's because she's seen him. I asked where, and she kinda shudders and says she can't tell me or somethin' bad will happen. She said it like it was really true."

"I believed her," his wife said. "Sally wouldn't lie."

"Did she ever tell you anything else about the Slasher?" Lydia asked.

Mr. Robinson shook his head. "Not that I can remember."

"Me neither," his wife said.

"If you ever remember anything else she said about him please call me at this number." Lydia pulled a card out of her purse and gave it to him. "If you don't mind my asking, where are you two staying tonight?"

"You're looking at it," he said, gesturing at the back of his van. "We got two little ones takin' a nap back there now."

"I'll be happy to find you a shelter for tonight," Lydia said.

"Thanks but we checked this morning. The family shelters are all full. The only ones with extra beds are for women and kids only." He shrugged. "It's important for us to stay together. Sleepin' here's the only way to do that."

"Then I've got a suggestion." Lydia took a pen and note-pad out of her purse and wrote on it. "If the family shelters are full again tonight then here's the address and phone number of some friends of mine. They're a husband and wife who let homeless families stay with them until they can get into a shelter. If they already have a family staying with them tonight, then call me and I'll be very happy to have you stay at my apartment."

Lydia tore out the piece of paper and handed it to him. He took it and exchanged a surprised look with his wife. "Thank you very much," he said. "We'll call your friends. We sure appreciate the help."

A small boy wearing pajamas and a White Sox baseball cap suddenly appeared and climbed into his mother's lap. "I heard you talking about Aunt Sally."

"That's right, Sean," she said to him. "We were talking about her with this nice lady here."

"Sally told our little ones to call her 'Aunt Sally,'" Mr. Robinson said to Lydia. "It makes her happy when they do. She sure is a nice lady." He stroked his chin. "We ain't seen her now for a few weeks. Have you seen her lately?"

"Could you step outside the van for a second?" Lydia swallowed hard. "I need to tell you something impor-tant."

"Sure," he said with a concerned expression and opened the door and stepped down onto the street next to her.

"I don't want to tell you this in front of your son," Lydia said to him quietly. "Sally died last month. She was mur-dered by the Homeless Slasher."

"Oh, no." He stared at her with horror. "We didn't hear nothin' about that. I don't read newspapers everyday and when I do I just look for jobs in the classified section."

"I'm sorry to have to tell you."

"She was such a wonderful lady. It just ain't fair."

"It certainly isn't. Look, I've got to go now. Remember, if my friend's house is full tonight then you can stay at my place."

"Thank you," he said, glancing at the piece of paper in his hand.

Lydia turned and waved to the police car down the street, wondering if both policemen were asleep now. There was no traffic so she walked down the middle of the street towards her car which was parked along the sidewalk. It would be nice, she thought, if poverty and homelessness could somehow be eradicated. She sometimes fantasized about what she'd do if she were miraculously elected to be dictator of the entire world. She'd create some brilliant incentive plan that would entice people to share their belongings with total strangers. No family would ever have to sleep in a van again.

She was ten feet away from her car when she heard a loud popping noise and the window on the passenger side suddenly exploded. There were two more loud pops and multiple bullets slammed into the side of her car. Another window shattered and she instinctively dove down on her stomach on the opposite side of the car from where the bullets were coming. She hoped her car would shield her as a bullet ricocheted off the pavement only a few feet in front of her. She pressed her face down on the street and felt her body stiffen with fear as she waited for the next shot.

Chapter Thirty

The other policemen agree with us," Officer Groth said to Lydia as he sat down in the front seat of the police car next to Officer Dadosky. "The shots came from the window of that abandoned building. After he put six rounds into your car he must have ran out the back and left the area because we searched the alley and all the surrounding buildings and couldn't find him."

"Did anyone see him?" Lydia asked, leaning forward in the back seat.

He shook his head. "I doubt it; it's pretty deserted back there, but the other policemen are asking everyone in the neighborhood just in case." He paused and looked at her with concern. "Are you sure you're OK?"

"Yes, other then a slight headache and I guess that's a minor problem compared to what could have happened to me."

"Did they find anything interesting?" Officer Dadosky asked.

No." Groth frowned. "He didn't leave any blatant evidence. They'll check around for prints, but if he wore gloves that won't do any good."

"I've been thinking," Dadosky said. "If this guy was aiming at Lydia then he's a pretty lousy shot, which is possible of course. But it's a lot more likely he just wanted to shoot up her car, because if he was good with a gun he could have picked her off easy."

"That's real comforting to think about," Lydia said with a hint of sarcasm.

"Sorry." Dadosky looked embarrassed. "I don't want to scare you. What I'm trying to say is, I don't think this was a murder attempt."

"Me neither," Groth said.

"It seemed like it was to me," Lydia said, sinking back into the seat. "Regardless of whether he was trying to kill me or just frighten me, he's definitely increasing the pressure. This was even more drastic than leaving a bloody T-shirt in my desk drawer."

The two policemen exchanged a glance and Officer Groth cleared his throat. "Uh, we're not exactly sure if this is related to what's been happening to you."

Lydia stared at him. "What do you mean?"

"Well, this might not be the same guy. He hasn't done anything this violent yet."

"Besides the bloody T-shirt, he sent me a dead kitten with its throat cut."

"This was a lot different from everything else he's done. He hasn't used a gun before."

"Until now."

"Look, don't get me wrong, this might be the same guy. But it could just as easily have been some lunatic or a couple of gang members who decided to randomly shoot up a car and just happened to pick yours."

"I don't believe that, it's too coincidental. I know it was him."

"We may never know for sure. But don't worry; we'll still keep you under twenty-four hour protection."

"I don't know anything about police procedures," Lydia said carefully, "and I don't want to insult you but I don't understand why he was able to shoot up a car and escape. How come you two stayed in here so long?"

Groth frowned. "Well, we heard the shots but we didn't know where they came from. If we just came running out of the car he could have gunned us down."

"We saw you dove for cover," Dadosky said. "It didn't look like you were hit."

"We called for backup like we're supposed to," Groth said. "When they got here we went out and searched for him. We had to be cautious because we had no way of knowing he'd already left."

They continued taking turns explaining why immediately rushing out of their car would have been the wrong thing to do, but Lydia stopped listening as her headache throbbed more painfully. She ruffled the pages of the newspaper on the seat next to her, wondering what Ryan would think of this incident and wishing she was with him now.

She remembered last night was his deadline for quitting their investigation and wondered if he had. And if so, would that mean the end of their relationship? She had to admit the thought of never seeing him again filled her with sadness and concern. How could she have allowed herself to care about him so much? She wanted to avoid getting emotionally involved with any man but caught herself thinking of Ryan countless times each day. Where did she go wrong?

She picked up the newspaper and noticed it was the late edition and when she saw the front page story she moaned with horror.

Ryan woke up with a pressing pain in the back of his skull, and when he swallowed it felt like his mouth was caked with sand. He glanced at the clock next to his bed and saw it was four o'clock in the afternoon. He certainly couldn't have slept this late if he hadn't come back to his apartment last night.

He sat up and his head hurt even worse but he reluctantly got out of bed and staggered out to the kitchen. He took some aspirin out of a cupboard and grabbed a container of orange juice out of the refrigerator. He put the aspirin in his mouth and kept gulping down the juice until he had to pause for a deep breath. *Same as always alcohol definitely dehydrates the human body.*

He carried the orange juice over to his dilapidated couch and sat down with a groan next to a half empty bottle of Scotch. He stared at the faded wallpaper across the room for a while until he heard a knock at the door. He slowly walked to his door and opened it. Lydia was standing there, her red hair blazing brightly in the late afternoon sunshine.

"I called a little while ago," she said, twisting a rolled up newspaper in her hands. "I got your answering machine so I figured you were home."

"Yeah," he said self-consciously. "Like I told you, I turn it off when I'm gone and keep it on when I'm here. I guess that makes me antisocial."

Lydia looked at his tousled hair. "Did I wake you up?"

"No. I've been up at least five minutes now." He noticed the police car that was parked at the curb. "Looks like you brought a couple of escorts with you."

"After today I'll be taking them with me everywhere." Lydia paused. "Aren't you going to invite me in?"

"Uh, sure." Ryan stepped aside and held the door for her. "Don't mind the mess. This place isn't exactly Buckingham Palace."

"You won't believe everything that's happened today," Lydia said walking past him into the apartment. "I'm so upset..." She paused, noticing the bottle of Scotch. She walked over to the couch and picked it up, not wanting to believe that Ryan was drinking again. "Did you drink this?"

Ryan nodded and forced a grin. "Yeah, but I saved a few drops. I didn't want to be a glutton."

"Oh." Lydia put the bottle down on a battered coffee table, surprised by the anger that was so sudden and intense it made her face feel feverish. So, she thought, this is the man I can't stop thinking about. Someone I've considered placing all my affection and trust in and he can't even be trusted alone with a bottle. "I thought," she said accusingly, "you made a vow to never drink again."

"I did. But I decided to forget about it for one night."

"You told me you always keep your promises. You said drinking nearly destroyed your life."

"My life was already destroyed. Anyway, I figured one more time couldn't hurt me."

"If it is only one more time."

"It is. It definitely is."

"A lot of alcoholics keep telling themselves that over and over, that every drinking binge is the last one, but it never is."

"You can spare me the lecture," Ryan said sharply, surprising both of them with his bitterness. "Last night was rough. I found a guy who claimed to be the Slasher but he turned out to be a phony."

"So you didn't solve the case by your self-imposed deadline. If you extend it a little . . ."

"If I extend it I'll go crazy," he interrupted. "I'm tired of sleeping in crowded shelters and eating bad food and seeing despair on so many faces. I can't live in the streets any more."

"Then sleep here at night and keep searching for him during the day."

"It would be a waste of time, I'll never find him. It's time to quit."

"But you've learned a lot about the murders."

"Yeah, a lot of cryptic clues that don't make any sense. The only thing I learned is that the Slasher is probably black."

"No he isn't."

"Of course he is. Sally Malloy told me he's black."

"No. She said he was the same color as Jackie Robinson. You assumed she meant the baseball player but she didn't. I went to a soup kitchen this morning and found Jackie Robinson. He's white."

"How do you know he's the Jackie Robinson she was referring to?"

"Because she ate there often and knew him well. He remembered Sally said she'd seen the Slasher and that he was white. She was just being evasive when she answered your question."

"So I was wrong." Ryan collapsed into a chair. "As usual."

"Why not look at the positive side? Now we know his race."

"But that doesn't help much considering how many white guys live in Chicago." Ryan gripped the chair's armrests tightly. "It's all my fault, though. If I didn't fall asleep that night and let Sally get killed we'd have found him weeks ago."

Lydia bit into her lower lip. "Will you please stop this?"

"Stop what?"

"Wallowing in self-pity."

Ryan flinched as if he'd been slapped in the face. "Wallowing? That's what you think I'm doing?"

"Yes. I'd say it describes you quite accurately." Lydia felt her cheeks reddening from anger. "It seems to me you spend the majority of your waking hours feeling sorry for yourself."

"Thanks a lot," he said sarcastically, squeezing the armrests even harder. "Nice of you to tell me."

"I'll tell you even more. Sometimes I think you must enjoy submerging yourself in self-pity or you wouldn't do it so often."

"I don't think it's self-pity to take your mistakes seriously."

"Ryan, we all make mistakes sometimes, but it's not healthy to torture yourself by constantly dwelling on them. Why not try to learn from them and then get on with your life?"

Ryan stood up. "Because I never seem to learn from my mistakes. I keep repeating them."

"There you go again. You can't stop saying negative things about yourself. Sometimes I think you'll drive me insane."

"You mean more insane, don't you?" He instantly regretted what he said but now it was too late. *Insulting the girl you love, Ryan the loser, is not very smart.*

Lydia stared at him, trying to control her emotions. "Did you just insult me or did I misunderstand you?"

Ryan felt himself grin sarcastically at her, knowing it was too late, he wouldn't even try to save himself even though he felt he was about to fall into a bottomless abyss. "That all depends. How do you define everything you just said about me?"

"Constructive criticism."

"Then so was my comment."

"There's nothing constructive about hinting that I'm insane."

"But you think it's constructive to say I'm negative and feel sorry for myself?"

"In your case, yes! Because it's the truth!"

"Maybe you'd like to hear my opinion of the truth," he said, his voice rising angrily, "which is, someone who has faults of their own shouldn't judge others!"

"And what's that supposed to mean?"

"You accuse me of having faults but never acknowledge your own."

"Such as?"

Ryan shook his head. "Never mind."

"No. Tell me."

"No."

"All right. Then I'll just have to assume you can't tell me because you're too busy feeling sorry for yourself again."

"At least I'm not living in fear!"

Lydia glared at him and tightened her grip on the rolled up newspaper. "I don't live in fear. Even though someone's trying to kill me I'm not letting fear control me."

"Yes it is, but I'm not referring to the guy who's stalking you." He paused and defiantly stared at her. "You're afraid of men."

"I am not!"

"Yes you are! You're afraid of having a relationship with a man. You're afraid to trust any of us."

"That's not true!"

"You know it is, Lydia. You're afraid of being hurt or betrayed."

"I'm not afraid of anything."

"Is that right?" He moved closer to her. "Then why did you run away from me that night on the ledges? Were you afraid of your own feelings?"

"No."

"Were you afraid of me?"

"No!"

"Then why did I see fear in your eyes?"

"Because I don't want any romance in my life!"

"With me?"

"With anyone."

"Not ever?"

"It's my right to live any way I want to. My lifestyle is none of your business."

"Lydia, I shouldn't have kissed you that night but for a moment I thought that maybe, just maybe, we felt the same way. I'm not just referring to being physically attracted to each other, but something far more important. I thought we'd reached the point where we cared for one another more than anyone else in the world, and I hoped we were finally willing to trust each other enough to admit the truth." He paused for a few seconds. "Was I wrong to think that, Lydia?"

Lydia swallowed and gestured to the bottle of Scotch. "Why should I trust someone who breaks a promise to himself?"

"I guess you can't." Ryan moved away. "Your fear won't let you."

"Here," she said, handing him the newspaper. "I thought you'd want to read about it." She hurried to the front door.

"Wait a second. Didn't you come here to tell me something?"

She paused at the door. "I don't have time now. The Homeless Slasher's still out there. If I'm ever going to catch him I've got to find a new partner."

Ryan winced as she slammed the door shut and he sat down on the couch, resisting the urge to run after her and beg her to stay. He felt light headed and slightly nauseous as the hurtful words they had both said echoed in his mind. How did they let things get so out of control between them?

He looked down at the newspaper in his hand and unfolded it, involuntarily groaning when he saw the front page story. The Homeless Slasher had claimed another victim last night but this time he didn't murder one of the homeless. He killed a legendary Good Samaritan named Robert Wills, also known as Bible Bob.

After reading the story several times Ryan dropped the newspaper with a moan. Bible Bob had invited him to come with him to Garfield Park last night, and he had been murdered there in his van. There were no witnesses.

Ryan sat down in a chair and put his head in his hands. He might not have been murdered if he'd gone with him. Everything he did always turned out wrong.

He remembered when he first met Bible Bob he wondered if he was a phony, or perhaps even the Slasher himself, but now he knew his faith was genuine. He talked about God with such confidence, as if he had a personal relationship with Him. He had also promised to pray for him and Ryan wondered if he'd had the chance before he died? Was Bible Bob right, that God was willing to forgive everyone, even him?

He noticed his Bible on top of the coffee table. If it truly was God's Word, it contained all the answers he was looking for. He reached over and picked it up. He'd been undecided about Jesus all his life. It was time to decide now, one way or the other.

Chapter Thirty-one

I'm going to find him myself," Lydia said confidently as she leaned forward in the back seat of the van. "I can't count on the police to do it."

"I hope you're not referring to the person who's harassing you," Carl said, sitting next to her. "You'll never find him and if you did, who knows what he'd do to you?"

"I disagree," Augie said, glancing back from behind the steering wheel. "With the right strategy Lydia can find this guy. All she needs is the brilliant insight of a certain co-worker who'll be happy to share his ideas."

"Thanks, Augie," Martin said with mock gratitude from the other front seat. "I didn't know you considered me brilliant."

Augie snorted derisively. "I think Lydia knows who I was talking about."

"Surely you don't mean yourself?" Martin asked with feigned surprise. "Do you actually consider yourself brilliant?"

"A fact is a fact," Augie grinned defiantly.

"If you are in fact brilliant," Martin said pointing at the dashboard, "then why are you speeding when we're being followed by a police car?"

Augie groaned and hit the brakes. "Just my luck!" He looked in the rearview mirror. "No, they're staying back."

"Maybe they don't give out tickets when they're protecting someone?" Carl said.

"Some protection." Augie shook his head with disgust. "Lydia could have been killed the other day and they just sat in their car like cowards while the maniac got away. Then they say it's not the same guy who's been stalking her."

"They didn't say that exactly," Lydia said. "They said it could have been him, but it might have just been a random shooting by some gang member."

"But what about the note you got from him yesterday where he admitted doing it?"

"They say his claiming responsibility doesn't prove he did it. If he knows me he could have heard about the shooting and decided to take credit for it."

"Their logic is infuriating," Augie said with disgust.

"What do you think?" Martin asked her.

"It was him." Lydia clenched her jaw tightly. "I know it was."

"Would you like to know the best way to catch this guy?" Augie asked her.

"Actually, I've already got a plan that I think will work, but at this point I'm willing to listen to any suggestion."

"Great, because I've been dying to tell you mine."

"I can hardly wait," Martin said sarcastically.

"Even skeptics like Martin and Carl will be impressed," Augie said to her with enthusiasm. "First you have to figure out why this guy is tormenting you. The obvious answer is that he's doing it because he's angry at you. He believes you did something unforgivable to him."

"No." Lydia shook her head. "I've thought about this a lot. I haven't done anything wrong to anyone."

"I'm sure you haven't, but in this guy's twisted mind he believes you did or he wouldn't want revenge. In fact, it might even be someone who frequents our shelter. Have any of you noticed the quiet, nervous guy who's been in for a few meals lately? He refuses to talk to anyone and sits alone in a corner with his food, staring at Lydia."

"Plenty of guys stare at her," Martin said.

"Yeah, but not like this guy," Augie said. "He watches her with a burning intensity and he looks angry, not lustful."

"I haven't noticed him," Lydia said, "and I think I'd be aware of someone glaring at me."

"Maybe you're too preoccupied to notice," Augie said. "Anyway, he probably has mental problems and might be dangerous. If he isn't the guy who's threatening you, it's someone like him, somebody who believes you did something terrible to him."

"What do you propose I do?"

"I think we need to come up with a list of potential suspects for the police to follow or bring in for questioning, beginning with this guy, and if they're not willing, I'll do it myself."

Martin groaned. "Augie Rosen, the world's greatest private eye."

"Hey, I can't do any worse than the police, and at least I'm willing to try." He glanced at Lydia's reflection in the rearview mirror. "Even though the police will keep watching you it wouldn't hurt for me or some of your other friends to be with you at all times."

"I'll volunteer, too," Martin said.

"What a surprise," Carl said sarcastically.

"Thanks for the offer; it's very kind of all of you, but two friends stayed with me last night and their snoring kept me awake for hours. I appreciate your advice, Augie, but I've already got a plan. I'm going to put a sign up on the shelter bulletin board saying I'm sorry for what I've done and to please meet me at the Sears Tower at three on Sunday, I'll be standing there alone on the observation floor. I'll also put an ad in the personals column saying the same thing, and I'll put a sign in my car and apartment windows saying 'Read the Personals!' He should notice if he's watching me. Then I'll keep going to the Sears Tower every Sunday until he shows up and approaches me."

"Not alone, I hope?" Augie glanced at her with astonishment.

"I'll be alone."

"Are you crazy?"

Lydia smiled. "I'll be standing alone, but plainclothes police will be waiting nearby to grab him. And when they do my nightmare will finally be over." She paused and looked out the window. "If my plan doesn't work then hopefully the police or someone like you, Augie, will find him soon. I'll be eternally grateful to anyone who finds him."

Augie slowed the van down and pulled over to the side of the street, parking behind a long row of cars. Martin opened the door but Augie put a hand on his arm. "Wait a minute." He looked in the rearview mirror. "OK, they're pulling in behind us."

"We'll get out first, Lydia," Martin said, getting out on the passenger side as Carl followed.

Lydia nodded reluctantly. She was already tired of being protected and having to listen to an unending barrage of suggestions. Some of her friends thought she should just stay in her apartment where the police could easily protect her, but if she did, when would it be safe to leave? It could be months or years. No, she would never know when it was safe to leave and in reality would be a prisoner in her own apartment. Other friends suggested she should leave Chicago and hide out in another city or country, but what kind of life would that be? What if he eventually tracked her down? Augie tried to convince her to at least wear a bulletproof vest but she refused, pointing out it wouldn't prevent the stalker from shooting her in the head. Besides, if she did any of those things she'd be letting her unknown enemy intimidate her, something she was determined to never allow. She fully intended to stick to her normal work schedule and take minimum precautions. The person tormenting her wouldn't kill her. She was literally betting her life on that.

She got out of the van and stood on the sidewalk, shivering in the damp air as the two policemen approached. Augie, Martin, and Carl surrounded her protectively as they glanced around nervously at the dilapidated houses on both sides of the street. Carl rubbed at his shaved head, Martin kept clearing his throat, and Augie chewed on his lower lip.

"Relax, guys," she said. "Isn't it unlikely that he'd guess exactly where we'd park?"

"Yes," one of the policemen said, "but he probably expects you to show up here for the funeral."

"Anything could happen," Carl said.

"I don't care," she said. "Bible Bob was a good friend."

They started walking down the sidewalk together, the men anxiously looking at every car that drove by. Lydia saw the huge crowd standing outside the large brick church, the cross on top of the steeple pointing up towards heaven.

Men and women of all ages and races stood there in the cold, many dressed in worn clothing and holding bags or knapsacks. These people, Lydia thought, are the ones Bible Bob would have appreciated the most for attending his funeral.

She could still picture Bible Bob towering over her with his tall, thin frame, imploring her to turn back to the Lord. "Trust in God," he would often say. "There's a reason He allowed your mother to die. You won't know why till you get to heaven, but in the end He will make everything right."

It would have made Bible Bob happy to know she had read the book of Job last night. She was astonished at how much Job had suffered, yet even though he lost his children, his possessions, and his health, he still never turned away from God, yet God allowed all those terrible things to happen to test his faith. Lydia wondered if her mother's death had been a test of faith for her, if it was then she had certainly failed. So be it.

Lydia swallowed hard when she saw Ryan standing over by the church's white stone steps, his eyes downcast and his hands shoved into his pockets like a small boy who had just been scolded by his teacher. She resisted the urge to go over and hug him, realizing with amazement that their argument had not diminished her concern for him. When he noticed her he stared at her with obvious remorse but she turned away.

"Lydia, we better get inside right away," one of the policemen said, gently taking her arm.

Lydia walked past Ryan, quickly climbing up the steps and fighting off the impulse to turn and say something kind and conciliatory to him. As she walked through the front door of the church she told herself that since she planned to live her life alone, this was probably for the best.

Chapter Thirty-two

This time it's going to be different, Ryan told himself, the answer to everything is here in Garfield Park. Ryan walked past the rows of theater seats, all empty now except for a coating of clean white snow. It doesn't matter, he thought, that my theater audience deserted me. I'm going to succeed without them.

He walked through swirling snowflakes towards an orange and yellow swing set and briefly wondered why someone chose to paint it such a garish color. He wasn't at all discouraged even though he hadn't learned anything useful the last two days. For once he was going to have faith. He'd eventually find the killer's identity here; there was no question about that.

He'd been in a good mood the last two days, ever since he had made his decision. He had sat there in his apartment reading the Bible. He read about the prodigal son, numerous verses about forgiveness, and finally concluded God wanted to forgive everyone, even a loser named Ryan Dolan.

He finally put the Bible down and prayed to Jesus that he believed He was the Son of God. He asked for forgiveness and invited Him to come into his life.

He was not hit by a bolt of lightning and did not feel any different physically, but he did feel a certain peace inside. He believed he was forgiven.

Ryan sat down on a swing and wondered what he should do next. He prayed a few times each day, he didn't know any formal prayers so he just spoke to God conversationally as if He were nearby. He also read a little from the Bible each morning before breakfast. He had so much to learn but he also needed to catch a murderer.

He had told himself the same thing last night as he sat in his uncle's police car.

"This Bible Bob," Kevin Dolan had said, pausing to take a huge gulp of coffee. "He's definitely the key."

"Why's that?" Ryan asked, even though he already knew the answer.

"Because for the first time, the Slasher deviated from his pattern. He killed someone who wasn't homeless. The guy had a dumpy little apartment in West Town, although he hardly ever stayed there. He usually slept in his van or a shelter. He actually spent all his time helping the homeless." He shook his head in disgust. "He must have been an idiot."

"I met him and I liked him. I'd appreciate it if you'd refrain from criticizing him."

Kevin raised his eyebrows. "A little touchy are we? OK, I'll try not to insult your buddy."

"Did you find anything at the murder location?"

"Nothing useful. This Bible Bob guy was asleep in the back of his van and didn't lock it. The Slasher came in and probably did his thing before the guy even woke up." Kevin grinned. "I hope I die in my sleep someday, but not like that."

"What's the theory on his motive?"

"There's a few we're tossing around, but that's been about as productive as tossing our cookies." Kevin Dolan gulped his coffee again. "Some guys think the Slasher had a personal vendetta against this Bible Bob. Some think he just came across him and assumed he was homeless."

"What do you think?"

"The Slasher plans everything out in advance and picks his victims carefully. He would have known this guy wasn't homeless. I've got a gut feeling this Bible Bob knew something and the Slasher had to kill him to protect his identity. The page the Slasher left from that homeless book kind of indicates that, he circled the words 'He knows'."

"If that's true then you can catch the killer by finding out what Bible Bob knew."

"Yeah, but that won't be easy." Kevin Dolan glanced at him, eyes narrowing slightly. "How's your investigation going?"

"The same as always. Nowhere."

Ryan blinked as a wet snowflake floated into one of his eyes and he slowly swung back and forth on the swing, watching the descending snow softly cover the area near the park's entrance. He knew he should have told his uncle that he'd been with Bible Bob the night he was murdered, and that he believed the Slasher had approached some people in Garfield Park. Obviously, Bible Bob had been right or the Slasher wouldn't have killed him. But instead he'd remained silent.

A man trudged across the snow to a nearby bench and sat down. Ryan immediately got off the swing and walked towards him. Eventually he'd find someone who had talked to the Slasher or Bible Bob, all he had to do was continue searching.

"Hello," Ryan said enthusiastically as he approached the man on the bench.

The man looked at him suspiciously, he was a black man in his sixties with white hair protruding from under his knitted cap and his shoulders were hunched against the wind. "I already talked to you yesterday," he said impatiently. "Nobody round here been askin' me no questions and I don't know no Bible dude so take a hike, chump."

Way to go Cryin' Ryan, a voice cackled inside his mind. He turned away and walked deeper into the park. It certainly would have been easier if he'd learned something at Bible Bob's funeral, but no one he talked to there knew anything.

Thinking of the funeral reminded him again of Lydia and he felt the usual piercing pain. He remembered that she had seen him outside the church and then quickly looked away and went inside without saying a word. He had resisted an overwhelming urge to run after her and tell her that he cared about her more than anything else in this world, and they were both fools if they let one argument destroy such a meaningful relationship. Someday, he thought, I'll tell her that. After I find the Slasher and prove I'm not a self-pitying quitter. *That may take you forever, Ryan the loser.*

"Oh say can you see," a man's voice sang out of key, "by the dawn's burly light. What so proudly got mailed, with somethin' else gleaming."

Ryan approached a familiar looking white man in his fifties, standing under a tree holding his baseball cap reverently over his chest and peering up at the bare branches. "And the rockets red glare, the bombs bursting somewhere…"

"Hello, Cleo," Ryan said.

Cleo stopped singing and looked at him with a puzzled expression. "I can't remember the rest of the words. Do you?"

"Some of them. Nothing personal, but why are you singing to a tree?"

"I'm not singin' to a tree," Cleo chuckled and shook his head. "That would be kinda looney. I'm singin' to the squirrels," He frowned and glanced up again, "but I guess they don't like this song or somethin' cause they won't come out and listen."

"It's cold out. It's probably warmer in the tree."

"Maybe," Cleo said thoughtfully. "'Cept you can't be sure unless you been inside one yourself."

"Do you remember me?"

"No," Cleo studied him, "unless you're my cousin Marty."

"I'm Ryan."

"Good, cause my cousin Marty is real spooky. Years ago I seen him eat a beer bottle."

"I met you last month at Humboldt Park. It was after Hector Lopez was murdered. You showed me the picture he drew of the Homeless Slasher."

Cleo shivered and put his hat on. "I still get bad dreams about Hector."

"I'm sorry to hear that." He paused. "Has anybody approached you lately and asked if you're tired and unhappy about being homeless?"

"No, but I am."

"Did you ever meet a tall, skinny African-American guy named Bible Bob? He was real friendly, always giving out food and stuff."

"Uh, yeah, maybe I do know him. I think he gave me food once and some food for the squirrels, too."

"Did you see him here last week?"

"No, uh-uh."

"Did you know the Slasher killed him?"

"No." Cleo took a step backwards and moaned. "You talk spooky."

"I'm sorry, but I had to find out if you knew anything." Ryan took a step forward. "The day after we met I had a social worker look for you but you were gone. Where did you go?"

"Away." Cleo took another step backwards. "I found another place to stay."

"Another abandoned building?"

"It's not banded now cause I live there."

"Some night you'll freeze to death."

"I keep warm by makin' a big fire in a trash can."

"Then sooner or later you'll accidentally burn down the building."

"Uh-uh. I'm real careful."

Ryan exhaled loudly. "Listen, Cleo, I want to help you. If you come with me I promise I'll take you someplace where you'll be happy."

"No, I'm not goin' to no shelter. Somebody'll beat me up again."

"I'll take you somewhere safe and warm. I'm willing to drive you all over the city until we find a place you like."

"Uh-uh." Cleo started backing away. "You're scarin' me. I gotta go!" He turned and ran towards the park entrance.

"Cleo, you don't have to be scared of me!" Ryan shouted after him. "I just want to help you!"

He watched Cleo reach the distant sidewalk and keep running. He shook his head and walked towards a park bench where two people were sitting. At this rate, he thought, it will take all of eternity to discover something important.

An African-American couple in their twenties watched him approach. The man wore sunglasses and the woman had headphones on which she took off as he got closer.

"A little cold today, isn't it?" Ryan said in a friendly voice.

"Colder than a morgue on a Saturday night," the woman said matter-of-factly. "But it's kinda refreshin' to sit out for a few minutes."

"Do you two come here often?"

"Yeah we come here lots; our apartment is only a few blocks away." She looked at him curiously. "How 'bout you?"

"I've only been here the last two days. I'm trying to find someone."

"A friend?"

"No. I'm looking for someone who's been here recently talking to homeless folks. Asking where they're staying at night and if they're unhappy or sick, things like that."

The woman glanced at the man next to her who was grinning and nodding enthusiastically. "Yeah, I knows just who you talkin' about," he said emphatically in a deep, raspy voice. "I was sittin' by the park entrance 'bout a week and a half ago near some homeless folks. And this strange dude was talkin' away to them just like you said, sayin' stuff like, 'Do you ever wish this nightmare would end?' and other weird stuff like that." He paused and cleared his throat. "You may think I'm crazy. But I gotta strong feelin' that maybe this here's the dude who goes around killin' all those people. That maybe he is the Homeless Slasher."

Chapter Thirty-three

YOU WILL DIE TOMORROW. After Lydia finished reading the note she angrily crumpled it up, fervently wishing she could confront her unknown tormentor. When she gave the note to the police they recommended that she stay in her apartment for the next twenty-four hours where they could easily protect her. Even though the writer of the note might be bluffing it wasn't worth the risk to test him by going out somewhere. Besides, they felt the shelter would be an ideal place for him to try to kill her, he only had to disguise himself as a homeless man to get close to her. Lydia agreed with everything they told her, but then boldly announced that she was going to work the next day anyway, no matter what the note said.

"Lydia, you're not being logical," Martin said as he entered the kitchen and interrupted her thoughts.

"If I was a logical thinker then I wouldn't be a social worker," Lydia said, continuing to stack sandwiches on a platter.

Martin turned to the policeman sitting in the corner. "Don't you think she'd be safer at home?"

"It would certainly make our job easier," the policeman said, "but she wouldn't listen."

Martin pointed a finger at Lydia accusingly. "Why are you so stubborn?"

"First of all, if I hide out today he might decide to mail me a death threat every day. Then what do I do, spend the rest of my life in my apartment?" Lydia began to make another sandwich. "Secondly, I don't think I'm in any danger today. I think he's bluffing, just like the day he asked me to meet him at the Sears Tower and didn't show up."

"How do you know he's bluffing and why take the chance? He already shot at you once and that police lab test confirmed it was an animal's blood on that T-shirt he put in your office. He's obviously a maniac."

"But he's a maniac who doesn't want to be caught. So far he's been very careful to conceal his identity in everything he's done. He must realize that the police will be guarding me here, so if he comes charging at me with a gun they'll catch him."

"Unfortunately," Carl said, coming into the kitchen with some dirty dishes. "They'll probably catch him after he shoots you."

"No. If he wanted to do that he could have shot me in the street that day instead of shooting my car. He just wants to frighten and intimidate me."

"Then why not let him?" Martin asked.

"Because I'm not going to let him get what he wants." Lydia began spreading mustard on some bread. "I'm going to keep working like this was just a normal day. Besides, we're shorthanded with Augie taking that elderly man to the hospital. Which reminds me, he should have been back by now."

"We can handle things here without you and Augie." Martin moved closer to her. "Therefore I'm giving you an ultimatum. Go home with the police right now, or else you'll have to go out with me tonight."

"There goes Romeo again," Carl said to the policeman, rolling his eyes.

"Martin, don't your hormones ever take a day off?" Lydia said. "I'm not going out with you."

"Then as punishment I'll come around to your apartment tonight around midnight and serenade you with romantic love songs and I warn you, I sing extremely loud. I'll probably wake up all your neighbors."

"And they'll probably lynch you." Lydia picked up the platter of sandwiches. "I'm staying here all day."

She walked out the door into the crowded eating area and set the platter down on a table. She picked up one sandwich and carried it over to a man who sat alone at a corner table.

"Here you go," she said, placing the sandwich on his empty plate. "You look hungry."

He stared at her impassively with his huge brown eyes, an African-American man in his thirties wearing a patched up overcoat. He picked up the sandwich and took a small bite.

Lydia sat down next to him. "I hope you like ham and cheese."

He stared at her, silently chewing his food.

She leaned forward expectantly. "I sure wish you'd talk to me." He took another bite of the sandwich.

"You see," she continued pleasantly, "Bible Bob was a friend of mine. Someone told me you hang out at Garfield Park and that he talked to you the day he was murdered."

Lydia looked up as a tall, angry looking man wearing a raincoat came in the front door. He glanced in her direction, frowned, and then sat down near the door and slowly unbuttoned his coat. What if he was her tormentor? What if he had a gun under his coat?

She forced herself to look back at the man sitting next to her. "If Bible Bob talked to you I'm sure he brought up God at least once. He always did with me, he used to drive me crazy, but I'll miss him. He would always smile at me and say something like, 'Miss Lydia, God is waiting with open arms to welcome you back.' I actually memorized a verse in the Bible last night where Jesus said 'Come to me, all you who are weary and burdened, and I will give you rest'. I could sure use some peace and rest. But I'll probably never turn back to Him. Did Bible Bob talk about God with you?"

The man stared at her impassively. "Well," Lydia said after a long pause. "If you tell me anything he said to you it might help the police find his murderer. I'm going to let you finish your meal in peace."

She stood up and saw the man in the raincoat watching TV with apparent interest, but what if he was ignoring her now to avoid suspicion? What if in a few minutes he stood up with a gun and charged at her?

The man next to her cleared his throat. "My name is Isaac," he said in a soft whisper. "I'll talk to you now."

"Thank you, Isaac." She sat back down. "Did you know Bible Bob?" He nodded at her. "Did he talk to you the day he was murdered?"

He nodded again. "Gave me food. Talked about how to end up in heaven and stuff."

"Did he mention being in any kind of danger?"

"No."

"Did you see him talking to anyone else that day?"

He shrugged at her with a puzzled expression. "Maybe. I gotta think about that."

A firm hand suddenly clamped down on her shoulder, Lydia screamed and turned to see two policemen standing there. "I'm sorry," she said, conscious of everyone staring at her. "I guess I'm a little nervous today."

"Lydia, we just got a call," one of the policemen said. "We found out who's been stalking you."

Chapter Thirty-four

Why did you think he was the Homeless Slasher?" Ryan asked innocently, struggling to disguise a sudden surge of excitement.

"I just knowed it." The man nodded so enthusiastically his sunglasses began to slide off his nose and he pushed them back in place. "I'm a good listener. When you listen real carefully to what folks say, you can understand what they're thinking; you understand who they are."

"My man Raymond, here," the woman said nodding in agreement, "is gifted. He can listen to a person talk and tell you everything you want to know about them and he's almost always right." She smiled at him. "Course it would be better if he was that good at pickin' lottery numbers."

"I'm a listener, not a psychic," Raymond said defensively.

"Raymond," Ryan said. "I'd really like to hear about this guy you think is the Slasher."

"You serious?"

"Absolutely. What did he look like?"

The woman glanced up at Ryan with surprise. "Raymond can't tell you that. He's blind."

"I'm sorry. I didn't know."

"Hey, that's OK," Raymond said. "That didn't insult me none."

"Well, I'm glad of that." Ryan sat down on the bench next to him. "A preacher named Bible Bob helped me the other night, probably saved my life. He told me someone was asking the homeless some suspicious questions in this park. He came here to investigate and was murdered by the Slasher that same night. That makes me think the Slasher really was here and he killed Bible Bob to protect his identity." Ryan paused. "If I don't find him he'll kill more innocent people unless someone helps me."

"Be glad to," Raymond said. "I can't tell you what he looks like, but I'll tell everythin' else."

"Thanks. When was this guy here?"

"One day, bout a week and a half ago. My woman went to get us some coffee."

"It was around noon," the woman said.

"That's right, and I was sittin' on a bench near the front of the park. Even though I couldn't see this guy I can tell a lot by the way he talked to a couple of homeless dudes. He was definitely white. Well educated I'd guess, and he didn't have no accent so he must have grown up around Chicago."

"How old do you think he was?" Ryan asked.

"It's hard to figure cause he had a deep voice. I'd say he was probably in his thirties."

"Did you know the homeless guys he talked to?"

"No, they was just two guys sittin' on a bench near me talkin' about where to find a shelter that wasn't all filled up."

"What exactly did he say to them?"

"He just come up and says 'Hi' and stuff, makin' small talk at first. Then he asks them how long they been homeless and where they stay at night and if they wished the nightmare could end for them."

"How did they answer that?"

"They say sure, but their nightmare won't end till they find a job. Then he says somethin' like have they ever wished they could help end the homeless problem in this country? And they say sure, but what could they do about it? And he says life is full of surprises, someday they might get the opportunity." He paused, nodding with obvious excitement. "That's when I thought he could be that Slasher guy, cause he would probably talk to folks that same way. I felt like I could see into his mind and I saw him thinkin' bout all the other homeless people he killed. Then I got real cold all over and started shakin'."

"Then what happened?"

"He just gave 'em some advice and told them good luck and walked away. But I knowed who he was. He was the Slasher."

"What was the advice he gave them?"

"He said there's a shelter on California that gives job counselin' and trainin' and stuff."

Ryan stood up so quickly he almost fell forward onto the ground. Suddenly everything made sense. He looked up at the gray sky and remembered the picture Hector Lopez had crudely drawn on a box with the words, "One that takes" written above. He thought again of what Sally Malloy had told him on the night of her murder, that the Slasher was supposed to be good, and to find him he should think of Malibu Beach and the end of summer. Finally he understood exactly who she was referring to. He knew who the Homeless Slasher was. Now all he had to do was prove it.

———

Chapter Thirty-five

Lydia, it looks like your nightmare is over." Officer Groth smiled at her proudly from behind his desk. Ed Scott, a homicide detective, sat next to him nodding in agreement. Augie reached over from a nearby chair and patted her arm reassuringly.

"I hope you're right," Lydia said with just enough doubt to cause all of them to look at her with surprise.

"Don't worry, it was definitely him," Detective Scott said. "Al Wilson was found with an envelope addressed to you that contained another threatening note."

Lydia glanced again at the note on the desk that was written with familiar block letters saying, "YOU WON'T SURVIVE MUCH LONGER! I'M COMING FOR YOU NOW!"

"He also had a picture of you," Officer Groth said, "and several sheets of paper that had your name written hundreds of times."

"He also had a .38," Detective Scott said. "The same caliber as the bullets that were fired at your car."

"But you told me it may have been a random shooting," Lydia said.

"Yeah," Groth said reluctantly, "but now it looks like it was this guy."

"Are you sure you don't remember this Al Wilson?" Detective Scott asked her.

"Yes, I'm sure, and I don't recognize him from the picture you just showed me."

"Then we'll let you view the body. Photos can be deceiving, especially with a corpse."

"Do you really believe he died of natural causes?" Lydia asked.

"Sure. The coroner says he died of a heart attack. The autopsy will confirm it."

"I just don't understand why somebody I don't even remember would be so obsessed with me."

Groth shrugged. "He was a nut case."

"Uh, excuse me," Augie said. "I think the proper term is mentally ill."

"Whatever," Groth said. "We checked him out. He'd apparently lived alone in that abandoned building for quite a while. He was angry and hostile, babbling to himself half the time. A guy that crazy doesn't need much to set him off with an irrational obsession. You may have accidentally insulted him at the shelter one time, or more likely he just imagined you did."

"I remember him, Lydia," Augie said. "He's the guy I told you about when we went to Bible Bob's funeral. He came in for a few meals recently and always refused to sign in or answer any questions. I noticed he always stared at you with intense anger, so that's why I asked some of the others where he lived and went to talk to him."

"Lucky for you he was dead when you found him," Groth said. "He might have used that .38 on you if you asked him about Lydia."

"If you didn't find him," Scott said, "that body would have been lying there till spring."

"Well, I'm glad I was able to help." Augie smiled at him scornfully. "Especially since your investigation of this wasn't going anywhere."

"Maybe when I view the body I'll remember him," Lydia said. "But most of all, I want to know why he was tormenting me."

"You'll never know that now," Groth said.

"And that," Lydia said with a frown, "is what bothers me the most."

Chapter Thirty-six

Ryan knew the logical thing to do was to go to the police and tell them who the Homeless Slasher was. They'd be skeptical at first and he would have to explain everything he'd learned and why it all pointed to a certain individual, but they'd finally agree to set up surveillance on him and obtain a search warrant for his living quarters. Then they'd eventually catch him by following him to his next victim or by finding some irrefutable evidence he'd hidden away somewhere. Going to the police was definitely the logical thing to do. The only problem was he had never been a logical thinker. So he intended to capture the Slasher by himself, or die trying.

He walked down the slushy sidewalk, the snow melting quickly from the warming temperature, and suddenly he saw the imaginary rows of theater seats on the sidewalk across the street, stretching into the distance as far as he could see, all filled with people staring at him with rapt attention. He shook his head with disdain and ignored them, pausing in front of a crumbling brick building with boarded up windows. Hopefully, this was where he'd find his new partner. *Maybe you're making another mistake*, a harsh voice whispered at him, *and you'll cause someone else to die like the little girl you shot, or Sally Malloy.*

Ryan walked up and pushed the creaky door open. This time, he said to himself, I'm going to succeed. He paused in the doorway and prayed silently for a moment, asking for guidance. When he finished he remembered that he used to look down on people who prayed. Now it seemed like a natural thing to do.

He turned on his flashlight and stepped inside, aiming the beam around the large, dusty room. Floor boards from the second floor above groaned as footsteps pounded on them. Ryan hurried across the trash strewn floor to a rusty metal stairway in the corner and ran up to the second floor and headed down a dark hallway in the direction the footsteps had gone. He heard a shuffling noise in front of him and went through the doorway cautiously and stopped when he saw him crouching down in a corner by some empty shelves.

"I've been to twenty abandoned buildings today," Ryan said as if he were scolding a child, "looking for you."

"You scared me when you came in," Cleo said, standing up hesitantly.

"I didn't come here to scare you. I came to ask you for a favor." Ryan moved closer. "I need you to help me catch the Homeless Slasher."

"No! Uh-uh!" Cleo backed up into the corner.

"You won't be in any danger. I promise I'll protect you. All I want you to do is tell him something."

"Forget it! Don't wanna go near no slasher guy; he might start liking my throat. I'm not listening no more!" Cleo stuck a finger in each ear. "Go away!"

"You just have to tell him one thing. It'll only take ten seconds."

"No." Cleo closed his eyes and began humming.

"Don't worry," Ryan said, raising his voice, "you'll approach him in public so he can't do anything to you."

Cleo hummed louder.

"It won't work, Cleo, I'll just speak louder," Ryan shouted, leaning closer. "I need you to do this for me. The Slasher probably observed your buddy Hector Lopez for days or weeks before he killed him, so he must know who you are. Maybe he even talked to you once or twice. He won't suspect a trap if you set him up for it."

Cleo kept humming.

Ryan grabbed onto Cleo's wrists and pulled his hands away from his ears. "More people will die if you don't help me!"

"Oww," Cleo said, stopping his humming. "You're hurting my ears. You don't have to shout."

"OK," Ryan said in a normal tone. "I could have come here and tricked you into helping me but I'm not going to. I'd feel guilty if you helped me because I lied or offered you a bribe."

"What's a bribe?"

"It's when you offer someone a gift for doing something."

Cleo looked thoughtful. "Bribes don't sound so bad."

Chapter Thirty-seven

Do you realize," Lydia asked, "that in a few minutes we may find out what the Homeless Slasher looks like?"

"I hate to sound negative," Augie said, peering over the steering wheel as the windshield wipers brushed away the soft rain, "but the message you got from this Isaac guy is pretty vague. He supposedly has something important to tell you, but how do you know it's about the Slasher?"

"Because when we were interrupted at the shelter yesterday he was trying to remember who he'd seen Bible Bob talking to in Garfield Park. Maybe he'll give us some descriptions and one of those people could be the Slasher."

"Why can't you wait until he comes to the shelter again?"

"Because this is too important. That's why I asked around to find out where he's been staying." She squinted out the rain streaked passenger window. "I want to talk to him as soon as possible."

"Well at least we don't have to worry about your stalker shooting at us," Augie shook his head, "although in this neighborhood somebody else might."

She glanced at him. "Are you sorry you volunteered to come along?"

"Not at all. Where we're going isn't a very safe place for you to be wandering around by yourself at night." He turned the van onto a side street lined with dark, ominous buildings. "Besides," he said, pausing to clear his throat. "I have a little surprise planned for later."

"What?"

"Well, I hope I don't sound like Martin, who never stops hitting on you, but I made some dinner reservations for us tonight at a certain romantic gourmet restaurant."

"Seriously?"

"Yes, definitely, and if you have a good time we can do it again soon." Augie drummed his fingers on the steering wheel. "We've worked together for a while now and we get along so well. I thought it might be fun to get to know each other in a different setting."

Lydia stared at him for a long moment. "I'm very flattered that you want to take me out to dinner, Augie, but I can't accept your invitation."

"Well, if you already have plans we can make it some other night."

"No, I can't," Lydia said carefully. "Augie, you're my friend and mentor, but I wouldn't be comfortable going out with you. It may be hard to understand but at this point in my life, I don't want to go out with anyone." She immediately thought of Ryan and realized her statement wasn't quite true.

"I see." Augie slumped down in his seat. "I must have been temporarily insane to think you'd go out with me, but

I remember you said you'd be eternally grateful to whoever found the guy who was stalking you."

"I am grateful for your help, Augie. I'm just not ready to change our relationship."

"I don't blame you," he said bitterly. "I'm an ugly guy. If I were you I wouldn't want to be seen with me."

Lydia looked at him with surprise. "I don't consider you ugly."

"Of course I am," he said, his voice rising slightly. "My nose is too big, my ears stick out, and my hair's too curly. I look like some kind of demented cartoon character."

"I disagree," Lydia said sincerely. "When I look at you I see an intelligent, idealistic person who I greatly admire. Besides, I think it's pathetic that our society places so much emphasis on physical appearance."

"Me too, for obvious reasons."

"Augie, you know I'd never lie to you, right?"

"Yeah."

"Then believe me, I think you look fine and I greatly respect you. Now, how about if we just forget we ever had this conversation and are friends forever?"

Augie hesitated and then smiled. "Good idea. Let's forget all this and find the Slasher, just like I found your stalker."

"Yes, at least I hope you found him."

"What do you mean?"

"I have some doubts now that Al Wilson was stalking me."

"Why?"

"Martin said a street person came in this morning who knew Al Wilson well. Wilson had apparently told him on several occasions that he would never set foot in our shelter because for some irrational reason the sign on our building terrified him. I want to talk to this guy myself."

"But I saw Al Wilson in our shelter several times."

"Maybe it was someone else who looked like him."

"Maybe," Augie said doubtfully.

"Then there's the picture of me that was found on him. How did he end up with that?"

"He probably stole it from your apartment when he took that T-shirt he put in your office desk."

"I don't think so." Lydia frowned. "I have very few pictures and that wasn't one of them. I'm going back to the police to look at it again. If I can remember when and where that picture was taken I may have a new theory."

The street came to a dead end and Augie stopped the van. "They told you he lived in an abandoned building at the end of this street, but I see buildings on both sides."

"Then we'll search both of them. I'll take the one on the left."

Augie picked up a flashlight from the floor and grinned as he handed it to her. "Figures. You give me the one that looks like a haunted house."

"Mine doesn't look any better." Lydia stared out at the brick building with boarded up windows and graffiti spray painted all over the first floor.

"Yeah, but with my luck the Homeless Slasher is in my building looking out at me right now and deciding he'll pick me for his next victim."

"But you're not homeless."

"Neither was Bible Bob."

"Be careful." Lydia got out of the van, grateful the rain had stopped and that it was unseasonably warm, a record high temperature for this time of year.

As she approached the decrepit three-story building she wondered if there were any rats in it. Once as a child she had been terrified when she saw a rat scurry out from under her bed. Even now she shivered with revulsion whenever she saw one.

She stepped through the open doorway, tentatively pointing the flashlight around at the cement floor and grimacing as she saw dozens of huge cockroaches scramble for cover under a few rotting two-by-fours.

"Isaac?" She called out and waited for a response. "Isaac?" She heard a slight creaking noise from upstairs. "Isaac, this is Lydia from The Helping Hand."

She walked determinedly to the nearby stairs. Isaac should have answered, but what if he was sick or injured? She hurried up to the second floor and walked down the hallway, quickly scanning all the rooms with the beam of light and finding them empty.

Lydia wondered if this was how a shepherd felt on a dark night searching for one of his lost sheep. She had read Jesus' parable last night, about how happy a shepherd is when he finds his missing sheep, which illustrated how much joy there is in heaven when one person repents. Would God be happy if she returned to His sheepfold?

She went up to the third floor and worked her way down the hallway without finding anything and finally came to a closed door. She thought she heard a noise from behind it.

"Isaac?" She opened the door slowly. She aimed the flashlight into the room and several furry forms raced away towards a dark corner. She groaned with disgust and slammed the door shut and dropped her flashlight. The beam of light went out and she was in total darkness as she bent over and fumbled around until she finally found it and discovered the light wouldn't come back on. She walked down the hallway, touching the wall for guidance, firmly telling herself that she wouldn't panic again. She made her way downstairs in the darkness and hurried out of the building, relieved to see Augie waiting for her.

Augie was holding a cup of coffee and leaning against the van. "Looks like you didn't have much luck either."

"No luck." She handed him the flashlight. "I dropped it. I think it's broken."

"Don't worry about it." He reached into the van and brought out a thermos and poured some coffee into another cup. "Fortunately, I always travel with coffee. You look like you can use a cup."

"You're right, thanks." She accepted the cup from him and took a huge swallow. "Hopefully Isaac will show up at the shelter tomorrow."

"He must have found somewhere else to spend the night." Augie tossed the contents of his cup down onto the ground. "How about if I take you back to your car now?"

"Good idea." Lydia walked around to the passenger side and got in. "I wish our shelter was bigger."

"Me too." Augie started up the van and turned it around. "When you open your shelter someday you need to find a bigger building."

"I plan to," Lydia sipped her coffee, "and I hope you can give me some input when I start looking."

"Be happy to." Augie drove slowly down the street. "I'm not infallible, but at least my advice is free. In fact I made some mistakes in selecting our location."

"Like what?"

He chuckled. "You got a few hours?"

Lydia settled back into her seat and drank the rest of the coffee, staring out the window as Augie kept talking about the bureaucratic hassles he endured while opening The Helping Hand. She barely listened, thinking instead a series of disconnected thoughts about the murders, Bible Bob, and most of all, Ryan. Where was he tonight and why couldn't she stop herself from thinking about him and wishing they were together?

She felt a powerful drowsiness envelope her and she blinked rapidly to keep her eyes open. It seemed like everything inside the van was spinning slowly around and then suddenly began spinning much faster. She looked over at Augie who had apparently pulled over because his hands were off the steering wheel and he was watching her. She noticed anger in his eyes, something that had never been there before whenever he had looked at her. But it was there now, a fierce burning anger. She began to wonder why when suddenly everything stopped and she felt as if she was drifting helplessly in impenetrable darkness.

Chapter Thirty-eight

What if he kills me?" Cleo looked fearfully at the entrance door.

"He won't," Ryan said in a reassuring tone. "I'll only be a few feet away."

Cleo's lips quivered slightly. "This is a pretty weird idea you got."

"Do you remember what you're supposed to say to him?"

"Yeah, we gone over it a million times." Cleo stared at Ryan. "You look kinda spooky wearin' that mask."

"I don't want him to recognize me." Ryan adjusted the wool ski mask, wishing it didn't make his face itch so much. "Let's go, Cleo. The sooner we start the sooner we'll be finished."

"Finished." Cleo's eyes widened. "Like dead?"

"No, like accomplishing our goal." Ryan patted him on the shoulder. "Let's go in now."

"You sure you don't wanna come back tomorrow or somethin'?"

"You'll feel better after we're done."

Cleo looked at the door and moaned. "As soon as I see him I'll probably have to go to the bathroom."

Ryan pushed the door open and Cleo reluctantly went in ahead of him. The Helping Hand was more crowded than usual, all the tables in the eating area were full and some people were eating their meals standing up. Ryan didn't see Lydia anywhere and felt a sharp pang of regret. He hoped to see her before he left. She wouldn't recognize him with his mask on so he'd be able to watch her openly. He saw Martin in the TV area talking with someone and Carl came out of the kitchen carrying a tray of food. Ryan noticed Cleo had taken his hat off and was twisting it in his hands with a worried expression.

Carl set a platter of sandwiches on a nearby table. "Hey," one of the men sitting there said to him. "Where's Lydia today?"

"We don't know," Carl said. "She didn't call in sick and she's not at her apartment. We're all a little concerned."

Ryan cracked his knuckles and tried to think of a logical reason why Lydia hadn't come in for work or even called. It just wasn't like her.

Augie Rosen entered from the hallway and Ryan noticed Cleo's face was twitching. Augie stopped by an elderly man, affectionately clapping him on the shoulder and talking to him quietly. Cleo put his hat back on and looked at Ryan with a pleading expression but Ryan shook his head. Cleo nodded as if he'd expected a negative response and walked slowly towards Augie.

Ryan went over to the TV area and sat down in a chair that was near Augie. He touched the outline of his .38 tucked under his pants belt and well hidden by the heavy coat he was wearing. He watched Cleo approach Augie as the elderly man walked away smiling. Cleo stood in front of Augie, his face contorted with apprehension. Don't run, Ryan said to himself, hang in there, Cleo.

Cleo mumbled something inaudible.

"What did you say?" Augie asked him in a friendly tone.

Cleo looked down at the floor and mumbled again.

"I'm sorry friend, but I can't hear you."

Cleo looked up at him. "I was just sayin'," Cleo said in a loud voice, "that I saw you kill Hector Lopez!"

Augie stared at him. "What are you talking about?"

Cleo took a step backwards. "In the building," Cleo said in a quieter tone, "where Hector lived near Humboldt Park. I saw you that night from across the hallway. You cut his throat with a knife."

Augie's mouth dropped open. "You're talking non-sense."

"I'm livin' there now," Cleo's voice quivered, "and I promise I won't tell anybody if you promise never to hurt me."

Augie glanced around, noticing that a few people nearby were watching curiously. "What's your name?"

"Cleo."

"OK, Cleo," he said politely. "Why don't you calm down and I'll get you some hot chocolate then we'll go back in my office and talk over this little misunderstanding of yours."

"No." Cleo flinched and took a few more steps backward.

"It's all right. You have nothing to be afraid of. No one is going to hurt you."

"Are you gonna promise not to kill me?"

"You're babbling, my friend." Augie moved forward and tried to put his hand on Cleo's shoulder.

"No!" Cleo turned and sprinted away, bumping into several people before he ran out the front door.

Augie shrugged at the onlookers. "The poor guy hallucinates. He needs his medicine."

Ryan looked away from Augie and remained seated as his pulse pounded wildly. He'd wait a few minutes to leave so it wouldn't be obvious he was going to follow Cleo. Judging from Augie's reaction most people wouldn't have believed Cleo's accusation, but Ryan knew differently. Augie was the one. Hector Lopez had scrawled "One that takes" over the drawing he'd made of the Homeless Slasher and may have been referring to Augie as the antithesis of a giving social worker. Sally Malloy had said he was supposed to be good, which could point to the same occupation, but the most important clue was when Sally had told him he could be found by thinking of Malibu Beach and the end of summer. When he learned the Slasher had mentioned a shelter on California Avenue to some homeless men in Garfield Park, the meaning of that statement suddenly occurred to him. Malibu Beach was in California and The Helping Hand was on California Avenue. Augie's complete first name was Augustus. The last full month of summer was August.

Sally Malloy was not a logical thinker, and since she was too frightened to reveal the killer's identity any clues she gave would be difficult to figure out. Without any incriminating evidence it was just a theory, but Ryan was determined to prove that Augie was the Slasher. He knew that the next part of his plan could fail; Augie was extremely intelligent and therefore might do something unexpected. All the various possibilities of how Augie might react made him dizzy just thinking about it, and even though he should be pleased that Cleo's confrontation had gone so well, one disturbing question kept interrupting his thoughts. Where was Lydia?

Chapter Thirty-nine

The worst part was waiting and wondering what Augie would do to her when he returned, if he ever did. Lydia stubbornly pulled at the handcuffs as hard as she could, ignoring the flaring pain from her bruised and swollen wrists. The metal handcuffs on both wrists were attached to a pipe under a cast iron sink in the small dingy utility room of an abandoned building. She knew it was probably impossible to break free but giving up meant certain death. Her feet were tied together but she swung them around and pushed hard against the sink, arching her back and grinding her teeth as the handcuffs dug further into her wrists. She paused to catch her breath which was exceedingly difficult because the tape across her mouth only allowed her to breathe through her nose.

Whenever she stopped struggling fear almost strangled her. It seemed logical that Augie was either going to come back and kill her or simply leave her to starve or freeze to death. She shivered and continued to rapidly inhale the damp air through her nose. Fortunately, she was still wearing her coat and the warmer temperature last night had been a near record, or she might already be dead. She wondered what part of the city she was in as she looked around the dark room for the hundredth time still seeing only four bare walls, a closed door and a pile of rags in the corner. The only sounds she heard were from the rats scurrying around inside the walls. The crack of light under the door was brighter now so she assumed it was daylight.

Lydia had never felt so alone. She knew it was by choice, though. She always had the option of praying, even in an abandoned building. She wondered how different her life would have been if she hadn't turned away from God. What if instead, she thought, I had turned to Him for help? Maybe He would have eased the pain.

Her back ached and she tried to shift her weight in a futile attempt to get more comfortable. I'm in pain now, she thought, but it will only get worse. I'm going to die here. I can't take this much longer.

She remembered her grandmother used to say you can do all things through Him who'll strengthen you or something like that. I need strength, she said to herself, and I need help and time is running out. Maybe it's time now, it's got to be now or never.

She bowed her head and prayed silently, *Lord, you know I became a Christian when I was little. I'm sorry now that I blamed you for my mom's death. Please forgive me.*

Lydia raised her head and looked around the dingy room and smiled. What an unlikely place to have reconciliation with God. Better here than nowhere, she thought, and now what would happen?

What else? She bowed her head and prayed again, *Lord, please get me out of here. Please help me.* Lydia hesitated for a moment, *but if that's not your will I still need your help. Give me the strength to die with courage,* Lydia paused again, *and please help Ryan, wherever he is.*

She heard a faint sound and her body tensed as she listened to distant footsteps from somewhere inside the building. If it wasn't Augie it might be someone who would free her. She began rattling the handcuffs on the pipe loudly, stamping her feet on the ground, and moaning as loud as she could through the tape over her mouth.

"Hello?" An indistinct voice called out softly from beyond the door and Lydia rattled the handcuffs even louder. "Where are you?" the voice called. "Is that you, Lydia?"

The door burst open and Augie stood there with a sardonic grin. "Sorry to disappoint you, but it's only me."

Lydia stopped making noise and slumped against the cold, hard sink as Augie approached her.

"Lydia, it didn't have to end this way." He stood over her shaking his head. "You have only yourself to blame, though. This is all your fault." He crouched down in front of her and she pressed back under the sink. "It's a shame though, it really is." He reached out and softly caressed her hair. "You are so pretty, Lydia. Martin always talked openly about how attractive you are but I deliberately kept my opinion to myself," he paused, "until now."

She flinched as he dropped his hand down to her neck and she lashed out with her bound feet, kicking him in the knee and knocking him backwards.

He chuckled as he stood up and rubbed his knee. "Still playing hard to get, aren't you," his grin faded quickly, "although I've followed you some nights when you met with that Ryan guy. Are you in love with him?" He moved closer but stayed out of range of her feet. "I had to hide my feelings for you then but now I don't. And now I get to decide what to do with you. There are a few interesting options, but first, we'll talk." He leaned forward and quickly ripped the tape off her mouth.

Lydia's lips stung as if they'd been scalded. "Augie," she said, her voice cracking with anger, "you better let me go right now."

Augie snorted derisively. "That's not possible."

She licked her sore lips. "Why are you doing this to me?"

"You mean with all the time you've had to think about it, you haven't figured it out yet?"

"You're the one," Lydia said accusingly. "You've been sending me the notes all along."

"Congratulations," he said sarcastically. "I knew you had it in you."

"You sent the notes," Lydia said bitterly, "and you left the dead kitten on my doorstep and put the bloody T-shirt in my desk and all the other sick things."

"And don't forget I shot up your car. That was my biggest gamble but I got away with it."

She looked at him with amazement. "You framed a homeless man so the police would think he was the one."

Augie smiled. "That was certainly brilliant. All along I intended to find someone I could frame."

"You murdered an innocent man."

"Oh, no," he said, pacing back and forth in a small area. "I didn't murder him. That was the part fate played. One of our regulars told me about a street person who lived like a hermit in an abandoned warehouse. I actually went there to see if I could help but when I found him, he was dead. I realized then it was an ideal opportunity to complete the final part of my plan. So I planted a picture of you on him, along with all the other things and of course, I lied about having seen him at our shelter and suspecting him as your stalker. I didn't have to worry about the police being suspicious because the autopsy would show he died of natural causes."

"I can't believe what you've done, Augie."

"You don't know me as well as you thought. Most of us never really know what others think and feel, even though we all like to believe we do." He moved closer. "But like I said earlier, you have only yourself to blame."

"Why, Augie?" She shouted. "Why is all this my fault?"

"Because you didn't turn to me. If you had, then none of this would have happened." He jabbed a finger at her. "I sent the notes and left the dead kitten and did everything else to scare you enough that you'd need my help. It was my dream that when you turned to me our relationship would blossom into something deeper, but even after you finally told me and the others what was going on you still refused most of my suggestions. So I knew if I wanted to impress you I had to find someone to frame. I figured then I'd be a hero in your eyes." He laughed bitterly. "Then last night when you wouldn't even accept my invitation to dinner I knew I was wrong. You could never be attracted to me."

"And that's why you drugged my coffee?"

"No. I probably would have just taken you back to your car and kept hoping for the impossible." He shrugged with regret. "You'd still be free except that you told me you were going back to look at the picture I planted on that dead guy. I was afraid you might remember that I took that picture of you a couple of months ago when I brought my camera to the shelter. I couldn't gamble that you or the police wouldn't figure it out. Too much is at stake."

"I still don't understand, Augie. We were friends and co-workers. We had a terrific relationship. Why wasn't that enough for you?"

"Because I wanted more." He began pacing again, faster than before. "Not only are you beautiful, you're the most honest, idealistic woman I've ever met. I wanted to do more than just work with you for a year or so, I wanted to spend the rest of my life with you," he paused, "and I wanted you to love me like I love you."

"Augie, I've been thinking while you were gone," Lydia said carefully. "I know how we can resolve this situation."

"Really?" He smiled and moved towards her.

"No!" Lydia recoiled and moved as far as the handcuffs allowed. "Listen to me. I've worked out a perfect solution for both of us."

"Oh?" He frowned. "And what solution is that?"

"You've made some mistakes but I'm willing to forgive you," she said, trying to sound positive. "If you let me go now and agree to a few conditions then I won't press charges."

He stood up and folded his arms. "What conditions?"

Lydia swallowed hard. "You must agree to regular counseling, and I'll select the doctor. I'll go to work at a different shelter until I open my own someday. You have to agree to never come near me or follow me again." She paused. "That's it. If you agree to this and let me go, then the police will never know what happened." She looked up at him with sincerity. "You know I don't lie. I give you my word you won't have to go to jail."

"I had a feeling I wouldn't like your conditions."

"I'll never tell anyone, I promise."

"But you'll always remember," his eyes hardened, "and I'll have to live without seeing you, always knowing that you despise me."

"I won't despise you if you let me go. It's the only solution."

"No. There's one other solution." He reached inside his coat and pulled out a long knife.

"Augie," she said as calmly as possible. "Put that away and take these handcuffs off."

"That's not going to happen."

"It can if you want it to. Put that knife away now."

He gently fondled the blade. "I'm sorry, Lydia. I really am."

"You're deluding yourself. You won't be able to use that on me, you've never killed anyone before."

"You're so wrong." He laughed harshly and crouched down, holding the knife in front of her face. "I've killed many people with this knife." He paused. "I'm the Home-less Slasher."

Chapter Forty

All Ryan had to do now was wait. He had read something about waiting last night. Wait on the Lord and have wings like eagles or something like that. Ryan shifted his position on the blankets and leaned against the wall. The windowless room he had chosen was up on the second floor so he would have plenty of warning when Augie entered the abandoned building. He'd smashed numerous bottles downstairs and scattered the pieces around to make sure he'd hear him enter. He sat in total darkness in a corner with his .38 next to him on the blankets. He had a flashlight on his lap, but he wouldn't turn it on until the moment Augie stepped through the doorway.

Cleo had said he lived in this building, so Augie would be coming here tonight to kill him. He really had no choice once Cleo said he'd seen him kill Hector Lopez, but when Augie arrived it would be the worst mistake he ever made.

Ryan pulled off Cleo's baseball cap and scratched his head. He knew it wasn't necessary to wear Cleo's hat and coat but it added a certain theatrical touch to capturing the Homeless Slasher. When he'd dropped Cleo off at his apartment he was reluctant to part with his coat but Ryan promised to buy him a new one and that made him happy. Ryan frowned, wondering what Cleo was doing at the moment and if he'd obey his stern command to stay there until he returned, but this wasn't the time to think about Cleo, conjure up an imaginary theater audience, or pine for a drink. It was time to stay awake and ready, or die.

It was easy to block out all those other thoughts, but not about Lydia. He groaned in frustration, wishing he could stop thinking about her for a few hours, just until he captured Augie. But he couldn't stop wondering why she hadn't been at The Helping Hand that morning. She loved her work and was so incredibly conscientious; it didn't make sense that she wouldn't show up without even calling to explain why. Carl had said she wasn't at her apartment. What had happened to her?

It was 6:30. He pulled out his cell phone and called Lydia's apartment but only got her answering machine again. He tried her cell phone and only got her voice mail. He called The Helping Hand and was told she wasn't there. Maybe he should leave and go look for her. Then again, what if Augie happened to show up while he was gone? *It would be just your luck, to ruin everything.*

Ryan idly tapped the handle of his .38. After he'd caught Augie and coerced a confession from him he'd make some phone calls and search for her. Then, when he found her he'd tell her the exciting details of how he'd trapped the Slasher. Maybe that would convince her that he had some worth as a human being. Maybe she'd even be impressed enough to consider having an ongoing relationship. *Don't count on it,* the voice whispered with sadistic glee.

Ryan vigorously scratched his head again, suddenly wondering if Cleo's hat contained any lice. If it did it was too late now. What if he left for a couple of hours? Maybe Augie wouldn't show up until later, but what if he was already out there watching the building? If Augie spotted him leaving and recognized him then the entire plan was destroyed. Lydia would agree that trapping the Slasher took precedence over anything else. Except, he thought to himself, I'm more concerned about her.

He turned on the flashlight, reached into his pocket, and pulled out a quarter. He studied it intently for a moment. Heads, he thought to himself. He flipped the coin up into the darkness and heard it land on the floor with a soft thud. If it was heads he would go look for her. He stood up and aimed the beam of light at it. It was tails.

Lydia knew he was going to kill her, when he told her he was the Homeless Slasher it had finalized everything. He wouldn't let her go now, even if she kept promising not to tell anyone. Of course her initial strategy of a compromise was completely ruined. Her only hope now was to escape and to do that she needed to immediately create a brilliant plan.

She considered her limited options and decided if she convinced him to take off her handcuffs it would be a good start. Her mouth was dry and her throat tightened as she looked at the knife he held in his hand and wondered with morbid fascination what the blade would feel like when he slashed it across her throat.

"Lydia, are you listening to me?" Augie asked her impatiently, sitting a few feet away.

"Yes. Of course," she said, having not paid any attention for several minutes. She realized though that she had to keep him talking, as long as he talked she'd be safe. In the meantime she had to fight off the fear that threatened to paralyze her and figure out a way to escape. "It's just that my wrists hurt so much it's hard to concentrate on what you're saying."

"Try harder."

"I have been, but I'm in too much pain to listen."

"You're going to have to, so quit whining."

Lydia frowned. "I do believe you now, that you are the Homeless Slasher."

"It's about time."

She hesitated. "Do you know what surprises me the most?"

"No."

Lydia took a deep breath. "That you're such a coward. I never knew you were one until now."

"What do you mean?"

"You have to admit it is cowardly to murder defenseless people."

"No." His eyes narrowed with anger. "Every time I kill I risk being seen, and if they catch me I'll get the death penalty. A coward wouldn't risk his own life."

"But you're acting like one right now," Lydia said confidently, ignoring the pain as her stomach tightened from fear.

"How?"

"By keeping me handcuffed. You're obviously afraid I'll try to escape or something. Even though you have a knife and are twice my size you're scared of me."

"I'm not scared of you."

"Sure you are. If I wasn't in such pain I'd probably laugh."

"You'll just have to endure the pain a little while longer."

"Why can't I be a little more comfortable before I die? I'll be able to pay attention better."

"You better pay attention regardless of how uncomfortable you are."

"I can't, my wrists hurt too much."

"Too bad." He slapped the floor with his hand. "Now, I'll continue my explanation. It's probably . . ."

"Excuse me," she interrupted, "but if you just set me free for a moment so I can rub my wrists I'm sure I'll be able to concentrate better. After a few minutes you can put the handcuffs back on."

"I'm tired of being interrupted."

"Then why not take these off? Unless you really are scared of me."

She flinched as he got up and knelt down in front of her and inserted a key into the handcuffs. "Lydia, I've taken psychology courses and I know you're playing mind games with me, but I'm taking these off anyway; for two reasons."

"Thank you." Lydia pulled her stiff arms forward and rubbed at her numb wrists. "What are your two reasons?"

Augie pointed at her with the knife as he crouched next to her. "First of all, I want you listening to me and not complaining or interrupting because you've got to understand why I've done all this." He paused with a serious expression.

"Secondly, if you suddenly realize you're in love with me you'll be free to hug me."

Lydia recoiled against the sink. "That won't happen."

"I know, I was only joking," Augie said, shaking his head. "You were never attracted to me before, how could you be now?" He reached out and grabbed her chin firmly. "But don't forget no matter what I decide to do, you won't be able to stop me." He released her chin and got up, moving back to the center of the room. "Now, are you ready to pay attention?"

"Yes," she answered softly, her heart vibrated wildly as she stretched her arms upward. She knew she had to convince him to untie her feet now, and then she'd have a chance.

"I want you to understand why I had to start killing the homeless." He began to pace in a small circle. "It's not like it used to be, ten or fifteen years ago. Do you know what I'm talking about?"

"Do you mean this country's attitude?"

"Exactly." He nodded at her, impressed. "Everyone is less sympathetic towards the homeless now. Most people believe they're all lazy alcoholics. They don't see what we do; the children, the families, the mentally ill, and the unemployed who want to work. Homeless people are no longer a hot topic in the news media. National apathy has set in."

"And you're trying to change that."

"Yes, I'm desperate to change it, aren't you?" He gestured wildly with his arms. "You see the despair in their eyes everyday too! I know it bothers you!"

"Yes it does."

"As long as I'm front page news they can't be ignored." His voice cracked slightly. "The life story of every one of my victims is read all across the country. Everyone is forced to see that there are still too many poor and needy people out there. Hopefully, those who have a conscience will want to help."

"Thanks to you."

"Yes. I'm risking my life to show this country that the homeless problem hasn't gone away."

"Augie, my legs are cramping up." Lydia rubbed at her calves. "Could you take this rope off and let me stand up? Please?"

"Lydia, I hope you're not planning something foolish like trying to escape."

"I doubt I can even walk, how could I escape? I just need to stand up for a few minutes."

"No."

"I can't listen to you when I'm in this much pain."

"You're really testing my patience."

"I'm sorry, because I really want to listen to you." She hesitated. "I agree with some of the things you said. I want to hear more."

He looked at her for a moment. "All right then." He moved over to her and cut the rope off with his knife. "I want you to lean against the wall. If you try to run away it's all over for you."

"Thank you, Augie." Lydia stood up on her unsteady legs, surprised at how weak she felt. She leaned against the cold wall, wondering if she'd be able to move quickly when the opportunity presented itself. I'll move fast, she told herself, I'll have to.

"Now that you're more comfortable," he said, resuming his pacing, "you can give me some advice. What else can I do to convince the American public that homelessness needs to be eradicated?"

"Well, you can make suggestions." She felt slightly dizzy and was annoyed at herself because she knew it was from fear.

"I have been. With every victim I leave a page from that book on the homeless and circle a key word or phrase."

"But maybe you need to leave a letter so you can give more details. Instead of just circling 'more low income housing' you can explain why that would alleviate part of the problem."

"Not bad." He nodded. "I have some ideas that aren't mentioned in that book. For example, the federal government thinks the cities and states should spend more on the homeless, but they want Washington to handle it. The only thing they all agree on is wishing the general public would help more. There needs to be a national consensus of how the costs are divided up."

"You're right." Lydia's heart throbbed so hard it felt like it would explode. She had to try something soon, before he was finished talking.

"And better job training and counseling is needed."

"That's true."

"And we need new laws for institutionalizing the mentally ill street people. Too many of them can't take care of themselves." He stopped and smiled at her. "There's something else I'm trying to teach the public. Can you guess what it is?"

"I don't know."

"Lydia, Lydia." He looked disappointed. "All you have to do is pick up a newspaper any morning and read about wars, famines, robberies, husbands killing wives, and political scandals. It's depressing enough to make you up-chuck your breakfast, and do you know why all these things are happening?" He paused and jabbed a finger at her. "I'll tell you why! It's because most people only care about themselves. They don't care enough about their fellow human beings. Selfishness. That's the main problem in this world."

"I agree, Augie, but is killing the homeless really going to change that?"

"I can only hope the publicity will convince some people to help the poor and the homeless. Maybe that'll give them enough satisfaction that it will carry over into their relationships with others. Sally Malloy, as confused as she was, tried to influence people to be kinder. I'd love to see a chain reaction begin some day with one person overcoming their selfish nature long enough to help another and then that person helps someone else and a tidal wave of human kindness starts building up. I know it sounds far fetched but it's a noble dream to strive for."

Augie was pacing in a small circle and sometimes came within a few feet of her. Lydia decided her only option was to suddenly lunge at him when he came near and shove him hard enough that he'd lose his balance for a second while she sprinted towards the door. Then she'd have to run out of the building before he caught up. She didn't know what neighborhood they were in so she'd just have to hope there would be some people or cars passing by when she got outside.

"Augie, there's something I still don't understand," she said, thinking that it would help to distract him. "How can you justify murdering innocent people?"

His eyes widened. "Haven't you been listening? They're all dying for a worthy cause!" His voice rose and a large blue vein protruded on his neck. "I pick my victims very carefully; most of them were helpless and would have died soon anyway! Remember Hector Lopez? He was out of his mind with grief and had a cough and a fever; he would have died of pneumonia this winter. Burt Wojik was incontinent and incapable of caring for himself. Another one of my early victims told me beforehand his life was so miserable that he wanted to die. All of the others led pathetic, unhappy lives."

She felt adrenaline pumping throughout her body and hoped it would give her the strength to push him hard. "What about Sally Malloy?"

"Sally believed evil spirits were communicating with her, does that sound normal to you? Besides, I had her and Burt set up to be a double killing one night. I told him where to find a new coat and told her that the spirits wanted her to be in a certain alley at a certain time. She apparently hid and saw me kill Burt and when she told me that later I had no choice."

Lydia decided it would help to already have her hands out in front when she charged him so she extended her arms and casually rubbed one of her wrists. "What about Bible Bob?"

"That's different. Late one night in Garfield Park I was talking to a potential victim and realized someone was eavesdropping. I turned around and Bible Bob was standing there. I could tell from his expression he'd heard enough to suspect me. So, I had to kill him to protect myself. It was unfortunate because I really respected him, but no individual life is more important than what I'm accomplishing."

"Even my life, Augie?"

"Yes," he said sadly as he continued to pace. "Believe me I wish it could be otherwise, but it can't. You should understand that by now."

"But I don't."

"Seriously?" He raised his eyebrows. "You should realize I have no choice." He circled closer to her. "I can't let you turn me in . . ."

Lydia dove forward and pushed hard against his shoulder and he spun backwards, almost falling over. She ran around him and sprinted through the open doorway and raced down the long hallway towards a stairway, moaning as she pumped her stiff arms and legs as fast as she could. Behind her she heard Augie yelling angrily as he ran out of the room and chased after her, his shoes pounding heavily on the hard floor. It sounded like he was gaining on her.

Chapter Forty-one

Ryan waited impatiently as the phone rang six times before he finally heard Martin's voice. "Helping Hand."

"Yes, is Lydia there yet?"

"No, I'm sorry she's not."

"Have you heard from her today?"

"No. Who is this?"

"A friend of hers. Do you have any idea where she is?"

"No, I wish I did."

"When was the last time you talked to her?"

"Before I left last night."

"Is Augie there?"

"No." Martin sounded annoyed. "Listen, we're in the middle of dinner and we're short handed and I don't have time to talk."

Ryan hung up and put his cell phone down. He knew he should stay in the abandoned building and wait for Augie. He picked up the phone and quickly dialed Lydia's number

324 • Kindness Kills

and again got her voice mail. Where was she? He dialed information and asked for Augie Rosen's home number. He then quickly dialed but there was no answer there either.

He was convinced something bad had happened to Lydia, and the mere thought of her being in danger made him feel physically ill. The problem was she could be anywhere in Chicago. How would he find her? Unless of course someone at the shelter might have seen her leaving last night or she'd mentioned where she was going, but if he went there now to ask around it might ruin his chance to trap Augie.

"Lydia, can you understand what I'm saying?"

Lydia opened her eyes and saw Augie's face, which seemed blurry and out of focus even though he was close to her. Behind him the room appeared to be tilted and when she tried to move her arms the handcuffs dug into her wrists. She remembered making it downstairs and sprinting towards the front door when she was tackled from behind and her head banged down on the cement floor. She must have blacked out because she didn't remember being brought back to the same room from which she'd just escaped.

"Answer me, Lydia." He slapped the side of her face.

She glared at him, her vision suddenly clearing as if her anger had pushed away the fog that had enveloped her. "I'm listening."

"Good." He nodded with satisfaction. "You better listen carefully before it's too late." He stood up and began pacing again. "No one really knows me. I've been hiding things all my life. I used to be one of them, you know."

"Who?"

"The poor, the homeless."

"Really?" She struggled to concentrate, ignoring the pounding pain inside her head. To stay alive she had to keep him talking. "But you've always said you came from a wealthy family back East. You've told us a lot of funny stories about how selfish and materialistic they are."

"My parents were always poor." He smiled sadly. "My dad was an alcoholic who couldn't keep a job, and we lived in a seemingly endless parade of dumpy apartments right here in Chicago. He left us when I was twelve. My mother was out of work so we ended up in a shelter downtown."

Lydia began shivering. I'm going to die, she thought, in a few minutes he'll cut my throat and there's nothing I can do to stop him.

"We'd lived in that shelter for a few months when my mother died one night of a brain aneurysm."

I want to stay alive, she told herself, and to do that I have to control my emotions and I have to keep him talking. "I'm sorry to hear that, Augie."

"It's OK." He shrugged. "I never felt any affection for her anyway. All she ever did was belittle me; nothing I did ever pleased her. After she died I took off and lived alone on the streets for a few months. After a while I learned that you don't even feel like a human being anymore, you feel more like a stray dog or cat that nobody cares about. When the weather got cold I turned myself in and lived in a series of foster homes, some of which were OK. I got some student loans to go to college and became a social worker." He paused and grinned. "I'm not boring you am I?"

"No," Lydia said quickly.

"Good." He moved closer. "Because our conversation is almost over."

326 • Kindness Kills

It can't be, she told herself; I'll find a way to keep him talking. "Augie, who was the first person you killed?"

His eyes brightened. "Now that's an interesting story."

She thought again about Ryan, fervently wishing she could tell him he was right about her. She had definitely let fear keep her from getting involved with him. She could no longer deny the affection and attraction she felt for him, ever since they'd argued she kept thinking about him.

"Would you like to hear about it?"

"Yes," she said enthusiastically, thinking she had to convince him not to kill her. There had to be a way.

"One summer during my college years I worked in a slaughterhouse." He laughed harshly. "Ironic isn't it? Anyway, I decided to find my beloved father. Remember him? The drunk who deserted us? I devoted all my spare time to playing detective and about a month later I found him. He was homeless, which I thought was very appropriate. He lived in a cardboard shack under a bridge, panhandling for booze money. When I saw him sitting in front of his flimsy shack I started shaking with anger and couldn't even speak. I had all this rage I wanted to vent at him and I'd already memorized a glorious speech designed to make him feel guilty. But as I stood there, paralyzed with fury, he started drooling and babbling nonsense at me. I realized he was completely insane, living in a world of his own, and he had no memory of any son. I walked away disgusted and feeling cheated out of my revenge, but later I had a flash of inspiration." He paused. "Can you guess what it was?"

"To kill him," she said, annoyed that her voice had quivered, telling herself that fear would not stop her now.

"That's right." He nodded, pleased. "I came back the next night and cut his throat with a knife. It was a beautiful moment and it gave me great satisfaction without any guilt. Because even though I was avenging all the misery he'd caused me, I was also doing him a favor. No one should have to go on living like he was." He pulled out the knife and touched it affectionately. "So now you know everything. There's nothing else to talk about."

"Sure there is. You haven't told me why you're killing the homeless."

"Of course I have. Haven't you been paying attention?"

"I mean the real reason."

"What are you talking about?"

"You love it." Lydia swallowed hard. "You can keep telling me you're doing this to help the homeless, but you know that's not the main reason. You've discovered killing people gives you pleasure, so much that you don't want to stop."

Augie stared at her for a moment. "You're very perceptive, Lydia. One of the many things I admire about you. It's true that I get an indescribable feeling of joy from all facets of these murders. The planning, the anticipation, the publicity, and the physical act itself. I do enjoy it, but I'm not sure I would do this if I wasn't helping a worthy cause."

"Yes you would."

"You'll never know for sure."

"I know you're a sick person, Augie. You need help."

Augie laughed. "You shouldn't insult a person who has a knife in his hand."

"Augie, you might as well put that away." Lydia said, staring at him confidently. "I just figured out why you can't kill me."

Chapter Forty-two

Ryan pushed open the front door of The Helping Hand and hurried inside, glancing around desperately at the large crowd that was eating dinner. Martin and Carl came out of the kitchen carrying platters of food but he didn't see Augie anywhere.

Ryan quickly walked over to the middle of the eating area and grabbed an empty chair and stood on it. "Hey!" He shouted loudly and the murmurs of conversation abruptly stopped. "Lydia Dupree is in some kind of trouble. Did any of you see her leave last night?" He paused expectantly, scanning the faces that silently stared at him with confusion or annoyance.

"Anyone?"

"Why don't you sit down and put a cork in it," an elderly man called out from a nearby table.

A few people laughed and Ryan glared at them. "Listen to me!" He shouted again. "Anyone who's met Lydia knows she's a special person and right now she needs our help." He paused. "So I'm asking you again. Was anyone here at closing time last night?"

He waited hopefully as the room full of faces stared back at him in silence.

"You're wrong, Lydia." Augie shook his head sadly. "I'm going to kill you now."

"You can't. Don't you remember? You said you love me."

"I do love you." He frowned, standing over her and slowly turning the knife in his hands. "But I have to kill you to protect myself and my noble crusade."

She wanted to scream but she fought back the urge and looked up at him defiantly. "How do you define love?"

"Well, I think love is caring about someone more than anything." He paused thoughtfully. "It means wanting to be with that person as much as possible and trying to do nice things for them so they'll be happy. It means never wanting to see them hurt."

"Is that how you feel about me?"

"Absolutely. Always have and always will."

"You're a liar."

He flinched. "No I'm not."

"Yes, you are! You just said if you love someone then you care about them more than anything and never want to see them hurt." She resisted the impulse to curl up into a fetal position and struggled to keep control of her shaky voice. "Don't you see how you're contradicting yourself? If you really love me you won't slash my throat!"

He slapped the handle of the knife against his open palm. "You don't understand!" His face reddened. "I don't want to kill you, but I have to. I have no choice."

"There's always a choice." She strained to breathe normally as her chest vibrated from her pounding heart. "If you murder me then that proves you never loved me."

"No. I'll never see it that way."

"I will," she said, her voice rising. "It will prove to me that you never loved me. I'll die believing your feelings were nothing more than a sick, twisted obsession that had nothing at all to do with love!"

"You're wrong!"

"That's what I'll believe! When you pull the blade across my throat I'll be thinking how phony you are. My last thought on earth will be that Augie Rosen never loved me."

"That's not true!" He moved closer and shook his knife at her.

"I'll die believing it!"

"No!"

"Yes, I will, Augie."

"Enough!" He hurried over to a corner and savagely kicked at a pile of rags. He slapped the wall with his hand and then paused for a moment to take some deep breaths. "Enough," he said in a softer voice as he turned and stared at her solemnly. "I don't care what you think, Lydia. You'll just have to die believing a lie."

"If you love me you should care what I think." She shivered violently and her teeth began to chatter. "You'll be haunted the rest of your life by my memory. You'll always remember that I never believed you loved me."

His eyes narrowed as he approached her and held up the knife. "Maybe I will suffer with that memory, but I'm willing to endure it to keep publicizing the plight of the poor and the homeless."

He's going to do it; Lydia thought to herself, there's nothing else I can say to stop him. I'll never get to see Ryan again. I won't be able to tell him how much I care. In a few moments I'll be with my mother and grandmother where there is no more death, grief, tears, or pain.

He knelt in down in front of her, holding the knife a few inches from her face. "It's time now, Lydia," he said quietly. "I'm sorry I have to do this."

"I don't believe you're sorry," she said bitterly. "You'll probably enjoy this as much as all your other murders." He reached out with his empty hand and held a strand of her hair, admiring it for a few seconds. She tossed her head back and the strand fell out of his hand. "Don't touch me like that."

"All right," he said with a somber expression. "I want this to be a pure and honorable act of duty."

"That's a joke," she said with disgust. Her entire body was shaking now, her heart and teeth were rattling away so hard it was difficult to talk. I won't give in to fear, she told herself, I shouldn't fear death.

"It will hurt if you struggle," he said in a calm voice, his breath warm on her face. "But if you close your eyes and keep still it'll be quick and painless."

She stared at him defiantly and then took a deep breath and raised her chin. "Go ahead," she said with a quivering voice. "Prove that you never loved me."

"I'm sorry you feel this way. But I have to do it."

It suddenly occurred to Lydia that dying a violent death had always been her biggest fear and if she could control herself in this last terrifying moment of life then that meant she would die defeating fear. For all eternity to come she'd be victorious over it. She quickly prayed for strength and self control. So as she felt the blade pressed against her throat she closed her eyes and fought back the urge to scream. She would die with courage.

Chapter Forty-three

Ryan awoke to the distant sound of crunching glass. He sat up in the darkness, his heart thumping wildly as he struggled to figure out where he was. As he shook off his drowsiness he remembered Lydia was in trouble, but no one at The Helping Hand knew where she had gone so he'd returned to the abandoned building to wait for Augie.

He heard more crunching sounds from downstairs. He couldn't believe he had fallen asleep when his own life depended on staying awake and alert. Sally Malloy had been murdered because he didn't stay awake the night he was with her in Grant Park. How could he be so careless and weak?

Augie continued to step on the broken glass he had scattered downstairs. Ryan grabbed his .38 with his right hand and his flashlight with his left. He would wait until Augie stepped through the door before turning on the flashlight.

"Hello?" A familiar man's voice called out from downstairs.

Ryan's stomach tensed and he gripped his gun tighter.

"Hello?" The man yelled again from downstairs. "Ryan, where are you hiding? Don't be scared! It's me, Cleo!"

Ryan groaned and leaped to his feet. "Cleo!" he shouted back. "What are you doing here?"

"You told me you'd be here at Hector's old place so I hitchhiked over." Cleo's voice drifted up to him. "I'm worried that the slasher guy will kill you."

"He won't kill me!" Ryan screamed. "But you might!"

"Why don't you leave and go tell the police about him?" Cleo shouted.

"Cleo, stay there! I'm coming downstairs!"

Ryan slid the .38 under his belt buckle and turned on the flashlight. "Why me?" he muttered to himself as he hurried out of the room and into the hallway.

"Oh, no!" Cleo yelled. "He's here! Run away, Ryan! Run away!"

Ryan raced down the stairs and stumbled as he reached the ground floor. He aimed the light towards the front door and saw Cleo gripped from behind by someone wearing a trench coat and hat. A knife was held against Cleo's throat.

"He's gonna kill me," Cleo said with a moan.

Ryan kept the light shining on them as he cautiously moved closer and saw that Augie was holding Cleo.

"I didn't expect this." Augie said. "I watched this place for a few hours and when I saw Cleo go in I assumed it was safe to come after him." He kept the knife at Cleo's throat while he shined his flashlight at Ryan and frowned. "You're Ryan. Lydia's friend."

"Yes."

"Well, I guess you're just in the wrong place at the wrong time," Augie said in a threatening tone.

"No, you are." Ryan pulled out his .38 and pointed it at him. "Let him go."

Augie dropped his flashlight and pressed the knife harder against Cleo's throat. "Put the gun down!" He shouted. "Do it now or your friend dies!"

Ryan hesitated, he used to shoot accurately but he hadn't practiced for years. If he took quick aim at Augie's head he might be able to kill him before he slashed Cleo's throat. Then again, he might miss.

"Put the gun down!" Augie screamed and Cleo moaned again.

Ryan thought of Lisa Thomas, the little girl he had accidentally shot, and how tiny and innocent she had looked wearing pajamas and lying face down in a pool of her own blood. If he shot and missed, then Cleo's death would be his fault, too.

"Put it down on the floor! Now!"

Ryan bent over and placed the gun on the floor.

"Good!" Augie shouted triumphantly. "Now stay where you are and kick it over towards me."

Ryan realized that once Augie had the gun there was no chance for them to escape. Near the front door there was a freight elevator shaft that he'd noticed when he'd entered the building earlier. He had looked down it and saw that it was open all the way down to the dark basement below.

"All right, Augie," he said calmly. "Just relax. I'll kick the gun to you now." He pulled back his foot and kicked the gun hard and it skittered across the floor and fell into the elevator shaft, clattering loudly as it landed in the basement below. "Sorry. I guess I have bad aim."

"Very clever," Augie snarled at him. "But it won't save either one of you."

Augie pulled the knife across Cleo's throat and Ryan charged forward and dove at him, but Augie threw Cleo down and leaped out of the way with surprising agility. Ryan fell onto the floor next to Cleo and immediately jumped up, ducking under the knife as it swept past him and barely missed his head. Ryan stepped back and the blade missed his face by an inch as Augie lunged at him and stumbled over Cleo's body.

Ryan backed up a few more steps and crouched down in anticipation of Augie's attack. Augie straightened up but instead of coming after him he moved off to the side and blocked the front doorway. Augie grinned and pointed the knife at Ryan. "I can't let you escape out the front door."

"I'm not going to run from you."

"OK, tough guy. We'll see how brave you are when I start slicing you up."

Ryan glanced around desperately but there were no boards or boxes nearby to grab and use as a weapon. "Augie, you disgust me!"

"I'm surprised you're insulting me. You should be more polite if you want me to tell you something very important. You see, I'm the only one who knows where your girlfriend Lydia is."

Ryan's legs trembled. "Where is she?"

"She's lying down, right where I left her." Augie held up his knife triumphantly. "I cut her throat with this very knife." He edged a little closer. "She was very brave. No screaming or pleading. She must have truly loved you. She died whispering your name."

Ryan suddenly felt like he was on fire from the uncontrollable rage that exploded within him. He screamed and charged at Augie, who quickly lowered himself for the impending collision. Ryan slammed his forehead into Augie's nose with a sickening crunch and simultaneously felt his ribs burn with searing pain as the blade slashed down his side.

Ryan's momentum drove Augie backwards and they both fell out the front door onto the sidewalk. Ryan rolled over Augie and landed in the street, as a passing car horn blared at him. Before he could get up Augie came at him and he felt the knife cut into his arm. Then Augie was suddenly on top of him slashing away wildly until Ryan finally grabbed hold of his wrist. They rolled over a few times and Ryan somehow held on. Augie pressed down hard with the knife and they pushed against each other with all their strength as a pair of headlights illuminated them and the deep sounding horn of a truck bellowed. Ryan kneed Augie in the stomach and in the same motion pulled down the hand holding the knife along the side of his head and used Augie's momentum to roll him over towards the middle of the street. As the truck rumbled by Ryan tightened his grip on Augie's wrist and thrust the hand with the knife in front of a huge wheel and Augie screamed as the tire ran over it.

Ryan released his wrist and watched Augie writhe in agony as he held up his crushed hand. The knife was lying next to Augie on the street and Ryan picked it up and grabbed him by the collar roughly and held the knife to his throat. "Now," Ryan snarled at him, "tell me where Lydia is!"

Ryan ran inside the abandoned building and stumbled over some broken crates as he sprinted for the stairs. He ran up the stairway, gasping huge gulps of air and ran down the hallway with his flashlight beam shining ahead. He turned into the utility room and saw Lydia handcuffed to a pipe under a cast iron sink. She was alive.

He hurried over to her and knelt down, carefully taking the tape off her mouth, noticing with concern how exhausted she looked.

"Oh," she said as he pulled the tape off the corner of her mouth. She licked her lips painfully. "Thank you." She looked up at him and smiled weakly. "I was praying you'd be the one to find me."

"Are you all right, Lydia?"

"Now I am."

"I was so upset," Ryan said, still struggling to catch his breath. "He told me he'd killed you. He lied, hoping I'd lose my temper and do something reckless which would make it easier for him to kill me."

"He was going to kill me," her smile faded, "but I kept saying that would only prove that he never loved me. So instead of murdering me himself he decided to leave me here to die of exposure or starvation as final proof of his love."

"The police will be here in a minute. They'll help me get these handcuffs off." He paused and swallowed hard. "I'm so glad you're alive."

"Me too." She closed her eyes for a second to ward off a wave of dizziness and then looked at him with curiosity. "It looks like our case is solved. What happens now?"

Chapter Forty-four

Tﾑhey better send out the salt trucks soon." Kevin Dolan squinted through his windshield at the huge snowflakes cascading onto his car as he slowly drove down the street. He glanced over at the passenger seat where Ryan sat. "Are you sure you're feeling OK, kid?"

"Never felt better," Ryan said truthfully as he stretched out his arms and only felt a mild stinging sensation from the minor wounds Augie had given him. "I'm glad I was wearing a heavy coat when we fought."

"How's that homeless guy doing today?"

"Cleo? He's getting better. Fortunately Augie missed a major artery when he slashed him."

"You must have hurried him when you charged at him."

"I guess so. I'm glad Cleo's alive, and I'm going to find him a nice place to live when he gets out of the hospital." Ryan looked at him. "Which reminds me, can I borrow a patrol car for an hour or so?"

"What for?"

"I promised Cleo he could drive one, with the lights and siren going. It's his biggest wish in life."

"I'm sorry I asked," Kevin Dolan rolled his eyes, "but I'll see what I can do."

"Thanks. You're welcome to ride with us."

"No way. I want to keep all my body parts intact."

"All right." Ryan grinned and then paused thoughtfully. "Did Augie tell you guys anything new today?"

"No, he already spilled his guts yesterday so he's got nothing more to tell." Kevin slowly turned the car onto another snow covered street. "Anyway, we would have nailed him even if he didn't confess. We'd have gotten a search warrant and hauled away a truck load of evidence from his apartment. He had a detailed diary, maps, pictures, you name it. He was dead meat and he knew it."

"He told me he wanted to influence the American public to have more sympathy for the poor and homeless and he expects to continue being front page news while he's in jail."

"He's a wacko dreamer." Kevin Dolan snorted in disgust. "Yesterday he was front page news across the country. Today he was just a back page story and tomorrow he'll be completely forgotten. People are already using his front page story to line the bottom of bird cages. I bet he didn't even change one person's opinion of the homeless." Kevin cleared his throat. "Enough about him. How about you?"

"What about me?"

"Well, I happened to have a little talk with the Chief. You're a celebrity now that you caught the Slasher. He says there shouldn't be any problem getting you restored to active duty again."

"Really?"

"Absolutely, and if you don't want to come back to the force I'm sure any private detective agency in town would be glad to have you."

"That's nice."

"Well, here we are." Kevin stopped the car in the middle of the street. "So what are you gonna do, kid?"

Ryan opened the door and stepped out into the street. "I'm going to keep you in suspense for a while."

"Suit yourself." Kevin leaned towards him. "I just want to tell you something, Ryan. I'll only say it once though because I don't want you getting arrogant." He paused. "I'm proud to be your uncle and if your old man was still alive he'd be proud of you, too."

"Thanks. I appreciate that." Ryan nodded at him and closed the car door, glancing up at the soft, cold snowflakes floating down on him. Today will be a wonderful day; he thought to himself. From now on every day can be wonderful. He waited for his familiar inner voice to contradict him but instead there was only silence. For once his entire mind and being was at peace and in complete agreement.

He stepped over to the sidewalk and paused as he saw the theater seats again, thousands of them lined up in front of him as far as he could see. The seats were all filled and the huge crowd rose in unison and began enthusiastically applauding and cheering. He recognized a little African-American girl in the front row, now whole and unharmed as if he had never accidentally shot her. Her mother stood next to her and they both smiled at him and applauded as if he were completely forgiven. Ryan smiled back at them and then opened the door to The Helping Hand and went inside.

A homeless man hurried up to him as he came through the doorway. "Give me five, bro'!" Ryan gave him a high five and the man turned and shouted to the others seated at nearby tables. "Hey, this here's the dude that caught the Homeless Slasher!"

They all began applauding and Ryan noticed that even Martin joined in. Then he saw Lydia standing by the kitchen door and he walked over to her.

Lydia watched Ryan approach and decided it was time to be honest with him as well as herself. She moved towards him and put her arms around his neck and kissed him affectionately for a long moment as the crowd cheered in approval.

"Come on, let's talk," she said, taking his hand and pulling him towards the kitchen.

She closed the kitchen door behind them and turned to him. "Guess what? I'm not angry."

"I figured that." Ryan grinned. "You wouldn't have kissed me if you were in a bad mood."

"I mean I'm not angry at God anymore. I prayed to Him the other night and I know He welcomed me back. It's just like the parable Jesus told about the father welcoming home his repentant, prodigal son. In some ways I'm like that son." She smiled at him. "Someday when I'm in heaven He'll explain to me about my mom's death. My anger is gone."

"I'm glad to hear that. So what are you going to do now that you've returned to the sheepfold?"

"Trust Him and try to make up for lost time. I want to find out what He wants me to do with the rest of my life." She looked at him with curiosity. "How do you feel now that you're a Christian?"

He put his hands on his stomach. "I feel the same. About one eighty-five."

She patted him on the shoulder playfully. "Come on."

"There is no guilt."

"You're sure?"

"Jesus said if you believe in Him you're forgiven. He didn't mention my name as an exception."

"That's great. So now what?"

"I want to learn more about being a Christian, and like you I want to find out what to do with my life." He shrugged. "But in the meantime I need to find a job. I heard a rumor that you have some openings here."

Lydia's eyes widened. "Are you serious?"

"Definitely. I might as well get a job where I'm helping others. Plus, I make a mean omelet."

"The pay is terrible and the hours are long."

"Sounds perfect. When do I start?"

"How about now?" Lydia gestured to a counter stacked with loaves of bread. "We've got a ton of sandwiches to make."

"Then what are we waiting for?" He took a step towards the counter but she put a hand on his shoulder.

"Wait. There's something I need to tell you." Lydia stared at him with complete conviction. "You were right. I have let fear keep me from having a meaningful relationship with a man. I've decided to change that."

"Really? How?"

"I'm looking for a man to take me to dinner tonight." She paused and smiled. "Do you know any one who might be interested?"

"Yes, I know someone," he said, reaching out for her, "but when he takes you to dinner he'll ask you to marry him."

A portion of the proceeds of this book will be donated to the Haven of Rest Ministry, a homeless shelter for men, women, and children in Akron, Ohio.

To order additional copies of

KINDNESS
KILLS

Have your credit card ready and call:

1-877-421-READ (7323)

or please visit our web site at
www.pleasantword.com

Also available at: www.amazon.com

Printed in the United States
32600LVS00002B/43

9 781414 103068